The Way You
Love Me

Also by Elle Wright:

The Wellspring series

Touched by You

Enticed by You

Pleasured by You

The Pure Talent series

The Way You Tempt Me

The Way You Hold Me

The Way You Love Me

Published by Kensington Publishing Corp.

The Way You Love Me

Elle Wright

Kensington Publishing Corp.

www.kensingtonbooks.com

DAFINA BOOKS are published by

Kensington Publishing Corp.
119 West 40th Street
New York, NY 10018

All Kensington Titles, Imprints, and Distributed Lines are available at special quantity discounts for bulk purchases for sales promotions, premiums, fund-raising, and educational or institutional use. Special book excerpts or customized printings can also be created to fit specific needs. For details, write or phone the office of the Kensington special sales manager: Kensington Publishing Corp., 119 West 40th Street, New York, NY 10018, attn: Special Sales Department, Phone: 1-800-221-2647.

The DAFINA logo is a trademark of Kensington Publishing Corp.

ISBN-13: 978-1-4967-2581-3
ISBN-10: 1-4967-2581-6
First Kensington Mass Market Edition: March 2021

ISBN-13: 978-1-4967-2582-0 (ebook)

ISBN-10: 1-4967-2582-4 (ebook)

10 9 8 7 6 5 4 3 2 1

Printed in the United States of America

For my daughter, Kaia.
Thank you for inspiring me. Love you!

Acknowledgments

It takes a strong person to love again after overwhelming heartache. Writing Paige's story was therapeutic, albeit a challenge. I struggled with her love story amidst the drama of life in the public eye. But Andrew . . . flawed, but so patient and so loving. He was her perfect hero, proof that love heals. And they both needed to heal.

I hope you enjoy their journey to happily ever after.

First of all, I want to honor God, who loves me even when I don't deserve it.

To my husband, Jason, I feel blessed to have you as my lover, my friend, my life. Thank you for *loving* me through everything.

To my children, Asante, Kaia, and Masai: I love you. Thank you for keeping me on my toes.

To my family and friends, thank you for supporting me. You make my life better. #TeamElle!

I can't say it enough! Sheryl Lister is my sister in every sense of the word. Thanks, sis, for everything.

I also want to say a special thank-you to Sherelle Green. Thank you for all that you do, for always making me smile even through my tears.

Thanks, Nicole Falls, for that kick in the butt I needed to get through. I appreciate you.

MidnightAce, you are a gem! Thank you for everything!

Thanks to my street team, #EllesBelles! You all hold me down. I truly appreciate you.

I also want to thank Priscilla C. Johnson and Cilla's Maniacs, A. C. Arthur, Brenda Kidd-Woodbury (BJBC), MidnightAce Scotty (MidnightAce Book Bar), King Brooks (Black Page Turners), Orsayor Simmons (Book Referees), Shannan Harper (Harper's Court), Wayne Jordan and Romance in Color, Jennifer Copeland (Jenny's Cozy Book Corner), Shavonna Futrell (Shay_Books Reviews & Recommendations), Stephanie Perkins (The Book Junkie), Loretta Murray (Chicago Public Library), and the EyeCU Reading and Social Network for supporting me. I truly appreciate you all.

And to my readers . . . thank you for rollin' with me! You're everything! I wouldn't be here without your support.

Thank you!

Love,
Elle

Chapter One

Another lawsuit, more media scrutiny . . . *Bullshit*.

Paige Mills tossed the court document she'd been reading aside. "What can we do?"

"Fight" was the one-word reply from Paige's divorce attorney, Demita Strong.

Fight. The notion seemed almost foreign in light of the circumstances. Perhaps it was Paige's reputation as Black America's Sweetheart that had colored her view of the entire process? Or maybe she'd been a naïve fool?

Paige had built an impressive career in television and motion pictures playing strong and relatable characters. Fans loved her because she was approachable and sweet, kind and giving, loving and loyal. She was a good daughter, a good friend, and a good wife. That wasn't an act for ticket sales and ratings. Paige was all those things in real life, not just *reel* life. She'd never been anything but herself. She'd never wanted to project an image that wasn't true. When she married Julius Reeves, she thought it would be forever. And when it wasn't, she'd assumed that he would let her go without a fight. After all, the deterioration of their marriage was *his* fault. Not hers.

"What if I'm tired of fighting?" Paige said.

Demi squeezed her hand, a comforting gesture that Paige appreciated more than her attorney knew. "Be tired. But don't stop. You can't let him win."

Divorce wasn't for the faint of heart, but Paige's soon-to-be-ex-husband had made the entire process a nightmare. Multiple court dates, restraining orders, and threatening texts were becoming Paige's new normal. But she should've known he wouldn't make it easy. Millions of dollars were at stake, and Julius had prolonged the proceedings with frivolous motions and crazy demands. He'd purposely painted her as an emotionally abusive control freak in the media. Julius had even intimated that she'd had major indiscretions of her own, knowing it could affect her brand and possibly destroy her reputation. Basically, he'd decided to try to pull her down into the mud with him. He was a petty, evil asshole.

Making the decision to split was hard enough, but watching it play out on the blogs, in the tabloids, and on television made it worse. Especially since she'd gone into her marriage with every intention of staying married. Paige had put her heart and her acting career on the line to support Julius, holding her head high and holding him down through everything. Until she couldn't anymore, until being there for him started to affect her own emotional and physical health, until she couldn't deny that her husband wasn't worth the energy or the effort.

The fact that he'd cheated on her through most of their short-lived marriage was hard to accept. Finding out that he'd fathered a child with her ex-publicist was a tough blow, too. Infidelity and a secret baby were huge, but not insurmountable problems.

But her breaking point came with his *alleged* history of

sexual harassment and assault, as well as the subsequent indictments against him. That made their already complicated situation unbearable.

Julius had humiliated her time and again. He'd turned what she'd once thought was beautiful into an ugly mess. And she needed it to stop. Now.

Taking a deep breath, she turned to Demi. "Okay. What's next?"

Over the next hour, they formulated a plan of action. More filings and more court dates, but Paige was resolved to do what needed to be done in order to move forward with her life. While Demi worked on the legal aspects, Paige communicated with her team about the specifics. Her publicist, Skye Palmer-Starks, would protect her brand, while her manager continued to handle her business. Her assistant would organize everything else and her agent . . . *Where the hell is Andrew?*

Paige dialed his number. *Straight to voicemail.* Setting her phone on the table, she tried not to read too much into Andrew's absence. After all, he was a senior agent at Pure Talent. And she wasn't his only client, she wasn't his only responsibility. Still, she couldn't help but feel frustrated with him.

"I need to step out for a moment, Demi." Paige walked out onto the patio. She'd requested that Demi come to her house because she didn't want to have to deal with the paparazzi. They'd been relentless in their coverage of her and Julius.

Taking a seat on her favorite chaise lounge, she stretched out and called Andrew again. *Voicemail.* This time, she left a message. "Andrew, I'm not sure what's going on, but I need to talk to you. Please. Call me."

When news of Julius's infidelity surfaced, Andrew had

dropped everything to come to Paige's aid. He stayed by her side through the release of her last movie. Then he disappeared.

From the very beginning of her career, Andrew had been there for her, working behind the scenes to facilitate her rise to stardom. Recently, he'd stepped back, allowing his assistant to handle most of the day-to-day work. And she had no idea why.

With a heavy sigh, she dialed Vonda.

"Hi, Paige. Give me one second."

Hushed voices and muted laughter in the background let Paige know the junior agent wasn't alone. Vonda had worked as Andrew's assistant for years before her promotion to junior agent. The younger woman had already garnered a reputation for being smart, thorough, dedicated, and very capable.

Vonda came back on the line. "Okay, I'm sorry. Just left a meeting and needed to get to my office. How are you?"

"Hanging in there. I'm trying to reach Andrew. Can you tell me where he is?"

Silence.

"My calls keep going to voicemail," Paige continued. "Is he out of town?"

"Let me check his calendar." Vonda cleared her throat. "Hm . . . He's in meetings all day and tomorrow. And next week, he's in Atlanta. Is there anything I can do for you?"

Paige gave Vonda a rundown of the latest development with the divorce. "I'm hoping the judge dismisses this motion, but if he doesn't, I'd like to talk about possible next steps. Shooting is supposed to start on my next project, and I'm wondering if the dates are firm or if they can be pushed."

"Let me make some calls," Vonda said. "I'll get back to you."

Paige swallowed past a hard lump in her throat. Vonda had done exactly what Andrew would have done, but as good as the junior agent was, she wasn't *him*. "Great. Thanks."

Ending the call, Paige typed out a quick text to Andrew. But she didn't hit the SEND button. Instead, she deleted it and stuffed her phone back into her pocket. It was way past time for her to stop depending on him or anyone else.

"Everything okay?" Demi asked when Paige walked back into the room.

Taking a seat at the table, Paige shrugged. "I'm okay."

"Got an email from one of Julius's attorneys."

Paige rolled her eyes. "Let me guess . . . another motion? Maybe he took out an ad about my double life as a prostitute and my secret affair with his father?" It was a bad joke. Paige knew that. And Demi knew it, too. The sad part? She didn't even put it past him to try to defame her in that way.

"They want another meeting," Demi said, without acknowledging Paige's sorry attempt at humor. She tapped her fingers against her keyboard, then closed her laptop. Turning to face Paige, she added, "They're requesting we move the settlement conference up."

Paige leaned back, narrowing her eyes. "After declining every single one of our requests to move the date up? Hm. Interesting." Goodwill gesture? *I think not.* Julius could not be trusted under any circumstance, which was why she'd filed for divorce.

"I'm not confident this isn't another attempt to get to you," her attorney said, echoing her internal thoughts. "I'm perfectly happy to tell him to go to hell. But I know you want this over, and I'm here for you."

Finalizing the divorce was Paige's ultimate goal. And it would be nice if they could settle things without going to court. The last thing she wanted were pictures of her leaving the courthouse every day plastered on every media outlet.

"If I agree, it has to be a neutral place, preferably my choice. No media. No cameras. Only *one* attorney." Over the last several months, Julius had trotted out countless attorneys for various things. He'd even hired a crisis management attorney at one point. "Four people. That's it."

"Of course," Demi agreed. "You know I don't play that."

Nodding, Paige exhaled slowly. She trusted Demi. The attorney's stellar reputation and impeccable record made the decision to hire her easy. And because she'd been recommended by Skye. Oh, and also because of the attorney's nickname—The Divorce Whisperer.

"Fine," Paige said. "Let me know when."

Demi stood and packed up her laptop. "I'll do that." She smiled. "In the meantime, I need you to relax."

That's easier said than done. "I'm trying."

"I know it's hard. What you're going through is difficult for any woman. Your celebrity status adds another layer of stress."

Before Paige met Julius, she'd tried to keep her relationships as low-profile as possible. She'd rarely dated men who worked in the industry, because she preferred to have an escape. But that charming bastard had wormed his way into her heart and convinced her to give him a chance. He'd wooed her and fooled her into thinking he was different, that he wasn't the average high-powered Hollywood director, that he'd protect her and keep her. And she'd believed him. Now she was paying the price for having faith in a man who'd basically lied to her every day of their marriage.

"You're going to be okay." Demi squeezed Paige's hand. "You will. That much I can promise."

"Thank you, Demi. I appreciate the work you've done for me."

"The work I'll continue to do until he's behind you in your rearview mirror, crying that he doesn't have a pot to piss in."

Paige laughed. "That's quite the visual." And, *damn it*, she wanted to see it.

"Then we'll celebrate." Demi picked up her bag and her purse. "I'll call you."

Walking her to the front door, Paige said, "If I don't answer, it's because I'm on set. If it's important, get a message to my assistant."

"I will. Talk to you soon."

A few minutes later, Demi was gone, and Paige was alone. She padded through the house to the kitchen and poured a healthy glass of merlot. Grabbing her iPad, she stepped back out on the patio to watch the sunset.

The stunning view of the Pacific Ocean had been the selling point for the purchase of her house. The Malibu property was everything she'd needed to put literal and figurative distance between her and Julius after the scandal broke. Whenever she felt angry or disappointed or sad, she'd sit outside and think of how blessed she was despite her current predicament. It was her little slice of heaven during trying times, an oasis away from the hustle and bustle of her public life. And she loved it.

Taking a sip from her glass, she picked up her phone and dialed Andrew again. *Voicemail*. Again. "Where are you,

Andrew?" she mumbled aloud. "And why do I feel like you're avoiding me?"

Paige glanced at the time. "He's late," she grumbled, staring out the window. "He probably won't show up."

The settlement conference had been rescheduled three times since Julius's attorneys requested it. That morning, Demi received an email asking to change the meeting date and location again. Demi sent the following response: Meet today or we'll see you in court.

Demi scribbled something on a pad of paper. "If he doesn't, he doesn't. That doesn't change our plans."

Standing, Paige stomped over to the window and peered outside. Strong Law had offices in a prime location on Wilshire Boulevard. She could see the Pure Talent Los Angeles office from the window and wondered if Andrew was back from Atlanta.

It had been a week since she'd talked to Vonda, and the talented junior agent had handled everything with the studio for her. She still hadn't heard from Andrew, though. The two-word text he'd sent explaining that he was "very busy" didn't count, in her opinion.

Paige crossed her arms over her chest. "Where is he?" she grumbled. But she wasn't sure if she was referring to Julius or Andrew. Or both.

"We're fine," Demi said. "It's a tactic that some attorneys use. They think it gives them the upper hand. It always gives *me* the edge."

Paige didn't understand what Demi meant by that, and she didn't really care. She had faith in her attorney. Tugging at her suit jacket, she leaned against the table.

My feet hurt. She considered kicking her shoes off and slipping on the flats she'd packed in her bag.

As the only child of superstar multiplatinum recording artist and actress Tina Mills, she'd been thrust into the limelight at an early age. She'd lived the bulk of her early years on the road, touring the world with her mother. Even then, she hated to dress up, hated to feel uncomfortable in her clothes. That hadn't changed, even now that she was a star in her own right.

Paige had been acting for years. She'd been dressed by top designers, made up by talented aestheticians, styled by brilliant hairstylists, but Paige was a jeans and T-shirts type of woman. Most days, she didn't even wear makeup or even do her hair. She'd intended to show up to the settlement conference in a pair of slacks and a simple blouse, but her assistant had nixed that idea. Chastity had shown up at her house early with a new suit, four-inch pumps, and matching accessories.

Pulling both shoes off, she walked over to the table and opened her bag. By the time she'd switched to the more comfortable flats, Julius and his attorney arrived.

"Ladies," the attorney said, strutting into the room like he owned it. He set his briefcase on the table. "I'm sorry we're late."

Demi didn't respond, so Paige took the cue from her.

"Good morning, Paige." Julius sat in the chair across from her and smirked. "You look tired."

Paige stared at him but didn't rise to the bait. Demi had warned her beforehand that Julius might try to piss her off, to get her to react in a negative way. And Paige didn't want to give them any leverage.

"Gentleman, you called this meeting." Demi shifted in her seat. "If you're not prepared to discuss a potential settlement, you can go. If you are, I will ask that you refrain from antagonizing my client. I will not have you disrespect her in any way."

Julius snickered. "Whatever."

"Don't try me," Demi said. "Trust me, you don't want to."

Julius's attorney, Michael, slid a leather folder over to Demi. "We've reviewed your proposed settlement and made several notes."

Demi made no move to pick up the folder. "I hope you realize there's no real room for negotiation. Paige and Julius signed ironclad prenuptial agreements. It is a waste of the court's time and my time to continue prolonging this, and it's in your best interest to settle."

"You don't know what you're talking about." Julius glared at Demi, before turning hard eyes on Paige. "Since we've been married, your net worth has increased tenfold—because of me." He pointed at his chest. "I made it possible for you to make the millions you did last year. I just want what's mine."

Paige's stomach turned. *How the hell did I marry this man?* He'd proven more times than not that he was incapable of acting like a human being.

"Okay, we're done." Demi stood and shoved the folder back toward Julius and Michael.

Paige peered up at her attorney, making sure she kept her face devoid of the shock she felt at the abrupt change in direction. "Demi?"

"Wait," Michael said. "Let's calm down and talk about this."

"I told you when you arrived—late—that I won't allow my client to be disrespected," Demi warned. "Either *you* control *your* client or get out."

The other attorney whispered something in Julius's ear before turning to them. "We're good."

Demi took her seat again. "That's what I thought."

"I just want what's mine," Julius muttered.

"What's yours is what was agreed upon in the prenuptial agreement *you* signed." Demi leaned forward. "And let's not forget the fact that you cheated on my client, you lied from day one, and more than likely, you will be going to jail soon. My suggestion? Sign the papers and focus on your criminal trials. Because I'm sure you're going to need all the help you can get there."

Instead of giving them the leather folder, Michael pulled out two documents and handed both to Demi. "Please, if you'll look at the proposed settlement, I think you'll find it fair."

Paige took the offered copy from Demi and scanned the document. As she turned the pages, she wondered when the other shoe would drop. So far, nothing looked out of the ordinary. It basically read like the proposed agreement Demi had forwarded to Julius weeks ago. Except . . .

"You want *my* house?" Paige yelled. Heat flushed through her body and her heartbeat pounded in her ear.

"Yes, I do," Julius sneered. "You purchased that house while we were still married. It's community property. And I want it."

"You've never even stepped foot in that house," Paige growled.

Demi called to her, "Paige?"

But Paige couldn't hear anything except the loud voices in her head that had warned her against marrying Julius. She couldn't see anything but the smug look on his face right now. Friends, colleagues, her mother . . . they'd all told her not to do it. They'd begged her to reconsider, to walk away from him. But she'd plunged ahead, floating on a cloud of lies and making the biggest mistake of her life.

"There's no way in hell," Paige said. "You think you can come in here and demand that I give you anything? After what you did to me?" Demi placed a hand on Paige's arm, but there was no calming the anger that had consumed her.

"I'm willing to have you buy me out." Julius leaned back in his chair, crossing his legs in front of him, like the smug bastard he'd always been.

Asshole.

"Pay me half of the value, and I'll sign the papers," he said. "And you can continue to be the stupid woman you've always been."

Paige turned to Demi. "Can I use your red marker?" she asked.

Frowning, Demi said, "You're not signing this."

"Please?" Paige held out a hand.

With a heavy sigh, Demi placed a red Sharpie in Paige's hand. "We should talk about this before you sign that."

"No need to talk. I'm done talking."

"As your attorney, I'm going to highly advise that you take a step back. We'll discuss everything later."

Ignoring her attorney, Paige bent low and scribbled two words in big capital letters on the front page: *FUCK YOU*.

Chapter Two

It had been two months since that disastrous settlement conference, and Paige was still married to Julius. After she'd scribbled those two big words on their proposed agreement, the meeting was over.

Before Julius could say anything, Demi had ordered Julius and Michael to leave the building. Since then, he'd tried to contact Paige several times, via text, via phone, via email. He'd even shown up to the studio when he knew she'd be there—and promptly got arrested for violating the restraining order she'd had on him.

Despite her objections, he'd sent a Realtor to her house to assess its value. The poor Realtor had no idea what was going on, but found out soon enough when Paige told the woman exactly what she could do with the clipboard she was holding.

With the divorce hearing fast approaching, Paige couldn't help but worry about the outcome. Even though Demi had assured her not to stress about it, she found herself obsessing about it, going over everything she'd done wrong in their relationship, blaming herself for her predicament.

Shifting in her favorite spot—her chaise lounge—she

peered out at the ocean. The September breeze felt like balm against her skin. Paige had always loved being near the water. Growing up, they'd always lived near a beach—Manhattan Beach, Topanga Beach, or even the Good Harbor Beach off of Lake Michigan. Living in Atlanta with Julius for that short time had been hard for her. She'd missed the sand between her toes, the crash of waves against the shore, and the scent of sea air in her nose. Now he wanted to take it from her, he wanted to steal her joy, he wanted to snatch her peace.

Paige's phone buzzed and she picked it up. She stared at the text from Andrew: How are you?

Disappointment filled the empty spaces in her heart as she contemplated her response to that question. Maybe he would know how she was doing if he'd been around to see the toll her divorce had taken on her life. They'd talked briefly over the past couple months about business, never about anything of substance. It was an obvious switch from the easy rapport they'd once had with each other.

Over the years, she'd come to depend on his guidance. More than that, she'd considered them friends. She'd grown to love him as a person and not just her agent. There was even a time when she'd thought it could be more than that. But his work obligations and her career trajectory had nipped that sentiment in the bud. Still, they'd remained close. And now they weren't. It pissed her off, because she'd hoped he would be standing with her. She'd yearned for his strong, silent support. He didn't offer it in the way she'd expected, and it pissed her off.

Instead of replying to his text, though, she turned her phone off. It was better she didn't answer. It was best that she put Andrew in the same category as most people in her life—*colleague*. Not friend, not confidante, not . . .

The doorbell rang, and she dragged herself out of her safe haven and hurried to get it. The security firm she'd hired wouldn't have let anyone get close if the visitor wasn't on her approved list. Peering through the glass, she smiled at the sight of her publicist, Skye.

"Hi, Skye," she said, opening the door.

"Hey, Paige."

"Come in." Paige stepped back, allowing Skye to enter. "What are you doing in town?"

Skye grinned. "Had to come check on you, lay my eyes on my favorite client."

When Paige discovered Julius's affair with Catherine Davis, who'd worked as Paige's publicist for years, she'd promptly fired the woman. Jax Starks, president of Pure Talent, had immediately sent Skye to her aid. It turned out to be the best thing he could have ever done. Skye had stepped in to fill the vacant role on Paige's team seamlessly.

They exchanged quick but sincere hugs. "I'm okay," Paige told her. "Just relaxing on the patio."

"Sounds like heaven."

"Come on out. Glass of wine?"

With a wide grin, Skye said, "A big glass, thank you." Once Paige had poured the wine, they retreated back to her oasis. Skye sat on the matching chaise. "So tell me . . . how are you really?"

Burrowing into the cushion, Paige took a sip from her glass. "It's been hard."

"I know it has. Julius is an asshole on his best day."

Paige giggled. "You're so right."

Paige and Skye had bonded over failed romance, but they'd quickly discovered other shared experiences in life. As biracial women, they'd spoken often about the challenges growing up and finding their identity. They both considered themselves to be black women, even though Skye had embraced her Filipino culture. On the other hand, Paige had struggled to identify with her white father and his family. She suspected that had more to do with their absence in her life than her willingness to try.

"I'm sure Demi has everything under control, though," Skye added.

"She's pretty awesome," Paige agreed. "Thanks for referring me to her."

They spent a few minutes talking business, upcoming appearances, new interview requests, and future events. Paige appreciated Skye's ability to cut through the clutter of her life. She never had to worry much about her career because she'd hired an amazing team—from her manager to her publicist to her . . . agent.

Swallowing hard, Paige admitted, "I feel tired, like I need time away. But I don't know how to make that happen."

"It's definitely something we can discuss. If you want, I can reach out to Andrew and set up a meeting."

"I don't think so," Paige grumbled.

Skye blinked. "Okay, that didn't sound good. No meeting with Andrew?"

Shaking her head, Paige said, "No. I don't need him. Vonda has been doing a great job in his stead. I'm actually thinking about staying with her."

Her publicist's mouth fell open. "Wow. I didn't expect that."

"Well, when your agent can't be bothered to call you back, what else can you do?" Paige finished her wine and set the empty glass on the ground beside her. "It's obvious his attention needs to be elsewhere right now." Paige didn't bother to mask the bitterness she felt in that moment. Because she fully intended to embrace her take-no-shit side for the foreseeable future. "And I'm shifting my focus to me, my health, my well-being."

Skye bit down on her bottom lip. "Sounds like a plan. But . . ." She sighed. "Somehow I don't think it's what you really want."

Paige averted her gaze and traced the pattern on her caftan. "My mother once told me that I would never get everything I want."

"True, but you can have some of what you want."

Meeting Skye's gaze again, she said, "Sometimes I don't even know what I want anymore."

"Because of Julius?"

"Because everything I thought I wanted is nothing that I need. If that makes any sense."

"It does." Skye reached out and squeezed her hand. "I've been in that space, not knowing what I want, not believing I could ever feel happiness again. But let me tell you . . . *you* can."

"Skye Palmer-Starks, when did you get so mushy?" Paige laughed. "Wait, I know. Garrett just melted all that ice inside you."

"Girl . . ." Skye smiled. "I love that man."

Paige had celebrated Skye's recent engagement to Garrett Steele a few months ago. It was a happy occasion, and a much needed reprieve from the drama of her own life. And she couldn't be happier for her friend.

"I can see that," Paige said. "How's the wedding planning?"

Skye told her about her venue woes, her mother's insistence on designing her wedding gown, and her bossy bridesmaids. "I keep telling Garrett that I want to keep it small. Zara just had the baby, so she's not feeling any of the dresses I pick out. She keeps saying her boobs look too big. And Rissa? Goodness grief, she just got married and has appointed herself the Wedding Queen. Even though I can plan a wedding in my sleep."

Paige had to agree with that. Skye had planned Zara's wedding to Xavier Starks in a matter of weeks and it had turned out perfectly. Paige had attended the Hawaiian ceremony with her mother and enjoyed the entire experience.

"In a minute, I'm going to fire them both and appoint Duke as my man of honor," Skye added.

"What?" Paige barked out a laugh. She didn't know Skye's good friend Duke well, but he didn't strike her as the "man of honor" type. "I would like to see that."

Skye waved a dismissive hand. "It will never happen. I know that."

"Well, you know I'm here if you need any help."

"You're too busy, Paige. I know because I have access to your schedule."

Shrugging, Paige said, "Which is why I need to take a step back. I need to reset, spend some time healing."

"You'll get that time. I promise. If I have to smack Andrew to get him in line, I will."

Paige's smile fell. "You don't have to do that. I meant what I said earlier."

"I hate to see you like this. I get it, though. Divorce isn't something I'd ever wish on anyone. But you'll get through this. And you will love again, too."

"I doubt that." Paige sighed. "I'm not sure I even want to."

"Trust me, it won't be like this forever."

"We'll see." Standing, Paige picked up her glass. "I need a refill. Hungry?"

"I can always eat." Skye scooted off the lounger. "Preferably some of your delicious collard greens. Yum."

Paige threw her head back with laughter. "Girl, you're a mess. But you're in luck. I made some for Labor Day."

"I was hoping you did."

An hour later, they'd eaten a delicious lunch and had more wine. Paige felt remarkably better, too. It felt good to chat with a friend, to unplug for a while with Skye. The doorbell rang again, and she excused herself to answer it. This time it was Demi.

When Paige opened the door, Demi stepped inside. "How are you?"

"I'm pretty good right now," Paige said. "Skye is inside. We just had something to eat. What brings you my way?"

Demi smiled, but it wasn't her normal bright smile. It was her serious, we-need-to-talk smile. "I hate to bring this to you when you're having a good day. But I felt like I needed to give you a heads-up."

"What is it?"

"Can we go in your office?" Demi asked.

"Sure." Paige let Skye know she had to take care of some business but would be right back. When they entered her office, Paige opened the window to let the air in. "What's up?" she asked, taking a seat on one of her chairs.

"Michael forwarded me a copy of their newest motion. Julius is asking for another forensic audit of your income."

Paige's stomach fell. "Why? We already went through this."

"I know. He's digging in his heels about the house. They

told me they'd be willing to drop this latest motion and sign the settlement agreement, if you budge on the house."

Closing her eyes, Paige let out a frustrated sigh. "He's only doing this to slight me. He only wants the money."

Julius's recent financial troubles were the subject of many blogs and news articles. The once impressive fortune he'd amassed as a movie producer and director had dwindled substantially in the past year. He'd spent thousands on legal fees and lawsuits due to his criminal activities. And he'd lost opportunities to earn additional income because no one wanted to work with him anymore. Going after her money was the reason this divorce had dragged on for so long. Their prenuptial agreement had saved her from a hefty payout but the income she'd earned since they married seemed to be fair game.

"I have something up my sleeve," Demi said, "something I just discovered. A game changer."

Paige didn't care anymore. She just wanted to be divorced. "Can I see the agreement again?"

Frowning, Demi pulled out the agreement and held it out to her. But she didn't let it go when Paige tried to take it. "I don't like that look in your eyes."

"I don't like how I feel right now," Paige admitted.

After a few tense seconds, Demi finally let the document go. "Don't give up on me yet, Paige."

"I'm not giving up on you," she assured the attorney. "You've been wonderful. And I appreciate all of your hard work, your diligence, and your patience." Paige turned to the last page of the document. "But it's just a house." Except it wasn't *just* a house to her. The one thing she'd wanted to fight for felt like a cage now, a reminder of everything he'd taken from her and still wanted to steal.

"Paige, don't sign that."

Paige asked for a pen. This time, she asked for the blue pen. A few minutes later, she signed the settlement agreement. "Here. I'm done."

"No, we're not done," Demi argued.

A tear spilled from Paige's eye and she wiped it away. What she was about to do was breaking her heart. But she would do it because then it would be over. And she needed it to be over more than she needed this house.

"There are other houses, different beaches," Paige said. "Right now, I just want this connection severed permanently. I need my life back. And I need my peace."

Andrew Weathers had been bogged down with contracts, long meetings, and blueprints for the past several months. The new audio division for Pure Talent was officially up and running, but it required more time than he'd considered when he had agreed to spearhead the endeavor.

It had also taken him away from his clients, from the day-to-day work that he'd once loved. Andrew had been a loyal employee of Pure Talent Agency since he graduated from college. He'd learned from one of the best men in the business—Jax Starks. And he'd mentored several talented agents himself.

The actresses and actors he'd worked with had fueled his passion for agenting. Helping them succeed, pushing them higher in their careers, had made his job worth the hard hours, the time at the negotiation table, the stress of travel, and the many PR nightmares.

After many years in the business, though, he'd felt the pull to do something else, to step away from direct client work. Which was why he'd jumped at the opportunity to create something fresh within the agency. Now he could see the fruits of his labor, now he knew that he'd made the right decision to step back from his clients. He just had to get his heart on board with his mind.

A soft knock on his door pulled him from his thoughts. A moment later, his mentee poked her head in. "Got a minute?"

He smiled. "Sure, Vonda. Come on in."

The petite woman grinned and stepped into the office. She took a seat across from him and set a folder on his desk. "Can you review this contract?"

He opened the folder and skimmed the first page, pausing at the name on the document: *Paige Mills*. "Is this the new Christmas movie?"

"Yes, I've combed through everything, triple-checked the clauses, and highlighted several changes I'd like to negotiate."

Andrew had no doubt that Vonda had handled everything exactly the way he would have. That was the reason he'd transitioned the bulk of his daily client work to her. But there was one client he couldn't completely let go. Although he'd let Vonda handle the direct communication, he still made sure he had the final say on everything that crossed his desk with her name on it. *Paige*.

"I also emailed it to you," Vonda added.

"Thanks." Closing the folder, he met Vonda's gaze. "I'm happy with the work you're doing. You've really stepped up to the plate."

Vonda grinned. "I just appreciate the opportunity to prove myself."

"You have nothing to prove. How is she?" He didn't need to say who the "she" was, because Vonda already knew.

"Actually, I haven't heard much from her. I've sent several emails, but Chastity has responded to all of them."

"That's strange," he murmured, almost to himself. "Have you talked to Tanya?"

Paige had been managed by Tanya Baldwin at TB Management for the last eight years.

Vonda shook her head. "I called Tanya, and she hasn't heard from her either."

"Not like her," he mumbled.

As Paige's popularity skyrocketed with every performance, every new film, every television special, she'd always made sure she handled most of her own business. He knew that had a lot to do with her mother's influence and her mother's experience in the industry. Tina Mills had always stayed on top of her own career, even though she was represented by one of the most trusted, honest agents in the industry—Jax Starks. Although Paige had trusted Andrew to handle her career, she'd always followed her mother's advice to the letter when it came to the business of acting.

"I figure she just needs time," Vonda said. "It's been a roller coaster for her."

Nodding, Andrew considered her statement. He'd read the articles, he'd seen the slanted media coverage, and he'd heard the rumors. Paige's divorce had turned into a media spectacle. Paparazzi had latched on to the story, probably hoping to expose anything that would make viewers question her Black America's Sweetheart status. But she'd prevailed, maintaining her reputation as the lovable real-life heroine she'd always been.

"I read the latest article," he said. "Divorce is final?"

"Yes. By all accounts, she walked away with everything she brought into the marriage."

"Good. Is there—?" Another knock interrupted his inquiry. "Come in."

Skye Palmer-Starks opened the door. "Andrew?"

While it wasn't uncommon for Skye to be in Los Angeles for business, he hadn't expected her to drop by his office. "Skye? What brings you here?"

Skye greeted Vonda with a warm smile before turning cold eyes on him. "We need to talk. Alone," she added with a raised brow.

Vonda quickly excused herself, leaving him with the obviously irritated Skye. Since she'd taken over publicity for Paige, he'd often been on the tail end of her ire, mostly because of his decision to step back.

"What's up?" Andrew asked.

"I need your help." Skye took Vonda's vacated seat. "Paige is off the grid."

Andrew frowned. "What do you mean she's off the grid?"

"What does off the grid mean to *you*, Andrew? She's gone."

"I know what it means."

Skye shrugged. "So why did you ask the question?"

He let out a heavy sigh, rubbing a hand over his face. "Because I'm trying to understand what happened."

"Maybe if you'd been talking to her like you should've been, you might be able to answer your own damn question."

Andrew paused. Skye was right. If he'd been there, maybe he'd know the details, maybe he'd know how to get through to Paige, maybe she wouldn't have disappeared in the first place. "When did she leave?"

"The day after the divorce was final."

"What happened?" he asked.

"Again. . . I. Don't. Know. Shit, I'm just as confused as you are."

He took a deep breath and counted to ten. Andrew had

known Skye for years, and he considered her a friend. But she had an uncanny ability to get under his skin. "When did you see her last?" he grumbled through clenched teeth.

"Two weeks ago" was her inadequate answer.

"Where?" he blared, surprised by his own outburst.

Skye's eyes widened. "Okay, damn." She crossed her legs. "I saw her right after the court hearing. She was happy Demi was able to save the house."

"The house?" he asked. "What does her house have to do with the divorce? She bought it after they separated."

"I can see you're out of the loop," Skye muttered. "Julius's ass tried to force her to sell and split the value of the house because they were still married when she bought it."

Muthafucka. Andrew could sit no longer. He stood, nearly tipping over his chair. Pacing the floor, he thought about how devastated Paige must have been. Especially since he knew how much she loved that house. Purchasing it had been a bright spot in the midst of the darkness.

"Andrew?"

He blinked. Sighing, he turned to meet her waiting gaze. "Yes."

"I know your mind is working overtime, but I need your attention right now."

"Go ahead," he said.

"Anyway, I handled the press release. We celebrated with a shot of tequila, I went back to my hotel. When I came back the next morning, she was gone."

"And that's the last time you talked to her?" he asked.

"Yes. She missed reshoots for the rom-com, she was a no-show at the MTV Awards ceremony, and she turned off her phone. Tanya can't find her. Chastity doesn't even know where she is."

Andrew shared what Vonda had told him about Chastity returning the emails. "She had to give her instructions to do that."

"Actually, she hasn't. Chastity is just good enough to know that business won't stop. She took it upon herself to handle Paige's inbox."

He massaged his temples. The migraine coming on would be a big one, and he had no one to blame but himself. "Okay." He took another deep breath. "Have you talked to Tina? What's your plan?"

Skye smacked her palms on her legs. "I got nothing."

"What the hell does that even mean? You always have a plan."

It was one of the reasons her new public relations firm had exploded the way it did. In a few short months, Skye had built an impressive clientele. High-powered actors and actresses, directors, authors, and producers had left long-standing relationships with established PR reps to join the Skye Light PR family.

"I've done everything I know to do. Tina isn't talking, her security team is in the dark, and I'm out of options."

"I find that hard to believe," he said. "We need to do something."

"Correction . . . *You* need to do something." She pointed at him. "I told you, I'm tapped out."

Skye was right. He needed to find Paige and fix this— the sooner, the better. He would hate for her career to suffer. He hated the thought of *her* suffering. Andrew approached the huge window. His gaze shifted to the street below, the countless people going about their day as if the world was just right. Except, there was one woman's world that hadn't been right in a long time. It had been so wrong that she'd disappeared.

Staring out at the LA skyline, he wondered if she was okay, if she was safe. He ignored the ache in his gut that had built to a dull throb with every moment that passed since he'd found out she'd disappeared without a trace. He ignored what he knew that meant. Because he had to focus on one thing right now. *Where are you, Paige?*

Chapter Three

"What's up, Drew?" Xavier greeted him with a dap.

Andrew had arrived in Atlanta an hour ago and contacted X right away. His friend agreed to meet him for a quick beer at a local sports bar. "Nothing much, bruh." He took a seat across from X. "How's fatherhood?"

Xavier and his wife, Zara, had recently welcomed Cicely Angel Starks to their new family. "I'm in love, bruh." X grinned. "She's beautiful and she's mine."

Andrew had been in town for the christening and got to meet the little cutie-pie in person. "She's adorable, man. How's Zara?"

"Beautiful and cranky. She's not feeling the extended maternity leave." Zara ran the sports division at Pure Talent. "I keep telling her to enjoy this time. Once she goes back to work, she'll miss being home with Cici."

"Exactly." He waved the waitress over and placed his order. "How's work?"

"Work is work. Getting ready for Dad's retirement."

Jax Starks had finally announced a retirement date, much to the chagrin of most of the Pure Talent employees.

Andrew had expected it, but he still felt a tinge of sadness when his mentor had let him know his plans.

"I still can't believe he's doing it," Andrew said.

"I can. He's ready to spend some quality time with my mother and my baby. She's two months old and already has him wrapped around her finger. You should see him with her."

"I bet he's proud."

"Absolutely." X took a long pull of his beer. "He's already asking for baby number two."

Chuckling, Andrew said, "I'm sure that didn't go over well with Zara."

"Hell no."

The waitress returned with his beer. Andrew thanked her, then turned his attention back to X. "I'm glad to see you happy, bruh. Marriage and fatherhood definitely agree with you."

"I wouldn't change a thing," X told him. "They are my life."

Andrew wondered if he'd ever feel that way about someone. Having a family had always felt like a pipe dream, something that *might* happen after he'd risen the corporate ladder. But the novelty of money and status had worn off, and he found himself wanting more out of life than hours in front of the computer, long meetings, and turbulent flights around the world.

"It's a good feeling," X continued. "But enough about me. What's going on with Paige?"

Andrew wasn't surprised X knew there was something going on with Paige. "I guess you've already talked to Skye?"

X shook his head. "No. But I've heard some rumblings."

Andrew smiled. "I swear you're becoming your father, man."

Jax Starks knew a lot about everything, from industry news and potential investments to office gossip. It was a gift that Andrew never really had. He tended to get so engrossed in his work that he missed a lot of the extra shit.

"What can I say? He taught me well. And so did you."

When Xavier declared he wanted to be an agent, Andrew had taken the former child star under his wing. X had been eager to learn and determined to prove himself to his father and the world. Now X was ready to step into his father's role as president of the agency. As much as Andrew would miss Jax, he was confident the company was in good hands with X.

"You'll fill his shoes nicely," Andrew said.

"Not likely. I'm wearing my own shoes. By the way, I read over the report you sent me the other day. Pure Talent Audio is surpassing expectations. I'm pleased."

Andrew thanked him. "I'm just doing what needs to be done."

Xavier finished his beer. "Ready to take it a step further? Are you interested in jumping in on a new endeavor?"

"You know I am." Andrew couldn't deny the appeal of working on a new venture. He didn't mind giving his time and expertise to the company that had given him so much. Jax had taken a chance on him and had sowed a positive seed in Andrew's life. And he wanted to see the company grow and diversify.

"I'm not ready to reveal my plan just yet," X continued. "But you'll be the first to know when I am."

"I'm looking forward to it."

"Which leads me back to Paige . . ."

Andrew didn't know how that led his friend back to Paige, but he'd roll with it. "You won't let this go, huh?"

"Not at all. What's up?" X asked.

"She left town." Andrew gave X a brief rundown of the situation with Julius and Paige's subsequent disappearance. "I'm handling it, though."

"Good. I'm glad you're on it. Paige is one of our best clients and a friend. I hope she's okay."

"She will be." Andrew cleared his throat. "I'm actually in town to talk to Tina. I heard she's renting a place in Buckhead right now."

"My father mentioned something to me about that. Hopefully, she can shed some light on it." X ordered another round of beer for both of them. "But let me ask you something. Why have you been so distant with her? I mean, I've known you for a long time. I've never seen you with any other client the way you are with her."

"I treat all of my clients the same way," Andrew lied. "And I felt it was necessary to shift some of my responsibilities to Vonda so that I could focus on Audio."

"Even Paige?"

Especially Paige. "Yes."

"I'm sorry, bruh, but I don't believe that shit."

Andrew barked out a laugh. "What the hell is that supposed to mean?"

"It means what I said." X shrugged. "You've devoted so much time to her career. Then, all of a sudden, you're 'stepping back'"—he threw up air quotes—"when she needed you the most? It's bullshit."

"I don't know what you want me to say. It felt like the right thing to do at the time." He paused, hesitant to finish his thought. In the end, he decided to say what had been on his mind. "Plus, it was killing me to see her hurt."

X smirked. "Finally, you're speaking the truth."

"After the L.A. premiere of her last movie, and prior to the divorce filing, I realized one thing. Being in the room with her and Julius made everything worse. I wanted to kick his ass up and down the street, paparazzi be damned. Which would have put her in an uncomfortable position."

"That's understandable. What's the problem now? The divorce is final. She's not with him and the chances of you being in the same room with Julius are pretty slim, since his ass will probably be in jail soon."

Andrew couldn't think of an answer to the question. Correction, he couldn't think of an answer that he wanted to share with X.

X must have caught on to Andrew's dilemma because he said, "No comment?"

Still, Andrew didn't respond.

Chuckling, X shook his head. "Okay, well . . . Let me know when you're ready to talk. Trust me, I've been there, done that. Got the T-shirt, the wife, and the baby to prove it."

Andrew blinked. "What the hell are you talking about?"

"You're a smart man, bruh. It's time to open your eyes and think about why you really haven't been there for her. When we both know you wanted to."

The waitress dropped the bill on the table and X told Drew he'd take care of it.

"I can get this one," Andrew argued.

"Nah, I got it. I'm sure there will come a time when you'll want to revisit this conversation. Then the drinks will be on you."

Once the bill was settled, they left the restaurant. The valet ran off to get his rental. "You heading back to the office?" Drew asked.

"Nah, I'm done for the day. Have to stop at the grocery store. It's my turn to cook."

"Are you sure you want to risk giving Zara food poisoning?"

"You're talking shit and you can't even make a pot of grits?"

Andrew glared at him. "You can stop bringing that shit up. It was years ago." He'd offered to bring grits to a breakfast potluck a long time ago. Unfortunately, they were too dry to eat.

"You'll never live that down, bruh." X cracked up. "And I can grill a damn hamburger and some asparagus."

Chuckling, Andrew said, "Tell Zara I said good luck."

His friend waved a dismissive hand. "Shut the hell up, man."

Andrew glanced at his watch. When he'd contacted Tina to ask if he could come over and talk to her, she'd let him know she wouldn't be home until late afternoon. He figured he'd go over around five o'clock—not too early and not too late.

"Give Zara my love, bruh."

"I will. Tell Paige we're here if she needs anything." X clasped Drew's shoulder. "Oh, and make sure you're honest with her. She'll spot your bullshit reason in a heartbeat."

"You get married and suddenly you think you know everything."

X grinned. "I always knew everything."

Andrew covered "bullshit" in a fake cough. "I remember plenty of times when you didn't know shit."

"I graduated to Jedi Master, man. Ask Skye. I've been giving some pretty good advice for the past year."

The valet pulled up. Andrew tipped the man and walked around to the driver's side. "Well, if I need some advice, I'll be sure to ask you."

X held up his arms at his sides. "I'm sure that will be soon."

"Talk to you later, man. Kiss Cici for me."

Later, Andrew knocked on Tina Mills's door.

"Andrew!" Tina grinned, opening her front door to him. "Long time no see."

Leaning forward, he placed a kiss on the older woman's cheek. "Tina," he said. "How are you?"

"I'm well. Glad to have a little time off."

At sixty-three years old, she looked as beautiful as she was when he'd seen her perform at the Fox Theatre in Detroit in her twenties. His mother had dragged him to the concert to see the legendary Tina Mills perform in the 1980s. It hadn't been his ideal outing then—because he would've rather been watching *Tom and Jerry* or *The Muppets*—but the experience had changed his life. It was the first time he'd thought about doing something in the entertainment industry.

He still remembered his mom taking his six-year-old self backstage to meet her, and he also recalled feeling starstruck. She'd seemed larger than life, like a goddess with smooth brown skin, long wavy hair, and a gold-sequined catsuit. Andrew had been smitten, and that crush had lasted all the way until his seventh birthday when he'd fallen head-over-heels for Denise Huxtable.

Tina led him to the gourmet kitchen. "What brings you

all the way to Atlanta? Because I know you're not here to see me." She winked. "Have a seat."

"Thanks." Smooth jazz played through the surround sound speakers, a cool breeze flowed through the kitchen, and a pot of something delicious simmered on the stove. It smelled like chicken and spices, fresh herbs and garlic. "Smells good." He slid onto a barstool.

"I decided to make dinner today," she said. "It's been a while since I've cooked."

Andrew watched as she poured chicken stock into a pan and stirred. Moments later, she added in heavy cream and seasonings. Then, she put the cooked chicken breasts back into the pan. They talked about surface things, like the weather and the latest political drama, while she finished up.

"How is your mother?" she asked.

Smiling, he replied, "She's good. Ready for retirement." Connie Weathers had put in forty-five years of hard labor at an automotive plant near Detroit, Michigan. She'd done so without a complaint so that he and his brothers could have a great life. "Thinking about coming out at the end of the year."

"About time. It's been long enough. She has three beautiful boys who are more than willing to take care of her."

Tina and his mother had attended the same high school in Detroit, Michigan, and had grown up blocks away from each other. It was one of the things that had sealed his bond with Paige when they'd met.

"I'm trying to get her to sell the house and move to Cali," he said.

Tina pointed a wooden spoon at him. "Now that, I can't

see happening any time soon." She laughed. "You know she loves the city."

"You're right about that."

Convincing his mother to leave Michigan seemed futile. She'd grown up riding bikes down 7 Mile, attending infamous block parties, and hanging with her cousins. Although none of his brothers live in the state anymore, she was determined to stay put.

Andrew couldn't say he blamed her. After all, his mother had purchased their childhood home herself, in cash. It was her first investment after the divorce and her safe place. The neighborhood had recently seen a resurgence in popularity, as more and more people moved back into the city of Detroit from the suburbs.

"I went back a few months ago." Tina poured him a glass of lemonade. "Took a tour of the old neighborhood. Looks beautiful."

"It is. The property values have tripled. She's happy."

"I'm glad to hear it." She fixed two plates and slid one to him. "Eat. And tell me what's going on."

He took a bite of a tender piece of chicken and held back a groan. It wasn't often that he was able to enjoy a home-cooked meal. His mother did not pass along her talent in the kitchen to him, so he'd pretty much survived on takeout, delivery, cereal, and sandwiches.

"Well?" she prodded. "Everything okay?"

Shrugging, he said, "I'm not sure. That's what I came to ask you. Where's Paige?"

Tina smiled. "Ah, you're here for my daughter."

"We've been trying to find her." Andrew had done everything he could to locate Paige. He'd purposely saved

Tina for last because he didn't want to alarm her. "Studio's calling."

Tina pinned him with her gaze. She didn't seem surprised that Paige was gone, though.

"Can you tell me where she is?" he asked.

"So you can try and drag her back here?" She folded her arms. "She needs a break, Drew."

Andrew sighed. "I understand that, but I need to be able to help her."

"You?" Tina raised a challenging brow. "Or Vonda?"

The question caught him off guard. Paige was close to her mother, but she'd limited the information she shared with Tina for a reason. He'd witnessed several disagreements between mother and daughter over Paige's career. The fact that Tina knew that he'd been absent was very telling. Because it meant Paige was angry enough—at him—to say something.

Clearing his throat, he mumbled, "Me. I want to help her."

Tina sat back and studied him. Andrew wasn't a nervous person by nature, but he found himself averting his gaze to escape the scrutiny. "My daughter is safe," she said simply.

"Can you tell me where she is?" he repeated. "Or how I can get in touch with her? I'd like to contact her."

With a heavy sigh, she said, "Honestly, I'm not in a hurry to give anyone access to her. She's been through a lot this past year."

"I'm not just anyone," he said.

"That's not what she told me." Tina leaned forward. "I'm not sure what's happened between you two, but she specifically told me not to tell you anything."

"What?" Andrew knew he'd made mistakes, but he

hoped he would be able to get through to her. He needed to let her know that he could still be trusted.

"She's hurting. After the divorce, she wanted to put her house on the market."

Frowning, he said, "Wait, I thought she was able to keep the house?"

Tina nodded, taking a sip of her drink. "Yes, but she said it didn't feel like a safe place for her anymore after everything. Then she heard that Julius was marrying Catherine Davis."

His eyes flashed to hers. "Are you serious? The divorce was just finalized."

"I'm dead serious."

"Catherine Davis is married."

"Not anymore." Tina explained that Catherine had divorced her husband of ten years quietly and moved in with Julius. The embattled movie director sent the news via courier to Paige the morning after the court date. "He's a fuckin' asshole. Always has been full of shit."

Shaking his head, he mumbled a string of curses. "She's sad that he's moved on already."

"No, she's just *sad*." Tina tapped her manicured fingernail on the countertop. "Partly because she feels like she wasted her time, but mostly because she feels alone."

"She has people who love her," he argued. "People who are rooting for her, people who support her."

"She's lost so much, Andrew. People who claimed to love her have repeatedly disappointed her."

He wondered if Tina counted *him* as one of those people. "What about Skye?" he croaked. "I know they've grown close. She didn't even tell Skye where she was going."

"Because she needs to disconnect from being Black America's Sweetheart."

Andrew decided to try another tactic. "What about her career? I would hate for her decision to affect her brand. She's already missed several key meetings and events. You know how hard it is to recover from a difficult-to-work-with label. "

Tina's brow creased, signaling that he might have pierced her armor a bit.

"I just want to talk to her, I need to know she's okay. We can come up with a plan to mitigate the scandal around Julius's upcoming wedding and protect her career. Then I'll make sure she can take the time she needs away from the spotlight."

A moment passed before Tina said, "If I give you the information, do *not* pass it along to anyone else."

"I won't."

"If you do, I'll find you and make you regret it."

He laughed. "I don't doubt it."

Tina wrote down an address on a small piece of paper and slid it to him. But before he could grab it, she said, "Andrew, take care of her. She doesn't realize it right now, but she needs you."

Andrew swallowed past the hard lump in his throat. "I won't let you down."

"Never mind me. Don't let *her* down."

Nodding, he said, "I won't." Andrew meant every word. Now he just had to make sure Paige knew it. "But can you do me a favor?"

Tina eyed him skeptically. "What is it?"

"Don't tell her I'm coming."

Chapter Four

"Boy, when did you get here?" Andrew's mother dropped her garden hose and grinned from ear to ear as she approached him.

Coming to Michigan and *not* seeing Connie Weathers would have resulted in a long lecture about visiting more often, letting her know what's going on in his life, and not bringing her any grandchildren to love on. Because, yes, she'd found a way to slide that in during every conversation.

He'd flown into the Detroit Metro Airport, instead of the Gerald R. Ford International Airport in Grand Rapids. And had planned to hit the road in a few hours.

"Hey, Mama." Andrew embraced his mother and placed a kiss to her cheek.

"You're full of surprises!" She took off her work gloves and patted his face. "I just talked to you."

He couldn't help but smile at his mother's enthusiasm. "I have business in Michigan and figured I'd visit my favorite girl."

Connie smiled, her eyes filling with the tears she always

shed when she saw him or his brothers. "Well, I guess I'm pretty lucky then."

"I'm the lucky one." He winked at his mama. Time had been good to her, but he noticed a few more gray hairs and worry lines than had been there the last time he'd seen her. "How are you, Mama?" He hadn't missed the slight limp she'd tried to conceal when she'd walked toward him.

"Oh, I'm doing alright." She stretched a little. "Aching in new places."

He frowned. "Are you okay?"

"Oh, boy, I'm good. Just tired."

"Hm." Andrew studied her. "Are you still working midnights?"

She waved a dismissive hand his way. "No, boy. I started back on days." Connie shuffled toward the colonial-style house he'd grown up in, talking the entire way about her lawn and the flowers she wanted to plant next year.

On his way to the house, he called to Mrs. Fulton, who was sitting on her porch knitting.

The elderly woman stood, hands on her hips. "Is that you, Drew?"

He stopped to talk to the former elementary school teacher. "Yes, it is, ma'am."

"Good to see you, boy. About time you came to see about your mama. She's too busy for her own damn good. I keep telling her to sit her tail down somewhere."

He chuckled. "I keep telling her the same thing. How are you?"

"I'm fair to middling," Mrs. Fulton said. "I'd be even better if someone could take a look at my thermostat. I think I messed around and pushed a wrong button or something."

Andrew knew a hint when he heard one. "I'll stop by and take a look."

"Oh, good. You're such a respectable man. Thank you."

Andrew managed to get away from Mrs. Fulton before she asked him to cut her grass, but *not* before she asked him to install the new kitchen blinds she'd recently purchased from the hardware store.

He hurried inside his mother's house. "Whoa, Mama. You've been busy."

Andrew's mother had mentioned hiring a contractor to do some home improvements, but he didn't expect the sleek, modern look that greeted him when he walked in. The old mint green walls were now gray. New leather furniture had replaced the worn brown couches he'd jump on with his brothers when his mom wasn't around. New cabinets and a granite countertop had been installed in the kitchen.

"You weren't playing around when you said you were ready for a refresh." He took a seat at the brand-new kitchen table. "Looks good in here."

"I'm in love with my new kitchen." She opened the refrigerator and pulled out two bottles of water. She joined him at the table. "Oh, and I retired yesterday. My last day is Friday."

He blinked. "What? Why didn't you tell me?"

Connie took a long gulp of water and shrugged. "I'm telling you now. They offered a buyout and I took it."

Andrew chuckled and squeezed her hand. "Once again, you never cease to amaze me."

His mother had sacrificed everything for him and his brothers. She was strong, determined, and genuine. She'd always walked with her head held high, even after his father had left her for one of the other workers at the automobile plant where they both worked. For years, his mother had to work alongside the man who had broken her heart and treated her like crap. But she'd never let anyone see her cry, never let his dad believe he'd gotten the best of her. And she'd instilled that same drive, that same determination in all of her sons.

Connie giggled. "I'm just me."

"You always say that." It was her favorite line when they were growing up. It was her excuse for everything from wearing huge pink rollers when she picked them up from school to doing silly dances in front of him and his friends at his birthday parties.

"It's true."

"Are you happy with your decision?"

Connie nodded. "Maybe. Kind of." She let out a heavy sigh. "I don't know. I'm just ready for something more. I've worked and now I'm ready to rest."

There was something about his mother's tone that didn't sit right with him. "And you're sure you're okay? I noticed that limp when you were walking."

"I'm fine. I broke my toe last week."

His mother was entirely too secretive for his liking. She seemed to make sport of hiding shit from him and his brothers. "And you just thought you'd keep that to yourself?"

"I told Connor," she explained. "And you better not try and lecture me like he did. I'm still your mother."

Connor was the oldest and self-proclaimed boss of everyone. She'd had his brother young, right out of high school. Andrew suspected his brother's arrival had influenced her decision to marry their father.

"And I'm not Connor," he tossed back. "No lectures from me, but I need you to understand how important it is to communicate with us. Since you insist on staying in Michigan, I need to know what's going on."

"I haven't reported my daily activities to any man

since your father, and I'm not going to start today." She snickered. "You're going to be waiting a long time on this *communication* you're talking about." She grumbled a curse. "I need you and your brothers to mind your own business."

He held out his hands in surrender. "Okay, Mom. I'm done."

"All three of you are too busy living your best life and not giving me any grandbabies," she muttered. "My friends keep showing me cute little grandbaby pics and stuff."

"Mama, come on now."

"I'm serious." She drummed her fingernails on the tabletop. "According to Connor, he's never getting married again. And Damon? He claims he's too busy for a wife and kids."

Andrew laughed. His younger brother had never denied he wasn't husband material. The financial analyst had moved to New York right after college, and had been singularly focused on work—and parties.

"You know you're not getting any younger," she said. "You're already in your forties. Don't mess around and have kids that you can't play with because you're too old to keep up with them."

Still cracking up, he said, "You're on a roll today."

Connie sighed. "Seriously." She slipped her hand into his. "I worry about you, all alone in California. At least Connor and Damon live near each other. They hang out a lot. You're by yourself. I have no idea what you do to stave off the loneliness."

"Mom, I'm not lonely." Which was mostly the truth. Andrew had always been content in his solitude. He never had a slew of friends like Connor, and he didn't date a lot of different women like Damon. He'd made a nice, quiet life for himself. If he found someone he wanted to marry, he'd do so. Until then. . .

His mom eyed him skeptically. "Are you sure?"

He offered her a smile. "I'm sure, Mama. Don't worry about me. And if you're so concerned about me being in L.A. by myself, you could always move closer."

Smacking his shoulder playfully, she said, "I'm not moving to no California. I'm happy right here where I am. I have my flowers, my new television, my friends, and my card nights." His mother had a standing card game every Friday night with her girlfriends. "I'm just fine."

"Well, the offer stands, whenever you're ready."

"What time is your meeting?" she asked.

He explained that his "meeting" was actually on the west side of the state, near Lake Michigan. He also told his mother that he'd be gone for a few days.

"Have time to eat lunch with me?" His mother stood and walked to the refrigerator. "I have your favorite."

Andrew glanced at his watch. He'd planned to get on the road within the hour, but he could never tell his mother no. And he could never turn down her food. So he agreed to stay for lunch. After he took care of Mrs. Fulton's blinds and checked her thermostat, he and his mother ate leftover lasagna and tossed salad, while they talked about all the things she wanted to do around the house in her free time.

"I have a request." She cut a big piece of lasagna and transferred it to a plastic container. She'd insisted he take some with him. "I want all of you home for Thanksgiving."

Andrew joined her at the kitchen sink and watched as she washed the few dishes inside. "Not Christmas?" They'd all made a point to return to Michigan for Christmas. It had been their tradition since they'd left home.

"Not this year. Me and the ladies decided to go on a trip

to Vegas." She smirked. "We thought it would be good to get away from the snow."

"Good plan." Andrew had grown up in Michigan, but he wouldn't move back there. He'd gotten used to the mild temperatures of Los Angeles. "It's not that far from me. Maybe I'll join you."

She frowned. "No. It's a ladies' trip."

"You just want freedom to go to the casino." He bumped her shoulder and she burst out in a fit of giggles. "You think you're slick."

Swatting him with a drying towel, she said, "Get out of here."

He took the container and kissed her cheek. "I love you, Mom. And if you want me here on Thanksgiving, I'll make it happen."

Connie beamed. "Thank you. Make sure you tell your brothers."

"I will."

"Are you stopping by before you leave the state?"

"I'll be sure to see you before I leave." He gave her another hug and waved at Mrs. Fulton before he took off.

Three hours later, Andrew turned down a private road. A mile up the street, he came upon the house. In all the years he'd lived in Michigan, he had never visited South Haven. But he'd done some research before he made the drive.

With a population of around five thousand people, South Haven was known for its beautiful beaches off of Lake Michigan, wineries, unique restaurants, and boutiques. As he'd driven through the city center, he almost felt like an intruder, like he didn't belong in the small town. But he'd come there for a reason and he wouldn't leave until he saw her.

He pulled into the driveway and parked outside of the garage. He stared at the sprawling lake house in front of him, before making his way up the stone steps to the large front porch. Knocking on the door, he waited. It took a few seconds, but he heard her unlock the door. Soon, he was staring into the eyes of the woman he couldn't stop thinking about.

Paige had on a pair of yoga pants and a tank. Her curls were pulled up in a high ponytail. *She's beautiful.* And safe.

The bright smile she'd donned when she opened the door turned to ice once she'd realized he was waiting for her on the other side. "Andrew," she whispered.

"Hi, Paige. Can I—?"

But before he could get his question out, Paige slammed the door in his face.

What the hell is he doing here?

Paige leaned her back against the front door and let out a harsh breath. She'd ordered groceries and had mistakenly assumed the delivery had arrived early. She'd also opened the door without even looking out of the glass like one of those naïve women in a horror flick. If there was a crazed lunatic on the loose, she'd be dead. Except, it wasn't a killer on the other side of the door. It was *him.*

"Go away!" she shouted. The windows were open, so she knew he heard her.

"Paige," he called through the door. "Please. Open the door."

"No."

"I came all the way here to see you."

Paige didn't dare turn around. If she looked at him, even through the glass, she would cave. If she met his brown gaze, she'd want to step into his comforting arms. And she couldn't do that right now.

After she'd found out about Julius's upcoming wedding to Catherine Davis, she'd made the decision to leave town. Partly because she didn't want to be the sorry, sad, jilted ex-wife in front of the entire world. Partly because she couldn't feel comfortable in her house anymore. But mostly because she was tired. She needed a change in scenery, she needed to unplug, she needed peace.

Retreating to the lake house had been exactly what she needed. She'd slept the first two days, then she'd moped for a few more. Paige had just started to feel her legs beneath her again, emerging from inside the other day to take a walk along the beach. Last night, she ventured into town for ice cream—in disguise, of course. This morning, she rode her bike along a public trail. No one had recognized her, and she'd been able to blend in. She had even chatted with some of the other riders. It felt good to talk to someone who didn't want anything from her.

"Drew, leave," she ordered. "I don't want you here."

"I'm not leaving until you talk to me."

Letting out a frustrated sigh, she walked over to the window. "What do you want?" Slow footsteps on the front porch signaled he was approaching the window. "How did you convince my mother to give you the address?"

Paige had made her mother promise not to tell anyone where she was, especially him. He'd obviously charmed her mother into giving up her location. To make matters worse, her mom hadn't even given Paige a heads-up on their call that morning. Shaking her head, she made a mental note to call her mother and let her know she was *not* happy.

"Paige, please."

Closing her eyes, she exhaled. It was the second time he'd said the word *please*, but *this* time it felt different. She heard the sincerity in his plea, imagined how he looked when he said it. Andrew had a good voice, deep and raspy. The low timbre coupled with her raging emotions did not make her confident she'd be able to resist him for long. The mere presence of him, the fact that he'd come to see her, made her want to let him in. Even if it was just to take in his scent. He always smelled like comfort and calm, like home. Which was why he needed to leave.

"Paige."

She jumped away from the window. Even though there was a wall between them, she felt him as if he was standing right in front of her. "Answer the question," she snapped, forcing the edge back into her voice.

"I asked her," he replied. "She didn't want to give me the address, but she did."

Paige huffed, folding her arms over her chest. "You worked her."

He chuckled. "You know your mother. When is the last time someone worked her?"

Staring at the ceiling, she sent up a prayer for patience. He was right. Her mother had been in the game for years and she didn't become Tina Mills, legendary R&B singer and actress, because she allowed people to charm her.

"Your phone is off," he said.

"There's a house phone here. The people who need to reach me have my number." That small group consisted of her mother and her attorneys. Paige had no idea why she'd explained herself, even a little bit.

"Can I come in? Can we talk?"

Paige slumped against the wall. Because, *Lord help me*, she wanted him to come in. She wanted to talk to him, hear from him. At the same time, he was part of her problem. He'd abandoned her when she'd needed him the most. He'd ignored her calls and sent someone else to handle her. The anger she'd felt at him a few days ago, or even an hour ago, sparked back to life.

"You know what?" she said. "I'm not doing this. No, you can't come in. We can't talk. Go. Away."

Paige walked away from the window, from him. He'd leave once he realized she was serious. He was a gentleman, and he always honored her wishes. She headed to the kitchen, straight to the bottle of wine on the countertop. After pouring herself a healthy glass, she took a long gulp. *Get it together, Paige.*

Briefly, she considered calling the police. But she wouldn't do that to him. He didn't deserve that. Picking up the cordless house phone, she stepped onto the patio off the kitchen. She sat down on a wicker chair. It wasn't her chaise lounge, but it would do for now.

Taking another sip of wine, Paige kicked her feet up and rested them on another chair. She dialed her mother. The stunning views of Lake Michigan centered her as she waited for her mom to pick up.

"Hey, babe," her mother said, in the same singsong voice she'd always had.

Growing with *the* Tina Mills had been quite the ride. While her friends were playing hopscotch or jump rope, Paige was traveling to London and Paris and sitting backstage while her mother wowed massive crowds. Instead of school recess and Girl Scouts, she'd watched recording sessions and put together puzzles.

"Hi, Mom. Are you busy?"

"Not at the moment. I do have to run in half an hour."

Tina told someone in the background to turn the music off and leave her alone. "What's going on?"

"Why did you tell Andrew where to find me?"

Silence.

"Mom?" Paige called.

More silence.

"Really, Mom. You're really doing this right now?"

Tina sighed. "Fine. I told him where you were because he asked."

Andrew had told her the same thing earlier. "But I specifically told you not to tell him."

"Well, babe, I figured you might need a friend. I don't like the idea of you up there all alone anyway."

Muttering a curse, Paige said, "You come here by yourself all the time." The house had been outfitted with a state-of-the-art security system. There were cameras everywhere. She could see every room in the house on an app that she'd downloaded to her iPad—an iPad that no one knew she had or else they would have been able to track it.

"Now, that's not exactly true," her mother insisted. "There's always someone with me."

"Fine, I'm not going to argue this point." Paige and her mother had argued often over the years. At times it felt like they were miles apart, physically and emotionally. Then there were times when Paige didn't know what she'd do without the woman who'd raised her to be independent, creative, and capable. "Just please don't tell anyone else where I am."

"Okay, I won't. Where is he now?"

"I told him to leave." Paige stood and paced the patio. By now, Andrew should be gone and she could go on with her life. "I don't want him here."

"Why, babe? He cares about you."

He has a funny way of showing it. "Whatever you say. I'm not convinced." A beep sounded, signaling she had another call. "Listen, I have to go. I'll talk to you soon."

"Call me if you need me."

Paige hung up from her mother and answered the second line. A young woman let her know she'd arrived with her groceries. She stepped back into the house and went to open the door.

"Thank you for coming so . . ." Paige yelped, nearly tripping on the welcome mat. Because the young woman wasn't alone. Andrew was standing next to her with a soft smile on his full lips. He waved at her. She tried to ignore him.

"I appreciate you," she told the young woman, handing her an additional tip.

"Thank you." The lady tilted her head, staring at her, almost like she recognized her. "Do I know you?"

"No." Paige grinned. "I'm new here." And thanks to her lawyer, she'd been using an alias since she'd arrived.

The other woman studied her. "You look so familiar."

Shrugging, Paige said, "People tell me that all the time. But I'm just a regular small-town girl."

"Okay." The lady seemed convinced. "Well, I'm pretty much the only person who delivers from the market." She handed Paige her card. "Call me if you need anything."

"Will do." Paige waved at the woman as she walked down the steps to her car. A few minutes later she was gone.

"Need help with those groceries?" Andrew asked.

Glaring at him, she grumbled, "You're still here."

"I told you I wasn't leaving until you talked to me."

"And I told you I didn't want to talk," she said through clenched teeth. Paige picked up two bags of groceries and set them right inside the door. Then she picked up another two, then another two.

He pointed at the bags. "See, I could've helped you with that."

"I don't need your help." She set the last bag inside. "I'd like for you to just go."

"Do you have a bottle of water?" he asked, as if she hadn't even spoken.

She snickered. "You know who has bottles of water? The store. In town. Why don't you go get one?"

Andrew cleared his throat, drawing her attention to him. She'd managed to pretty much avoid direct eye contact since she'd stepped outside, but now . . . he looked so large, so male. And he *did* smell good, like grapefruit and moss. Dressed in dark jeans and a long-sleeved shirt, he towered over her. His eyes were soft and focused on her. And she was . . . *Oh God*.

There was always something between them, more than an agent-client relationship, sometimes more than friends. But they'd never done anything about it.

"Paige?"

She blinked. "Bye, Andrew." She practically ran inside the house and slammed the door. Again.

Chapter Five

"He won't leave!" Paige whined, staring at the security camera feed of Andrew sitting quietly on her front porch.

"Really?" her mother said. "I knew he was a good one," she mumbled.

"What did you say, Mom?"

"Oh, I was just saying . . . he's a good friend. When did you tell him to leave?"

"Hours ago!"

In that time, he hadn't moved off the porch. He'd alternated between sitting down, stretching, and pacing the length of the porch. But he never walked away, not even to his car. She turned off the screen and walked toward the front of the house.

Peeking out the window, she sighed. "What am I going to do?"

"Let him in. You said it's been hours. He's probably going to pee his pants. Stop torturing the man already."

Paige considered what her mother said for a brief moment and immediately felt bad. He'd been sitting out there waiting to talk to her and she'd slammed the door in his face. Twice. What if he did have to use the restroom? What if he was really thirsty?

Turning away, she whispered, "I just need him to go." She stomped to the refrigerator and pulled out a bottle of water. "But he won't go. And it's your fault."

"How is it my fault for worrying about my only child? Paige, get it together, now. I don't think I've ever seen you this way."

"I have a lot of reasons to be this way, Mom." *A lot* of hurt, *a lot* of pain, *a lot* of mistakes, *a lot* of bad relationships. "I know you think he's good and all, but he's also part of the reason I'm here now."

"Fine, I get it. He acted a like a sorry-ass fool. But he's there now, he's trying to make it better."

Paige's stomach roiled as guilt took over, replacing the anger that had been simmering for so long. She grabbed an apple from the basket on the counter and sliced it. Next, she cubed a block of cheddar cheese. She set the cheese and the fruit on a plate.

"I have to go, Mom."

"Wait!"

"Bye, Mom."

"Paige Ann Mills, don't you hang up on me," her mother yelled. "Are you going to let him in?"

"Bye, Mom," Paige repeated. "Love you."

After hanging up, she took the plate to the front door. With a heavy sigh, she called out, "Andrew?" Seconds later, he was standing in front of the glass door. She opened the door and held out the plate and the bottle of water. "I figured you might be thirsty—and hungry."

He took the offered snack and water, and bit into one of the apple slices. "Granny Smith. My favorite."

Paige knew that. She'd grown up ignorant to the various types of apples. He'd turned her on to the many different options when it came to the fruit, and it had changed her world.

"There's a small bathroom behind the garage." She pulled a key out of her pocket and gave it to him. "Here."

He smiled. "Does this mean you're going to talk to me?"

"No." She backed away and shut the door again.

An hour later, Paige sat down to enjoy the beautiful spinach salad she'd made with the fresh produce she'd ordered from the market. She'd just poured her homemade Italian dressing on top when she heard a car door slam. *Maybe he's finally leaving?*

She stood and walked to the front of the house, just in time to see a pizza delivery guy step onto the porch. Andrew wasn't there anymore, though. Instead of the thrill of victory, she'd only felt the sting of defeat. He'd honored her wishes, yes. She should be happy about that. But it still felt like he'd deserted her again, given up without a fight.

For a few seconds, she stood there, torn between opening the door or not. The guy looked innocent enough, like a young school kid delivering pizzas for prom money. His blond hair fell just below his ear. The skater jacket, skinny jeans, and Vans were new, and he didn't strike her as the type who would watch a romantic comedy.

Paige had already made the mistake of opening the door to Andrew, though—without properly assessing the threat level. Luckily, it had been *him* and not a reporter or someone else. But . . .

Fuck it. Decision made, she pulled the door open and smiled. "I think you have the wrong address. I didn't order a pizza?"

The young guy's eyes widened. "You didn't?"

Shaking her head, she confirmed that she hadn't ordered anything to eat. "You have the wrong address."

The man set the pizza down on a chair and fumbled with his bag, shoving his hand inside and pulling a piece of paper out. He read her address aloud. "This is the address I have."

"But I didn't order a pizza," she insisted.

"I did." Andrew climbed the steps, wiping his hands with a paper towel. "I ordered the pizza."

Paige's mouth fell open. *What. The. Hell?*

"Thanks, man." Andrew handed the delivery guy several bills.

The young man grinned with wide eyes. "Wow! Thank *you*, sir!" He turned to her and waved. "Bye, ma'am."

Ma'am? Now, she felt "punked" *and* old.

Andrew opened the box of pizza and smirked. "Looks good."

Oh my God, it smells so good. But she wouldn't give him the satisfaction of telling him that. Instead she said, "What are you still doing here, Andrew? And why did you order a damn pizza?"

"I'm hungry," he said simply. "Figured I'd get something for dinner."

He held the open box out to her, but she didn't look inside. Pizza was not on her diet. She'd spent the last week eating a shitload of bad stuff. She needed to get back on her plan.

Glaring at him, she growled, "I told you to leave. Why are you doing this?"

"I told you. I'm not leaving until you talk to me." He bit into a slice. A slice of her *favorite* pizza.

The pizza looked like heaven smothered in cheese and sauce. The juicy tomatoes glistened, the chunks of feta cheese glimmered, and the thick pieces of chicken glowed like a beacon of bright light. The pizza called to her. The pizza wanted her to eat it. And the man eating it looked just as appetizing, with his smooth brown skin and his broad shoulders and his muscular arms and his long fingers.

Wait a minute . . . She shook her mind free from that wayward thought, because it had no place there. He was her agent. That's it, that's all. Yes, she used to count him among her small group of friends, but he wasn't even that anymore. Closing her eyes, she decided to try a different tactic.

"Look, thank you for coming to check on me. But I'm fine. If you want to help me, contact the studio and let them know that I need more time." She plastered a smile on her face. "Okay?"

Andrew narrowed his eyes on her as he chewed.

"Okay?" she repeated.

"Want a slice?" he asked, completely disregarding what she'd said. "It's good. It has—"

"I know what it has," she snapped, fighting the urge to stomp her feet. Or kick his shin. "I have a salad that I'm planning to eat for dinner. So, no, I don't want your pizza." *Or your smile, or your brown eyes, or your hugs.*

He grinned. "Sure?"

Damn him. "I'm so sure."

"Because I have enough to share," he said. "I know you love the Mediterranean-style pizza."

Every part of her wanted to invite him in, to enjoy the pizza she knew he'd purchased for her. But if she let him in to eat, she'd let him in for good. Because on July 23, 2005, he'd changed her life for the better, because sixteen years ago she'd met a man who had encouraged her to be herself, to take the roles she wanted, and to never settle for a part just to work. But mostly because his friendship, their connection, meant everything to her.

Paige was angry when she returned to her apartment after a particularly challenging audition. After countless hours memorizing her lines, she'd stumbled in front of the casting director. But that wasn't the worst part. When the director asked her to take her shirt off and show him her goods, she'd stalked off the set without another word. Maybe her mother was right? Maybe she needed a better agent? Maybe she needed her mother's help, after all?

Groaning, she took off the black slacks and silk blouse she'd worn to the studio and put on a pair of oversized sweats and a T-shirt. Tonight was about ice cream and reruns of A Different World.

Settling in on the couch, she turned on her favorite television show and tucked her feet into the cushions. Dwayne had just begged Whitley to take him back when her doorbell rang. Tossing her blanket off, she stomped to the door. "About time," she grumbled. The pizza delivery guy was late and she was starving.

She peeked through the peephole. A man stood outside, holding her dinner. Unlocking her door, she grinned. "Thanks!" She put a ten-dollar-bill in his hand and took the box from him. "Have a nice day."

Before she could close the door, he blocked it with his hand.

Frowning, she said, "What? I paid with my card."

"I'm not the deliveryman," he told her. "I just happened to get here when he did, so I took the pizza."

She stepped back. "Who are you?"

He held out his hand. "Andrew Weathers."

Paige stared at his hand, then back at him. And now that she'd gotten a good look, she could say beyond the shadow of a doubt that Andrew Weathers was super fine. Brown skin, brown eyes, strong physique.

A beautiful smile spread across the man's face when her gaze met his again. "Your mother sent me. I work for Jax Starks."

She blinked. "Oh." Her eyes fell to her attire. "Oh no. Um, come in." Paige gestured him inside and hastily straightened up her throw pillows and folded her blanket. "I'm sorry."

"It's not a problem," he assured her.

Pulling at her shirt, she said, "Have a seat." She remained standing, after he lowered his big body onto her small couch. "So, my mother sent you?"

"Yes, she thought I could help you. But we can talk about that after you eat your pizza." He smirked. "Smells good."

Paige couldn't help but smile. "It is good. My favorite. Want a piece?"

Andrew nodded. "Don't mind if I do."

Paige eyed the pizza and Andrew. After every successful audition, after every hard-won fight, they'd celebrated with pizza. Always her favorite, always together. What did they have to celebrate now?

Her stomach growled. *Pizza or salad?* Tomatoes on a bed of lettuce or tomatoes with mozzarella and dough— and garlic butter sauce? Eat alone or have dinner with him? Sighing, she let her hunger and her heart make the decision for her.

Without another word, she walked back into the house. Glancing at him over her shoulder, she said, "Come in."

Andrew followed Paige farther into the house. The lake house was large, but wasn't overwhelming. Windows offered stunning views of the lake. The furniture, decorative accents, and impressive woodwork filled out the space perfectly.

The kitchen was spacious, with white cabinets and a light granite countertop. He set the pizza box on the island and slid onto one of the barstools.

Paige opened the refrigerator door. Glancing back at him, she asked, "Want something to drink?"

Andrew told her he'd be good with another bottle of water. "The house is nice." He scanned the kitchen, noting the indoor-outdoor fireplace and the window seat near the patio door. He imagined her sitting there on cool evenings, maybe watching the sunset or daydreaming or reading a book.

"Thanks." She handed him a bottle of water and a plate.

Andrew took two slices from the box, set them on the dish, and slid it to her. She smiled softly and bit into a piece. His chest tightened when she let out a low moan. "Good, huh?"

She nodded, chewing her pizza happily and even doing a little dance. "So good."

Chuckling, he said, "I actually wasn't expecting it to be that good." He'd taken a chance with a local pizza parlor that had good reviews, and lucked up. "They had a cheesesteak pizza that looked good, too."

Her face lit up. "I know. I tried that one a few days ago. Delicious."

They ate in silence for a few minutes. He struggled to find the words to say, and he'd never been tongue-tied around her. But he didn't want to say anything that would disrupt the fragile peace between them. He took a moment to study her. Still stunning, beautiful from her bare feet to her wavy curls. But he couldn't help but notice the dark circles under her eyes and the way she stared off at some point behind him when she thought he wasn't looking.

"I've never been to South Haven," he confessed.

"Really? We used to come here in the summer. My father's family lives in town."

"Have you seen them since you've been here?" Andrew didn't know why he asked, because he was well aware of the tense relationship she had with her father and his family.

"Of course not. I thought about going up to my mother's house in Traverse City, but she's having it renovated right now. And I'm kind of in love with this house." She smiled wistfully, and pointed outside. "I mean, look at that view. Stunning."

Andrew couldn't tear his gaze away from the first genuine smile she'd blessed him with since he'd arrived. "Stunning is right," he whispered.

"My mother's brother had this house built last year. He was going to put it on the market, but I convinced him to let me lease it for a while. Who knows?" She shrugged. "I may buy it myself."

"Not a bad investment, and it would always be an escape for you when you need it."

"Yeah." Paige bit into another slice and moaned. "I can't believe how good this is."

Andrew laughed. She'd veered the conversation back to safe territory so he'd roll with it. "Right? I should have ordered a large."

"I know!" She giggled. "I'll probably eat more than I should."

"And that will be okay. How are you doing?" he asked.

"What are you doing here?" she tossed back, dropping her pizza crust on her plate.

The tension was back in her voice, her smile was gone. But he wouldn't let that stop him. "I needed to check on you," he said, his voice small to his own ears.

She raised a questioning brow. "Because of work?"

"Because I needed to see for myself that you're okay," he admitted.

Paige's beautiful brown eyes softened. "I'm okay. I just needed to get away."

"I heard about Julius."

She rolled her eyes. "I don't want to talk about him."

"Okay," he said. "We don't have to."

The room descended into silence. He wanted to ask her more, to beg her to talk to him. He missed her voice, her laugh, the way she danced when she was excited. The realization that she was more than a client, more than a friend, had been too much for him to admit. Even though the truth had been staring him in the face for a long time. But now that he was face-to-face with her, now that he could hear her breathing and smell her shampoo, he could no longer deny it.

"I don't love him anymore," she offered, in a voice so low, he almost missed it. Almost. "But, damn, he's an asshole. He took me through hell, prolonged the divorce only to sign the damn papers and get engaged to another woman. What the hell?"

"You said it right. He's a fuckin' asshole. He didn't deserve you."

Her gaze flew to his, stared at him, stared through him. Sighing, she said, "I guess work is calling."

The change in subject surprised him, but he nodded. "Yes. You have offers we haven't responded to. Appearances you didn't make."

"Can you handle it? Or tell Vonda to ask for more time? I can't go back right now, Drew. I'm in no shape to put on a happy face for reporters or directors. I just . . ." Averting her gaze, she picked at her nails. "I have so much on my mind right now. Work is the least of my problems."

"What else is going on?" He tilted his head, waiting for her to look at him again. "What is it?"

Paige stilled and she set her palms down flat on the countertop.

"You know you can tell me anything," he said. "What's on your mind?"

"You." Her gaze met his, but there was nothing soft in her eyes. No warmth shined back at him, only cold, hard fury. "And the way you deserted me."

Chapter Six

Time seemed to slow, while Andrew relived the past several months. Moments when he could have reached out to her but didn't. Phone calls that he should have returned, text messages he didn't respond to, time he didn't spend. He wished he could go back and make different decisions, so he wouldn't be in this position now—on the verge of losing one of the most important people in his life.

"Well?" Paige said, interrupting his thoughts.

He met her waiting gaze. "I . . ." *Shit*. He didn't have an excuse for hurting her. Well, not one that wouldn't make her angrier.

"And before you make up a sorry-ass excuse, I want to let you know that I have no problem kicking you out. Thanks for the pizza, but I can't be lied to again."

"You know I wouldn't lie to you."

She let out a bitter laugh. "I used to believe that."

Sighing heavily, he said, "I never have before, Paige. You know that."

"Whatever. Answer the question."

"I didn't desert you, Paige," he said. When she opened

her mouth to speak, he rushed on, "I needed to take a step back."

"I got that part, Drew. But I need to know why! We were friends. I deserve the truth."

Andrew got hung on the word *were*. As in past tense, no longer. "We *are* friends," he corrected.

"Then why did you disappear on me? If we're friends, why weren't you there?"

"Because I couldn't watch you with him!" he blared. Andrew dropped his head, scrubbing his hand over his face. The truth hurt. But it might heal. So, he forged ahead. "I couldn't sit there and watch you twist yourself into knots trying to be a good wife to that asshole."

"Andrew?"

He shot her a sidelong glance, noted the slight tremble in her chin. *He'd* done that. *He'd* hurt her. And the thought that *he'd* caused her pain made him feel like shit. "It was a struggle."

"A struggle for you. What about my struggle?" she asked. "You weren't married to him. You didn't live with him. You're not the one who had to go through a divorce in front of the world. You didn't have to watch your spouse disparage you on every media outlet. He tried to ruin my career, Andrew. Then he tried to take my house!" She tilted her head up, staring at the ceiling. "He tried to steal my soul."

Andrew stepped forward. "Paige, I—"

She held up a hand. "Don't. I don't want your comfort. I needed it a week ago, I needed it months ago. But you weren't there."

A lump formed in his throat, as shame rolled through him. He'd fucked up. Plain and simple. *Can I fix it?* "I didn't mean to make you feel abandoned." His voice cracked under the weight of his guilt.

"Make me feel abandoned? No, I didn't just *feel* abandoned, I *was* abandoned." She stalked outside, paced the patio in the back of the house.

Andrew followed her, making sure he stayed a distance away to give her space. Shoving his hands in his pockets, he said, "I thought I was doing the right thing."

She froze.

"That last time, during the meeting at Pure Talent?" He swallowed. "I wanted to hurt him."

Skye had arranged a sit-down with Julius to discuss their movie and the plan for announcing their separation. Things quickly went left and Andrew nearly pummeled Julius to the ground. He *would* have if Paige hadn't run out of the conference room, prompting him to run after her. But if he had stayed . . . *I might be in jail.*

"Every time I saw him, I wanted to choke him," he admitted softly. "The last thing you needed from me was *my* temper and *my* disgust. It would have messed everything up."

Paige turned to face him. "I hear what you're saying, but . . ."

A rumble of thunder cracked the sky. Andrew looked out over the water and noticed the wall of clouds building in the distance. He'd read there might be a storm, but hadn't paid the weatherman any mind. Especially since they'd forecasted storms for the last few days that had never happened.

She turned to watch the lake as well, and he inched closer to her. "Storm's coming," she whispered. "It looks like a bad one."

"It does," he agreed.

"I need to close the windows." Without another word, she left him standing on the porch.

Andrew waited there, turning over the conversation in his head again and again. The first drop of rain fell about ten minutes later, and he ventured back into the house.

Paige breezed past him toward the sunroom. Several minutes later, she walked by him again. The third time, he gently grabbed her arm to stop her retreat from him. Because he didn't want to watch her walk away from him again.

"Are we going to finish this?" he asked.

She wrenched her arm from his grasp. "We're done."

"We're not done."

"Andrew"—she blew out a hard breath—"I don't have it in me to have this conversation. I heard what you said. I'm done."

"So that's it?"

"Yes." She smacked her hands against her thighs. "Thank you for explaining, but it's not good enough."

"You asked for the truth." He inched forward. She retreated backward. "I told you the truth. I gave you my reasons for stepping back. In hindsight, I can agree it wasn't the best decision. But I did it for the right reasons."

Except he'd yet to disclose the rest. It was one thing to distance himself from her for noble reasons. If that had been all it was, it might have been easier to explain at the time. But there was more . . . More reasons, more confusion, more of everything.

Andrew couldn't stand to watch Paige with Julius because he wanted Paige to be with *him*. It wasn't a new feeling. It wasn't something that had just snuck up on him. It had been building for years, through shared experiences and quality time, through victories and trials. It had been all-encompassing and unconditional. It covered everything, faults and all. And it had scared the hell out of him, because he shouldn't have felt anything even close to that for her. He'd been trusted to handle her career, to guide her. What had blossomed between them wasn't supposed to be part of the plan. But it had happened. And he couldn't tell her. Not now. Not like this.

"Your reasons suck," she told him. "You basically confessed to leaving me in the lurch because you couldn't control your temper."

When she said it like that, it did make him sound like a selfish asshole. "That's not . . ." *True* died on his lips, because that's exactly what his explanation sounded like.

"Just stop." She shook her hands in frustration. "If that's your reason, fine. But I'm not about to keep letting people hurt me time and time again." She rose her chin and squared her shoulders. "I'm not that woman anymore. I'm not going to *be* that woman ever again—for any man, not even for you. So thanks for coming to check on me, but I'm good."

Another roll of thunder pierced the air and the sky lit up as lightning flashed in the distance. Rain fell, hard against the house.

"I better go," he said, after a moment of silence. "I should probably hit the road back to Detroit."

"Don't do that," she said. "I have plenty of rooms here. You can stay tonight, but you need to leave in the morning." Paige asked him to follow her, and he did as he was told. She led him up the stairs to a spare bedroom. Andrew looked around the room. The queen-size bed took up most of the room, but there was a television, a bedside table, and a large window. She pointed to the en-suite bathroom.

"Everything you need is there. Towels, soap, and an extra toothbrush."

"I have those things in my car," he told her. They both stared at the bed for a long minute. He'd never been in a "bedroom" with her before. "I should go get my bag out of my car."

She nodded. "Okay. Sounds like a plan. I'll grab the sheets out of the dryer." She hurried out of the room.

Andrew ran out to his car and pulled his bag out of the trunk. By the time he made it back up the house, he was drenched. Shaking himself off, he cursed the erratic and unpredictable Michigan weather. Once he entered the house, he kicked his shoes off and made his way up the stairs. The spare room was empty, so he peeled his wet shirt off.

A throat cleared behind him, and he froze. Turning slowly, he smiled. "Um . . ." He scratched his temple. "It's coming down pretty hard out there," he offered lamely.

Paige stepped forward, pausing in the doorway for a moment before she entered the room. Her gaze dropped from his face to his chest. "Yes," she said, her voice slightly shaky. "I turned on the news. Supposed to get worse."

"I'm not surprised."

"Here." Paige handed him the sheets, jerking away from him when their hands touched. "I'll be right back."

"Thanks." He stared at the doorway for a while after she'd left. It was an innocent touch, just a slight brush of skin, but it felt like more. Because that one touch had lit his body up like a live wire, awakening something in him that had been dormant for quite some time.

"Andrew?"

He blinked, surprised that she'd snuck up on him without him realizing it. That wasn't like him. "Yes."

Paige threw the comforter in her hand at him, then

disappeared around the corner again. Sighing, he dropped the heavy blanket on the bed. He opened his bag and pulled a clean shirt out. Then, he felt something soft hit the back of his head. Glancing down, he noticed a pillow on the floor.

"Good night," she grumbled.

Seconds later, he heard the slam of another door and smiled to himself. Andrew was happy she hadn't lost her spunk, that she was taking control of her life. He wanted to honor her wishes. But if he walked away now, it would confirm everything she thought about him. In that moment, he realized what his next steps should be. Paige needed to know the full truth. Then he needed to prove to her that he wasn't like everyone else.

Paige glanced back at Andrew when he entered the kitchen the following day. She allowed herself a quick perusal of his strong, lean frame before turning back to the task at hand. *Coffee*.

"Good morning," he said.

"Morning." She watched the coffee machine with interest. She'd had a fitful night's sleep, filled with dreams of Julius and paparazzi and the most beautiful eyes she'd ever peered into. The same eyes that were boring into her now. She didn't have to turn to know that Andrew was watching her. He'd always paid close attention to her. "Coffee?"

Footsteps neared her and she prayed he stayed a healthy distance away. She'd heard him showering that morning, and had to smack her own hand for imagining the water streaming down his strong back. Seeing him shirtless had been enough to kick-start fantasies that she'd tamped down over the years.

"Sure." His low voice settled in her gut and inched down to her core.

After last night, after he'd admitted that he had purposely avoided her all those months, she wasn't sure there was anything left to say to him. Choosing to ignore the warring emotions inside her, she made his cup in silence, adding a dash of hazelnut creamer to it, no sugar. Just how he liked it. She set it in front of him.

Andrew took a sip of the brew and groaned. That groan bypassed her gut and went straight to her core. *What the hell is wrong with me?* It wasn't like she'd spent an obsessive amount of time wanting him. Of course, there had been many times when she'd thought . . . *what if?* For the most part, they'd lived full lives, together yet apart. She'd met his snooty girlfriends and he'd golfed with her past boyfriends. *Why is his presence so unnerving now?*

"Good," he told her. "You always did have a way with coffee."

Paige cursed her rapidly lowering armor. "Thanks."

Her mother had thought of everything coffee-related when she'd sent a care package ahead of Paige's arrival. Although her uncle left a Keurig, her mother had included a French press along with an assortment of the best dark roast coffee, several mugs, cute stirring spoons, and a variety of creamers. Paige considered herself a coffee connoisseur. Her mood determined which type of coffee she drank every day. Whether it was cold brew or hot, Colombian or Jamaica Blue Mountain, lattes or macchiatos, there was always time for coffee.

"I can't wait to try out the French press," she added.

He smirked. "I remember when you bought your first one."

Paige dropped her gaze, unable to stop the smile that formed across her lips. "That was so awful."

When Paige had purchased her first house, one of the things she'd chosen to buy was a super-expensive French press. And she'd tried it out on Andrew. Unfortunately, she didn't really know what she was doing and made several mistakes in her quest to master it.

The first batch, she'd made the water too hot. On her second try, she'd brewed it too long. The coffee was so bitter she'd spit it out—on his shoes. It took a bit more trial and error before she'd made the perfect cup. And Andrew was right there the entire time.

"Maybe the first couple of times," he agreed. "But you didn't give up until you made a damn good cup of coffee."

Paige met his gaze again. "Drew, I—"

"I have to—"

They both laughed, and he gestured for her to go ahead.

"No, you go," she said.

"I'm sorry, Paige."

She gripped her throat. "What?" she whispered.

He cleared his throat, pinned her with those eyes. So intense, so sincere. "I'm so sorry."

Those three words latched on to her heart. She took a deep breath to steady her nerves, to slow her heartbeat. "For what?"

"For hurting you. I never meant to hurt you, Paige. I never wanted to be the man who made you feel like you didn't matter."

Tears spilled from her eyes. Because he got it. He *did* understand why she felt the way she did.

"I thought about it all night," he continued. "I thought

about everything I could have done differently. You know me. I rarely second-guess myself, but I am now. I did abandon you. I told myself that it was for the best, but I know now that it wasn't the best for you. My decision to push you away, to step back, had more to do with my feelings and nothing to do with you."

Paige held her breath. *His feelings?* She wanted to ask him why, she wanted him to tell her more, but she was scared. Scared of the unknown, scared of the known. Her pulse raced, her stomach . . . She pressed a hand against her belly, hoping to calm the wild flutters.

"Andrew."

"Let me finish," he said. "I'm your agent, but I'm also your friend."

That word *friend* hit Paige differently in that moment. He was her friend, but he wasn't *just* her friend. And it felt like a letdown, as irrational as it sounded. Paige averted her gaze, tried to gather her thoughts.

A sincere apology *should* have made her feel better. Yet, for some reason, it didn't feel like enough—or even what she really needed from him. In the past, Paige never had a problem expressing herself with Andrew or sharing her truth. But now? Opening herself up would make her vulnerable to him. And she didn't want to give anyone that much power over her again.

"I'm trying to leave." He blew out a slow breath and inched toward her. "I want to honor your wishes, but I can't. I need you to forgive me."

Well, damn. Andrew didn't come to play today. And . . . *when did he get so close*? Paige peered up at him, searching his eyes. She couldn't figure out what she read in them, but it seemed a lot more complicated than an apology. *Oh, he smells good.*

Andrew brushed a strand of hair from her forehead. The simple, yet lingering touch was so gentle she wanted to lean into it. It also set off a surge of sensations inside her—some recognizable, others dangerous.

"I can't think or even imagine walking away knowing that you might hate me," he whispered.

She shuddered as his words washed over her. The pained expression on his face made her heart ache for him. Even though he'd hurt her, she could never hate him. She cared about him too much. And she wanted to take the road that led back to peace between them.

"I don't hate you," she breathed. She was pretty sure she felt the opposite of hate for the man in front of her.

"You don't like me," he amended.

"You're right. I don't like you right now." She laughed when his eyes widened. She shoved him playfully. "I'm kidding."

Andrew let out a tense laugh. "I'm glad to hear that."

"Well, kind of," she added with a wide grin. "It was iffy for a while."

"I could tell."

Before she could respond, he pulled her into his arms. *Oh shit.* It wasn't the first time they'd hugged, but it felt like it. And she couldn't help but let herself relax into him. For a moment, she forgot about everything else. The only thing that mattered was how it felt to be in his arms, how it felt to be held so close. Because right now, she felt an abundance of peace, she felt comfortable, and she also felt . . . *hot.*

Oh God. Needing some distance, Paige eased out of his arms and backed away—all the way to the other side of the island. "Are you hungry?" He moved toward her, and she stepped out of reach . "I could make some breakfast—to go with the coffee."

Andrew laughed, flashing the dimple on his right cheek that she loved. "Why do I think you're running away from me?"

"I'm not," she lied. "I'm just hungry."

He scratched his jaw. "Okay."

Paige dodged him again, walked the long way to the fridge, and pulled out eggs. "I can make something simple." She slid him a sidelong glance and found him watching her intently. Turning back to the refrigerator, she blew that same errant strand of hair from her face. "Oh shoot. I forgot to order bacon."

"It's fine."

"I do have turkey ham?" She pulled the package from one of the drawers and held it out to him. "I can make you an omelet. I didn't buy enough cheese," she muttered to herself.

"You don't have to cook for me."

Paige faced him then and smiled. "It's nothing. Really. Plus, I'm hungry, too."

"If you say so." He tapped the countertop while she pulled several slices of ham from the package and set it on a cutting board. "I have a confession to make."

Her eyes flashed to his. "Oh no." They'd often broached uncomfortable conversations in the past by stating they had a confession. She hoped whatever it was wouldn't derail the progress they'd made. "What is it?"

"I thought I would be on my way back to Detroit."

A surge of relief flooded her and she laughed. "Well, the day is still early." She winked. "You may still have to hit the road soon. Especially if you don't like this omelet."

"I love your cooking," he admitted softly.

She waved a dismissive hand at him. "Whatever. But to address your confession, I'm glad you're not on your way back. I missed hanging out with you."

"Me too. Okay, so it's your turn."

Paige's confession lodged in her throat. She definitely couldn't tell him that she wanted to kiss him, that she wondered what his lips would feel like against hers. She wouldn't admit that she'd dreamed about him.

"I confess . . ." She hummed, trying to come up with something that wasn't so serious. "I'm sorry I threw the comforter at you last night."

Andrew barked out a laugh. "You did catch me off guard with that move."

"That's the point." *That* and the fact that she had to cover up his bare chest by any means necessary. "But I'm not sorry about the pillow. You deserved that."

They both cracked up. Half an hour later, they sat down for breakfast. They conversed about the latest binge-worthy shows, and the last political debate. She teased him about his refusal to give up on his Detroit Pistons. He didn't bring up Julius or work, which was exactly what she needed. For the first time in months, she felt grounded, she felt hope—hope that the past was behind them. And a small part of her hoped this might be the start to something better.

Chapter Seven

"I have a confession. A real one." Paige turned her head and glanced at Andrew. He'd decided to stay after their earlier conversation. They didn't do anything in particular, just spent time catching up. Now they were seated in front of a fire pit, roasting marshmallows, drinking wine, and staring at the water.

Andrew rotated the stick holding two marshmallows slowly. "What is it?"

"I think Julius married me to help his image." It was the first time she'd said it out loud to anyone. She'd thought it for a while, but it hurt too much to verbalize it.

Meeting her gaze, he asked, "Why do you say that?"

Leaning her head back against her chair, she said, "I just can't reconcile his behavior with the man that pursued me, followed me around, purchased extravagant gifts for me." She shrugged. "What other reason could it be? I mean, he obviously has feelings for Catherine. They have a child together."

He took his stick from the fire and handed it to her. "That doesn't mean he has feelings for her." He added two more marshmallows to another stick and started the roasting process again.

"Marrying me doesn't mean he loved me."

In hindsight, she could clearly see she'd married a narcissist. Julius was entitled. He didn't have any boundaries. There were times when he seemed to genuinely care about people, but he lacked true empathy. On the other hand, he could charm the pants off a person. Which was why he'd been able to have the career he had.

"He was so manipulative," she said into the night air. "And he could be so cruel."

Andrew turned cold, hard eyes on her. "Did he hurt you?" he growled.

"No." She shuddered as Julius's harsh words replayed in her head. "He never touched me physically. But the way he acted during the divorce process . . . The things he said . . . Why did I marry him?"

His gaze softened, but she couldn't figure out if she read hurt for her in them, or hurt for himself. Maybe it was both? *Is it wrong to hope it's both?* "You loved him." He averted his gaze. "You wanted your marriage to work."

"That's part of it," she agreed. "But the signs were there all along. The insults buried in praise, the way he'd always turn things around to make it my fault, the constant criticism. Those were things he always did. So why was I with him?"

Andrew took a drink from his wineglass. Convincing him to try the merlot was quite the feat. He was a beer guy, through and through. "You can't get caught up in the whys," he said, rotating the stick. "You have to focus on what you're doing now to fix it."

She sipped from her glass, admiring his patient technique. He was as careful and methodical at roasting marshmallows as he was with everything in his life. "You're pretty intense with marshmallows," she pointed out.

A small smirk played over his lips. "Marshmallows are nothing to play about, Paige." He nodded toward her stick. "Better eat those before they get too cold."

Paige eyed him for a moment before stuffing one whole marshmallow in her mouth.

Andrew laughed, and it sounded like a song—a sonnet. "I don't think I've ever seen you stuff anything in your mouth."

Giggling, she pulled the other one off the stick and ate it in one bite. "It's so good, though." She licked remnants of the treat off her finger. "See, you're a bad influence on me. Got me out here being greedy."

He gazed at her mouth, his eyes soft.

Paige swallowed. "What? Do I have something on my mouth?" She wiped her lips with the back of her blanket. "Tell me. Don't have me out here looking crazy."

"Actually, you look good in marshmallow lipstick."

Paige grinned. "And your marshmallow is on fire."

"Shit." Andrew lifted his stick and blew on the marshmallow. "Oh wait, this is salvageable." Eyeing him skeptically, she watched as he gently peeled off the skin. Once he was finished, he held it up. "See. I can re-roast this one." He turned his attention back to the fire and she turned her attention back to him.

When he was done, he took his marshmallows and squished them between the chocolate and graham crackers he'd prepared earlier. He took a big bite.

Nodding, he pointed at his s'more. "This is the bomb."

Paige didn't think she could stop smiling if she tried. She didn't want to, because he looked so damn hot doing simple things, like eating s'mores. "Now I'm jealous," she told him. "I want one."

"Want a bite?" He held the rest of his treat out to her.

"Nope, I'm doing good. Only marshmallows. No graham crackers. And definitely no chocolate."

"I don't know." He shrugged. "You're missing out."

Paige's glance flitted between his eyes, the teasing smile on his lips, and the gooey s'more in his hand. Grumbling a curse, she snatched it from him and bit into it. "Oh my God," she said around a mouthful of deliciousness. "I think you missed your calling."

Chuckling, he said, "Nah, I just happen to have a mother who liked to camp with us when we were kids."

She wiped her lips. "And here I thought you were a scout or something."

Andrew snickered. "Hell no. One month in Troop 838 was enough for me to know that wasn't my thing."

He leaned over, brushing his thumb over her bottom lip and stealing her breath in the process. Stunned silent, Paige traced the same spot with her fingers, as he went on about the business of marshmallow roasting. Basically, he'd seared her with one simple touch, igniting a fire in her as hot as the fire in front of them.

"Want another s'more?" he asked, pulling her from her thoughts. "Or just plain."

"Plain," she croaked, licking her bottom lip. "Extra golden."

He smiled. "You got it."

Leaning back against her chair, she stared at the water. "You're always like this," she said, on a sigh.

He chuckled. "Like what?"

"Calm, steady, logical. You never really lose your temper or even raise your voice."

"I did yesterday."

Paige smiled. "It was a tense situation."

"That's a way to look at it." He sucked in a deep breath, and handed her the stick.

Pulling a piece of her marshmallow from the stick, she said, "How do you look at it?"

Andrew closed the bag of marshmallows and relaxed into his chair. "Tense, but preventable."

Paige raised a brow. "If you'd not acted the way you did?"

"Mostly that."

She ate her marshmallow and picked up her glass of wine. Tucking her feet under her butt, she shot him a side-long glance, only to find him watching her. "What?"

"Nothing."

They locked gazes again. "Your turn," she said.

Frowning, he asked, "My turn to what?"

"I made a confession, now it's your turn."

With a sigh, he peered up at the clear sky. "Hm . . . Remember when you wore that floor-length pink gown to the Image Awards?"

"Yes." Paige had been nominated for Best Actress in a Motion Picture that year. And she'd agreed to support an up-and-coming designer by wearing one of her creations on the red carpet. Of course, she hated the dress when she'd seen it. But Andrew had convinced her she looked beautiful. "I definitely remember that dress. Why?"

"That dress was horrible," he admitted.

Paige gaped at him. "What?" She swatted him. "You told me it was beautiful."

"*You* were beautiful," he said, rubbing his jaw. "But that dress . . . awful."

"I knew it!" She laughed. "You are so wrong for not telling me the truth."

"Hey, you needed to get out of the car."

Narrowing her eyes, she said, "You know I'm never going to believe you when you tell me I look good, right?"

"That was the one and only time I've lied about how you look."

"Yeah." She sent him a mock glare. "I don't believe you."

He barked out a laugh, lifting up his hands. "I swear."

"Tell me anything."

"Okay. You look way better in sweats and that marshmallow lipstick you're wearing than you did in that dress."

Sitting up straight, she wiped her mouth. "Oh my God. You suck for letting me sit here with food on my mouth." She tossed her lap blanket at him. "Ugh."

"You love throwing blankets at me, huh?"

Paige tried to pull it back to her. They played tug-of-war for a moment before he finally let it go. She huffed, wiping her lips again just to be sure.

"It's all gone now," he said.

"Really?"

"Really," he repeated. "Look at me."

Paige finally glanced over at him. Raising a brow, she asked, "Yes?"

He held out his hand. "I'll never lie to you again."

It was a simple promise, yet it seemed so loaded. It made her want to ask him more questions just to see if he'd tell her the truth. She wanted to know why he looked at her like she was the answer to his prayers. *Why do I love it when he does that?*

"I'll hold you to it." She slipped her palm into his, entwining their fingers. "No lies."

The lingering stare that followed made Paige comfortable and uncomfortable at the same time. Because she still had so many concerns, so many reservations. Because she sensed that something had changed between them tonight. Hell, things had been changing since he'd arrived on her porch yesterday. And, *God help me*, she was both scared and excited to see where the changes could lead.

Andrew had spent a lot of money and time on education. Valedictorian, dean's list, magna cum laude were only a sampling of the honors he'd received in his pursuit of success. He'd prided himself on maintaining his composure in any and every circumstance. There wasn't much that rendered him incapable of making good decisions. But now? Today he only knew two things: Paige had a smile that took his breath away and Paige in sexy black lace panties might kill him.

He stood at the base of the steps, transfixed by the sight in front of him. The music blasted through surround sound speakers as his client—because, yes, she was *still* his client—danced in the kitchen. As The Notorious B.I.G. rapped about dreams and *Word Up!* magazine, Andrew wondered if he would dream about the woman reciting the famous lyrics tonight—and every night.

Andrew wanted to stop her, to get her attention so she knew he was back from his store run, but he couldn't bring himself to speak up. Because she looked so good. Instead of the messy bun she'd been rocking since he'd been there, her hair was wet and falling down her back like ebony waterfalls. Aside from the black panties, she wore a black tank and pink fuzzy socks. Oblivious to his presence, Paige did a cute little dip and a hip roll as she stirred her coffee. *Fuck. Me.*

Blinking, he shook himself out of his naughty musings. He wasn't a voyeur . . . normally. And he definitely wasn't a Peeping Tom or a creep. One thing he was, though? Hard as hell. *Shit.*

Andrew covered his erection with his hat and opened his mouth to speak. "Paige?"

Of course, she didn't hear him. Instead, she launched into the chorus of the song. Loudly. And a lot off-key.

"Paige?" he called again.

"You know—" She turned and yelped, stumbling back into the sink. "Ouch." Paige jumped forward, rubbing her back. "Oh my God! When did you get here?"

Andrew looked at the stove, the corny painting of a sailboat, and the white trim on the walls . . . Anything but her and her ass and those damn panties. "Um, I just got here."

She held her hand over her chest and blew out a deep breath. "You scared the shit out of me."

Turning his back on her, he said, "Sorry." *One. Two. Three. Four.*

"Drew?" He heard her approach him. "Are you okay?"

"I'm fine," he lied. After he'd told her he'd never lie to her again. *Good fuckin' job, Drew.*

She walked in front of him and peered up at him, a frown on her face. And he held on to his hat for dear life. "You said you'd never lie to me again."

Shit. "Paige, it's not a lie." Except, it was and he'd just done it again. "I'm good." *That part is true.* He was good. Good and hard. "You just shocked me."

"Why?" she asked incredulously. "What did I do?"

"Your rap skills." He nodded. "I didn't know you knew all the words to the song." *Okay, that's true, too.* Paige was more of a neo-soul, R&B woman. Hip-hop wasn't usually on her playlist. "And I didn't expect you to be rapping that song in your underwear."

He glanced down at her then, just in time to see her drop her head and then peer up at him again. "Oh, this. You've seen me in my underwear before."

Of course he had. She was an actress. He'd seen all of her movies and most of her television work. He'd even seen the Broadway play she'd starred in a few years ago. He'd also seen her without her underwear. Not that she did a lot of nude scenes, because she didn't. But she'd had to disrobe for a sex scene once. Even then he'd always tried to focus on anything else.

"I have," he agreed, giving her a tight smile. "I just didn't expect to today."

"Oh well. I'll get dressed." She patted him on his shoulder and sauntered over to the stairs, giving him a full view of her beautiful butt. *That ass, though* . . . "Oh." She froze, turning to him. "I thought it would be fun to watch a movie tonight."

"Okay," he grunted. "We can do that later."

"I'll make popcorn." She waggled her eyebrows. "Without butter."

He drew in a deep breath. "Good."

She tapped her chin. "Horror or rom-com?"

"Horror."

Paige rolled her eyes. "Fine. But you know I'm a screamer."

Shit. As if he needed another vision in his head—him on top of her, him inside her—while she was screaming his name.

She stared at him, a coy smile on her lips. Almost like she knew what he was thinking. "Okay, I'm done. I'm going to get dressed."

"Please do," he murmured. Paige cracked up. And he wanted to cry. *I'm dying.* "The milk you wanted is on the counter," he told her. "I have a few calls to make."

"Fine, I'm going."

Paige walked up the stairs, humming another hip-hop tune, and he slumped against the wall. Suddenly, watching a movie with her in the dark felt like a trap, one that he wouldn't mind walking into.

Later, they sat at the table in the sunroom, a board of Scrabble between them. After she'd walked downstairs with her hair still hanging loose, a ripped T-shirt and a pair of sweats—looking every bit as sexy as she did in panties and a tank—he suggested the game. No sitting next to each other on a comfortable couch, no sharing popcorn, no bur-rowing into him during the scary parts of the movie. And best of all, they were in a well-lit room. No sense in tempt-ing fate right now.

Andrew made a show of looking at his watch. "Um, you can make your move any day." It had been at least a minute since he'd played his last word and she still hadn't formed a word.

"Shut up," she grumbled, moving her tiles around. "Don't rush me."

"You can always pass," he teased. "I won't think any less of you."

Muttering a curse, she passed. "Don't think I'm giving up."

Grinning, Andrew swiveled the board around and placed two tiles on the board. "I would never think that."

Frowning, Paige peered at the board. "Wait a minute!" She smacked her palms down on the table. "That is not a word. You're cheating."

"How am I cheating?"

"AA is not a word!" She pouted.

Andrew barked out a laugh. "It is."

Paige pointed at him. "Stop lying."

He picked up his phone and googled the word. Then he showed it to her. "See?"

Leaning forward, she read the screen. When she was done, she pushed his hand away. "Get on my nerves," she grumbled.

Andrew's phone buzzed on the table. He glanced at the screen, noticed it was Skye, and turned it off.

"You're not going to get that?" she asked, her eyes still on the board.

"No, they can wait."

She lifted her eyes, held his gaze. "What if it's important?"

"It's not," he insisted. Skye had been calling him all day, and he'd yet to answer the phone because he wasn't ready to bring work into the little peace they'd found there. Andrew knew the publicist would want to talk about Paige, and he felt it was best to table any discussions about Paige's career for the moment.

Arching a brow, she said, "Really? I've heard your phone ring multiple times just in the last hour."

Sighing heavily, he shrugged. "Like I said, they can wait."

"It's about me, isn't it?"

Andrew didn't want to give her another vague answer, so he just answered the question. "Yes, it was Skye."

"Skye? What does she want?"

He took a sip of his beer. "She's concerned about you."

Paige perched her chin on her hands. "Why?"

"Because you disappeared. She's your publicist—and your friend. She wants to know if I found you, and if you're okay."

Tilting her head, she observed him for a moment. Finally, she sat back and rested her hands on the table. "You can tell her I'm okay."

Andrew nodded. "Okay."

"So, I'm putting two and two together."

Oh boy. He knew exactly what she was thinking, so he said, "Skye came to me and told me you left."

Paige finished her glass of wine and poured another. "Exactly what I thought."

"Let's not do this."

"Do what?" she snapped. "Talk about how you wouldn't have known I was gone unless Skye told you?"

Andrew opened his mouth to speak, then closed it. She was right. He would have known eventually, but it could have been a while. Especially since he'd started letting Vonda handle the day-to-day.

"I guess I shouldn't be hurt, but I am," she admitted. "You came here because she told you to. Not because you missed me or you cared about why I left."

He placed his hand atop hers and squeezed. "Paige, that's not true. I care."

"Just when I start to feel comfortable, just when I start to believe that I'm more to you than a client, something like this happens."

Andrew blew out a harsh breath. "I get why you would feel that way, but that's not why I'm here. If it was just about the job, I could have told Skye where you were. I didn't have to come here myself." Her shoulders fell, and he rushed on. "Yes, Skye lit a fire under my ass. Yes, I was wrong as hell for how I treated you. But no, you're not just my client. I thought we already established that."

She tucked a strand of hair behind her ear. "If we're going to be honest, I'll admit that I've been wondering when you would bring up work."

"I didn't bring up work. You asked."

"True. But you're my agent. My work affects your bottom line. It benefits you for me to do my job."

"Don't do that." Andrew wanted to move forward, but if she really felt that way, he didn't see how they'd be able to.

"I'm sorry." She tugged at her ear. "That was under the belt."

"Thank you." They sat in silence for a long moment. "Listen, I'm here because I care about you. I'm here because I want to be here—with you."

"I want to believe you, but—"

"Then believe me."

Paige hugged herself. "It's just that . . . I've been so wrong about a lot of people."

"One person," he argued.

"A lot of people," she corrected. "I want to move past it, especially with you. Because I'm glad you're here. I'm happy we talked. I don't want to burst this bubble we've created here."

"You didn't."

"If it seems like I'm a bit suspicious, I hope you understand why."

Andrew knew exactly why she'd reacted the way she did. He didn't fault her for it. He just wanted to assure her that he was there for her—not for work. "I do," he said.

"Good," she said. "And . . . I'll think about contacting Skye myself."

"That's your decision. Call her when you're ready." He

leaned forward and brushed his fingers over her furrowed brows. "And stop frowning. You always tell me worry lines are forever."

A smile spread across her full lips. "I can't with you."

"You know what I think?"

"What?" she asked, confusion etched on her face.

"I think you are so upset that I'm kicking your butt at this game that you had to distract me with an argument so that we could stop playing," he joked.

Paige's mouth fell open. Then she laughed. And it was like music to his ears, because they'd weathered another tense moment together.

"Drew, really?" She shook her head. "I should throw this 'L' at you." She held up a letter.

"What is it with you and throwing shit at me?"

She slammed the tile on the table. "You deserve it."

"Maybe, but it's your turn. Go ahead and play that 'L' so I can win the game." He raised a challenging brow. "Unless you're scared. You can always resign."

Paige scrunched her nose, staring at her tiles in concentration. As he watched her deliberate over her next move, he realized that it didn't matter if they were in the dark, in the light, walking down the street, or even in different houses. The woman in front of him was breathtaking, beautiful in every situation. Even when she was angry at him. And he wasn't sure he'd be able to resist letting her know just how much she affected him.

Chapter Eight

Three days ago, Andrew had a plan—to talk to Paige, convince her to go back to work, and go home. But he was still in South Haven with no idea when he would leave. *Or if I want to leave.*

In his line of work, he was paid well to anticipate things that could derail plans. Which was why he often had contingency and fallback plans—and potential workarounds to deal with unexpected issues that his backup plans didn't cover effectively. Most of the time, things worked out like he wanted. Then there were other times, like today, when he couldn't believe his current predicament.

"That looks so good." Paige pointed at a spot on the tree they were standing beneath. "I want it."

Andrew reached above her head and pulled the plump apple from the tree, then dropped it in their basket. Early that morning, Paige had announced she wanted apple pie. So they'd googled the closest orchard and headed out to pick apples. So far, they grabbed two different types—McIntosh and Honeycrisp.

"Hm." Paige nibbled on her bottom lip. Her baseball cap hid her eyes. "I think that's enough. Don't you?"

Shrugging, Andrew picked up the basket. "I still don't understand why we couldn't just buy the pie."

"You won't say that once you taste the pie." An older couple walked past them, nodding and wishing them a good day. "Aw, they're so cute."

Andrew watched the couple disappear behind a tree. They'd seen the same couple three times since they'd arrived. And each time, the couple smiled at them like it was their first time seeing them. "Yeah," he murmured, shifting the basket from one arm to the other.

"I wonder if they need help picking their apples?" she mused, her finger tapping her lips. "We should ask."

He glanced at her with a raised brow. "I thought you said you didn't want anyone to recognize you."

She scoffed. "I'm sure they won't. Can you see them watching any of my movies?"

"What about your soap opera?" he challenged.

"Oh." Her shoulders fell. "You might have a point."

Paige's first role, in the daytime drama *All of Our Lives*, had thrust her into the spotlight and had been a stepping-stone to bigger roles. She'd played the feisty young wife to one of the story's most popular characters. If the older woman watched CBS, they would recognize Paige. Even though she hadn't played that character in over a decade, people still recognized her because of that role.

"And if she watched the show, she might not like me," Paige added with a grin. "I still get hate mail from fans for coming between Malcolm and Harley."

He chuckled, remembering her first not-so-nice letter. The angry soap fan had raked Paige over the coals for being a "gold-digging hoe." People had taken her head-shot, added little devil horns to her head, and posted it on the message boards. Paige had been devastated, and he'd had to soothe her with pizza and coffee to get her to stop crying.

"If you ever want to go back for a visit, let me know," he said. "The network has put out feelers several times over the years."

Paige muttered something that sounded an awful lot like *Hell no*, and he laughed. She bumped him with her shoulder. "Don't laugh at me."

"That was a quick answer."

"Because I didn't need to think about it. Soaps are hard work, memorizing all that dialogue every day. I'm good."

The elderly couple rounded the bend again and waved at them. He leaned down, taking in the hint of jasmine in her hair. Swallowing, he fought the urge to bury his nose in her curls. He'd been there for days, and they hadn't so much as brushed arms since they'd held hands in front of the fire. And, *damn*, he wanted to touch her.

"I think they like you," he whispered, enjoying her sharp intake of breath.

"Um, I . . ." she croaked. "They're probably just lost."

Andrew rubbed his nose against her ear, closing his eyes when she melted into him. It felt a lot like permission. But he didn't want to get ahead of himself.

"Maybe she does recognize you," he murmured, "and that's why she keeps dragging her husband over here."

Paige whirled around, her eyes wide and her grin even wider. "I just thought about that." She tugged at his shirt. "We better get out of here now. We still have to stop at the store to get the rest of the ingredients."

They hurried to the store, and an hour later, they were back at the house. He took the groceries to the kitchen as she opened the windows. It felt like the most natural thing in the world. Over the past few days, they'd taken walks on the beach, played Scrabble, and watched movies. All of those things seemed innocent enough, but something not so innocent had been brewing, percolating.

"Sometimes, I wonder if I'm really hungry, or just greedy." Paige grabbed an onion from the fridge. "I didn't need that donut today. I'm baking an apple pie, for goodness' sake."

Andrew leaned down on the counter and peered up at her. *She's so damn beautiful*. Her hair was wild, her face was flushed, and she wore no makeup. And she was stunning. "One donut won't kill you." He popped a piece of broccoli into his mouth.

That morning, they'd decided on vegetable lasagna for dinner. She'd already started cutting up the vegetables when she'd thought of making an apple pie for dessert.

Paige pulled a pot from beneath the counter, filled it with water, and set it on the stove. As she worked, she told him about the five pounds she'd gained while in Michigan. "I can't gain another ounce, but I can't stop eating." She laughed, turning fire on to heat the water. "I've never been so undisciplined."

Andrew raked his gaze over her body slowly, lingering on the curve of her hips and her full breasts. *Damn*. He told himself he was doing it so he could debunk her theory that she looked a hot mess, but the only thing his perusal had accomplished was making him hard. As hell.

Shifting in his seat, he said, "You look fine."

Paige shot a disbelieving glance his way. "You're only saying that because you don't want me to kick you out again." She tossed a piece of broccoli at him and it popped him in the nose.

Standing, he said, "Oh, you're going to get it now." He rounded the island, grabbing a handful of the florets. "I accepted that pillow to the back of my head, but I draw a hard line at broccoli."

Paige threw a carrot at him and took off, laughing as he chased her around the island to the sunroom and outside onto the patio. She ran toward the beach, screaming the entire way. He caught her easily, scooping her up in his arms.

Yelping, she pleaded with him to let her go. "Drew, I'm sorry." She batted her eyelashes, the grin on her face beautiful and wide, as he carried her toward the water. "But if you throw me in that water, it's on."

"Now you want to threaten me," he teased. "I'm not scared of you, Paige."

"Don't do it," she begged.

Andrew paused mid-stride and stared down at her in his arms. He tried not to be affected by her nearness, by the fact that she fit in his arms perfectly. He tried not to concentrate on her contagious smile and her scent. And he tried . . . he really tried not to think about kissing her.

His gaze fell to her parted lips, then back up to her eyes. Something in the air shifted, sparked to life. His heartbeat pounded in his ears, his fingers tingled with the need to touch her mouth. *God help me.* Because he was tempted to close the distance, to press his lips to hers, to taste her.

"Damn," he murmured, his voice strained.

Andrew didn't want to let her go, to put her down. He was perfectly content with her in his arms.

She let out a shaky breath. "Drew?"

Unable to tear his gaze from her mouth, he nodded. "Yes?"

"What are you doing, Andrew?"

He leaned in, so close he could smell the cinnamon

from the donut she'd eaten on her breath. *I'm in trouble.* Because he had no power, no control to stop himself.

Paige peered at him under hooded eyes. "Are you going to put me down?" she whispered.

Shaking his head, he circled her nose with his. "No." Then he kissed her.

It was amazing how one simple touch of Andrew's mouth to hers had opened the box that she'd tried to stuff him in years ago. Years of sweet friendship, funny moments, and deep talks had forced her to forget about any stray thoughts of "*What if?*" she may have had. She'd imagined how it would feel to taste him, to feel his tongue against hers, to feel his hands on her body. But this . . . *Damn*.

His nose against hers, his scent wrapping around her, his heart beating beneath her hands, and his low groan had tilted her world on its axis. The moment was everything she didn't know she needed, but secretly hoped for—warm and soft, smooth and wet. Yet, even in her wildest fantasies, it didn't feel like *this*.

It was almost like he'd kissed her back to life. She'd never felt so alive. Every part of her buzzed with excitement. Her nerves were shot, her heart was beating hard, and her fingers tingled with the need to touch him. She ached for him.

Far too soon, Andrew pulled back from her, from the magic they'd just made together. She opened her eyes, met his dark orbs. Paige wanted to press her lips to his again, she wanted to hold on to the slice of bliss she'd felt a little longer.

He set her down on shaky legs. "Um," he murmured, scratching the back of his head.

"Um," she echoed. She couldn't stop looking at his mouth, at those talented lips. "What did you just do?"

"Nothing," he said.

"Nothing? It felt like something to me." *Something good.*

He nodded. "Right." He took a big step away from her.

"Andrew?" She inched closer.

She searched his face, warring with herself over what she wanted to do next. Paige had never been the type to make the first move, but that kiss had been a long time coming. The past few days, her desire for him had increased tenfold. She wasn't naïve. The close proximity, the knowledge that he'd been sleeping right down the hall from her, the flashes of his bare chest in her dreams, or even the way they were with each other had heightened her emotions. It could even be the fact that he was so attentive to her, so calm. So attractive. And she wanted him. Plain and simple.

"You should probably go inside," he suggested.

Paige closed the distance between them. "I could go inside."

"It would probably be the best thing to do right now." His voice was a low rumble.

The smart thing to do would be to stay far away from him, to do as he requested and walk her ass back up to the house. But the heat of his gaze, and the way he stared at her, made that impossible. "What if I don't?"

Andrew swallowed visibly. "Why wouldn't you?"

Standing on the tips of her toes, she brushed her lips over his. "Because I don't want to." Then she kissed him, slowly and tenderly.

He pulled back again. "What did you just do?"

"Let's go with it," she whispered, wrapping her arms around his neck and pressing her mouth to his.

She groaned when he nipped her bottom lip. *Or is that him?* They were out on the beach, where anyone could happen upon them. But she didn't care. She just wanted more.

"Paige," he murmured against her mouth, before deepening the kiss again, dipping his tongue back into her mouth.

How is he still standing? Because she definitely wanted to drop to her knees and pull him with her, she wanted to peel his shirt off and trace his muscles with her hands, she wanted to lick him. Everywhere.

Off in the distance, they heard a speedboat on the water. And soon, his warmth was replaced by a soft breeze as he released his hold on her. She gripped his biceps, to steady herself. "Impressive," she mumbled without thinking. With wide eyes, she stared up at him. "I meant, you . . ." *What the hell did I mean?* "Um. I'm flustered," she admitted. "B-because you just kissed me."

"Technically, you kissed me."

"*After* you kissed me," she corrected. She felt a blush work its way up her neck to her ears. "Let's set the record straight."

"Okay. What do you want to do now?"

As forward as she'd been a few minutes ago, Paige didn't think she could tell him exactly what she wanted to do. Even though she was sure he wouldn't object. But she didn't want them to do anything they'd regret in the morning. There was too much on the line to make a decision based on her horniness.

Tugging on her shirt, she cleared her throat. "Um . . .
I—" She exhaled. "I have to go."

Embarrassed at her frazzled state, Paige hurried back
to the house. Inside, she headed straight to the refrigerator,
pulled a bottle of water out, and guzzled it down. It did
nothing to erase his taste, or his smell, or his body from
her thoughts. It definitely didn't cool her down. Because
the more she thought about him, the more she wanted
to just go with her first thought. Sex. *Hot. Sweaty. Dirty.
Naked. Sex.*

Squeezing her eyes shut, she let out a slow breath.

"Paige?"

She jumped, startled by his voice. "Hi," she breathed,
grabbing a knife and an onion.

"Hi." He stepped forward. "Paige, I—"

"Don't." She chopped the onion, cursing when a small
piece rolled onto the floor. Quickly, she picked it up and
set it on the counter. Bracing herself against the island,
she said, "Whatever you do, please don't apologize." She
peered up at him. "No woman would want to hear an apology after a kiss like that. *Two* kisses." Especially since she
still felt it in every bone in her body.

"I wasn't going to apologize." He took another step.

"Oh." She released a shaky breath. "That's good."
Scraping the edge of the countertop, she peeked up at him.
"But *I* should apologize for turning all teen girl and run-
ning away the way I did."

He chuckled. "Don't apologize."

"Should we be adults and talk about it?" She straightened
her spine, attempting to appear cool and calm, although
nothing about this moment was cool or calm. Hot and

intense were more appropriate descriptions for the shift between them.

"Definitely." Andrew sat across from her. "I think if we ever decide to change the dynamics of our relationship, it's better to be open about what it means."

"It's that easy for you?" she asked. "I mean, if I told you it was a mistake and it could never happen again, you'd be okay with that?"

"Is that what you're saying?"

Paige sighed. "No, I'm not saying that."

"Good."

She flattened a hand over her stomach. "Good?"

"Yeah," he whispered. His gaze flickered down to her lips before traveling lower. *What the hell is he doing?* Oh, she knew. He was playing with fire, igniting a flame inside her with his intense stare.

She walked toward him slowly. "Just so we're clear. When you say *good* does that mean you wouldn't want me to think it was a mistake?"

He shook his head.

Now standing in front of him, she stepped between his legs. "Because it's not, right?"

Andrew wrapped a hand around her neck and pulled her to him. "No." Then his mouth was on hers again.

And damn . . . his hands were everywhere, touching every part of her—on her face, down her back, over her ass. His warm lips grazed her ear, her neck, and her shoulder before meeting hers again in a searing kiss. She sagged against him, unable to fight the torrent of emotions swirling inside her. Paige had never been held like this, kissed like this. His touch stoked the fire already threatening to consume her.

Paige tugged his shirt up and off, tossing it behind her. He stood then, lifting her in his arms and fusing his mouth to hers again. Wrapping her legs around his lean waist, she dug her nails in his scalp as he carried her through the house. She had no idea where he was going, but she hoped he would stop soon so she could ease the ever-growing ache in her core, so she could feel the erection pressing against her sex inside her.

She broke the kiss. "You don't need to take me to bed. I swear. I'm good wherever."

Andrew laughed, before he turned her suddenly. Backing her up against the wall, he pushed his hard length into her. "You sure?"

Paige groaned, rolling her hips into his. "I'm so sure. Please, just do . . . something."

"Shit." He nipped at her chin. "You're killing me."

Then they were moving again, just a few steps until he dropped her on the sofa. *Finally*. She sat up and had started to pull her shirt off when his hands stopped her. Her eyes flickered to his, praying that he wasn't having second thoughts. "What's wrong?"

He smirked. "Nothing. Let me."

Paige dropped her hands and arched a brow. "Don't take too long. Make your move."

Andrew barked out a laugh. "We're not playing Scrabble. Don't rush me."

He dropped to his knees and peeled off her pants. Then he kissed his way up her legs, to her thighs. "So beautiful," he whispered.

"Drew," she moaned.

"Yes." He blazed a trail of hot kisses over her pelvic bone, up her stomach, pushing her shirt up along the way.

He brushed his lips over the tops of her breasts and finally pulled the shirt off before pressing his mouth to hers again.

Paige couldn't feel anything but him, and the way they were in this moment. She didn't register room temperature or smell or even the cushion beneath her. The only thing she felt was the heat between their bodies.

But the shrill sound of a phone ringing burst through the haze of desire swirling around them. And Andrew froze, sitting up straight and pulling out his phone.

Paige blinked and perched herself up on her elbows. "What is that?"

"It's my mother." He explained that he'd set his phone up to allow phone calls from his mother even when his phone was set to Do Not Disturb. He jumped up. "Mom?"

Paige fell back against the cushion and willed her body to calm down, to slow down. He hadn't even pulled her panties off yet and she was on the verge of a delicious orgasm—just from his kisses, from his soft touches.

"Okay." He paced the floor. "Okay, I'll be there as soon as I can. Please, call me if something changes. I mean it." When he ended the call, he dropped his head and let out a deep breath.

Her stomach dropped as worry replaced desire. "What's wrong?" she asked.

Andrew glanced at her. "I have to go to Detroit."

She scooted off the couch and went to him. Grasping his hands, she asked, "Is your mother okay?"

"She fell and broke her ankle. They have to operate. I need to go to her. I'm the closest."

"Of course," she said. "Go now."

"I'm sorry." Andrew headed to the kitchen and pulled on his shirt.

"Andrew, don't apologize. I can pack you something to eat in the car on your way. Since we didn't really eat lunch."

Tracing her cheek with his thumb, he placed a gentle kiss to her mouth. "You don't have to."

"I want to." She kissed his chin. "Now, go."

He turned and took the steps two at a time until he made it to the top. Sighing, Paige hurried to make him something to eat. Andrew returned a few minutes later with his bag. He set it on the floor next to the staircase.

Glancing up at him, she gave him a small smile. "I packed a turkey sandwich, an apple, and chips." She set his food into a thermal lunch bag she'd brought with her. "I'm also going to put a couple of bottles of water in here for you."

He walked over to her and pulled her into a hug. "Thank you."

Leaning back, she framed his face in her hands. "No worries. I got you."

Andrew rested his forehead against hers. "Just so you know, nothing else would have pulled me away from you."

Giggling, she wrapped her arms around him. "That's good to know." She grinned up at him. "But maybe this was a good thing. A little time, a little distance might force us to really think before we act."

"If you say so." He kissed the tip of her nose. "I better go."

Paige nodded. "Call me when you get there." She followed him to the door, handed him the lunch bag. "I put the house phone number and my iPad number in your lunch bag. Oh, and a spare key in case you want to come back."

"Good."

She watched him jog to his car. and waited until his car disappeared from view before she closed the door. Turning around, she slumped against the glass. In her haste to get him the things he needed, she'd failed to ask if he'd planned to come back. Because she really hoped they'd have a chance to finish what they'd started.

Chapter Nine

Andrew stood at the hospital room door. His mother was lying there so still, eyes closed. During the three-hour drive, he'd called his brothers to let them know about the accident. Neither of them knew about the fall, but both of them promised to get the next flight to Michigan.

Closing his eyes, he drew in a deep breath. He entered the room and approached the bed, paying close attention to the soft cast on her left leg. The woman in front of him had sacrificed so much for them, working long shifts, coming home with calluses and dirty nails. Yet she'd still found a way to make it to most school events and sporting activities. She'd flown in to college graduations and sent holiday care packages every year. He hoped a fall was all it was, he hoped she wasn't hiding something more serious. Despite what she'd told him, he wondered if her fall had something to do with that limp she had when he'd visited.

His mother's eyes fluttered open, and she smiled when she realized he was there. "Hey, Drew. When did you get here?"

He kissed her brow and gave her a gentle hug. "A few

minutes ago. How are you feeling?" He studied her face. Brushing a finger over the bandage on her head, he said, "What's this? You told me you broke your ankle."

His mother swatted his hand and pulled back. "I fell, baby. I was trying to get something out of the closet and fell off the metal stool." She grimaced when she shifted to sit up.

"Mom, be careful." He helped her sit upright. "Take your time."

"This shit hurts," she grumbled. "I thought I was leaving here. I'm so glad I had the window open. Dort heard me screaming."

Andrew sent up a prayer of thanks for Mrs. Fulton. His former teacher had been a thorn in their sides growing up, reporting every misdeed to their hardworking mother. He'd often caught her snooping out her window, watching them talk to neighborhood girls or lighting firecrackers in the street. He'd been punished many times because of Mrs. Fulton. But this time, the older woman's nosey ways had paid off.

"I'm glad she heard you." He brushed his mother's salt-and-pepper hair off her forehead.

"She didn't fool me, though. I had some company over earlier and she was probably eavesdropping like she always does."

Andrew laughed. "I wouldn't doubt it."

"But I'm glad." She let out a heavy sigh and burrowed into the pillow. "Did you see that cute nurse I have? I told her about you."

He shook his head. "Why are you telling a stranger about me and you're in pain?"

"I'm always your mother—even when I'm in pain."

"Mom, you have to stop trying to hook me up. I need you to focus on getting better."

"Don't tell me what to do. That nurse is a cutie-pie. I worked with her dad at the plant. She has a good head on her shoulders, a good education. Perfect for you."

Now wasn't the time to argue with his mother, so he changed the subject. "Have they told you when they can do surgery?"

"Today or tomorrow." She winced.

"It's a good thing you decided to retire."

"I wanted to have fun when I retired." She pointed at the remote on her belly. "Can you push that button? I need the nurse to come in here."

Andrew did as he was told. "What's wrong?"

"I need pain medicine. Now."

It took a few minutes for the nurse to come into the room. "Hi, Mrs. Weathers."

"Ms. Weathers," his mother corrected.

The nurse smiled. "Sorry." She turned off the nurse alert. "What can I do for you?"

"She's in pain," Andrew told the nurse. "Can you give her something?"

"Don't be so rude, Drew," his mother told him. "Ariane, this is my son."

Andrew narrowed his eyes on his mother before turning to the nurse. He smiled. "Hi, I'm Drew."

Ariane smiled. "Hello. Your mother told me all about you."

He stared at his mother while answering Ariane. "I heard."

Sighing, Ariane said, "Ms. Weathers, I'll ask the doctor about more pain meds." The nurse took his mother's pulse, then started the blood pressure machine. Once she was done, she announced, "Good. One twenty over seventy-six."

"That's good, Mom," he said, while the nurse typed notes into the computer.

A few minutes later, Ariane told them she'd be back and left the room. When he met his mother's gaze again, she was giving him "the look." The same one she'd given him so many times before, a mixture of disappointment and admonishment.

Andrew sat down on the chair next to his mother's bed. "What, Mom?"

"I wish you'd be nicer. Isn't she beautiful?"

"Yes." He couldn't deny the nurse was attractive, but he wasn't interested in exploring a relationship with anyone but the woman he'd left behind in South Haven. "But I'm not going to ask your nurse out."

"Why?"

"Can we not talk about this right now? You're in pain and I don't like to see you in pain. So let's concentrate on getting you better."

She smiled and patted his hand. "Fine. You're right." She closed her eyes. "I'm tired."

Squeezing her hand, he told her to rest. A few minutes later, Ariane came back with pain meds. Once she administered the medication, she let them both know that the surgeon would be in to talk to them within the hour.

A little while later, it was dinnertime and his mother was cranky. "See!" she said. "This is why I don't like the hospital." She forked a piece of dry-looking fish and held it up. "This is probably not even real fish. I shouldn't eat it."

Andrew opened the bottle of juice they'd sent with her

meal and dropped a straw inside for her. "You have to eat something. Stop complaining."

"I'm not complaining. I'm just keeping it real. They should have called this 'fish substitute.'"

Laughing, he took his seat again. "You're trippin', Mom."

"Who you been texting on your phone?"

He blinked. "What?"

She pointed to his phone. "I've been watching you. Every time your phone buzzes, you smile. And you continue smiling while you're typing a response."

Andrew had no idea he'd been smiling, but he knew what his mother was talking about. Since he'd arrived, Paige had messaged him many times. The first time, she'd sent a GIF of a woman glaring at him because he'd failed to send an update once he'd actually seen his mother's face. The next time, she'd sent a picture of her sniffing the apple pie she'd baked. And the final text was a pic of her sitting on a new lounger she'd ordered online, staring out at the water.

"Well?" his mother prodded. "You might as well tell me who's got you over there grinning like that."

"How do you know I'm not on Facebook reading a funny meme?" he asked.

"What's a meme?" his mother asked, a frown on her face. "You know I'm not on no Fakebook."

Chuckling, he told her, "It's Facebook, Mom."

"I know what it is. My friends have been trying to get me to try it out, but I refuse to get on there. Apparently, men try and pick women by 'slidin' in the DM', or whatever that means. Ain't nobody got time for that. Besides, I don't like people knowing my business like that."

Andrew understood where his mother was coming

from. He had social media pages that he never used. But he kept them for work. "I get it."

"But don't change the subject. Are you seeing someone?"

Peering up at the ceiling, he weighed his two options. To lie or not to lie. In the end, he chose a variation of the truth. "It's Paige."

Her eyes lit up. "Beautiful Paige Mills. Me and ladies went to see her last movie at the theater. It was so good, and different from her normal roles. I was on the edge of my seat. So scandalous."

Paige had co-produced and starred in her last movie. Right around the release, the news of Julius's misdeeds had hit the media, thrusting Paige into a real-life scandal. It didn't help that Julius was the director of the film.

His mother went on and on about Paige's performance, raving about her growth as an actress and how stunning she looked in the film. Andrew couldn't agree more. He'd seen the movie with Paige earlier in the year and thought it was Paige's best role to date. In fact, she was up for several awards for her portrayal of a woman torn between very different brothers.

"I know you had a lot to do with this," his mother said. "I'm so proud of you."

"Thanks, Mom." He smiled. "That means a lot coming from you."

"I'm proud of all of my boys. You all have surpassed my expectations. I was just hoping you'd graduate from high school, get a good job, and move out. But all of you are self-sufficient, educated, powerful black men. Makes me so proud to be your mom."

"It's because of you that we had the chances we did."

She waved a dismissive hand in his direction. "You always say that."

"It's true. I love you, Mom. That's why I'm always on you to communicate with me. I need you to tell me the truth. Is something else wrong? Something other than your ankle?"

His mother shook her head. "No, boy. I wouldn't lie to you. I'm fine. Just a little clumsy, but fine."

Andrew let out a shaky breath. "Okay. I have no choice but to believe you. But I want you to promise me that you'll tell me if something is wrong."

"I promise," she grumbled. "I'm still the boss, though."

He gave her a mock salute. "You definitely are."

"So how is Paige?"

"Good," he replied.

Mom tilted her head. "Why do I feel like *you're* hiding something?" She cupped his chin and peered into his eyes. "Do you have something going on with Paige?"

He eased out of her grasp. "Mom, you're so nosey. That's why you and Mrs. Fulton get along so well."

"It's not nosey when it's my son."

"Okay, there is something going on," he admitted.

With wide eyes, his mother said, "Really? Does Tina know?"

He shook his head. "No one knows. Just you."

"Oh, 'cause I was gonna say . . ."

He grinned. "You were gonna say what?"

"Tina better not know anything before me." She laughed. "Anyway, when did this happen?"

"I went to see her when I left here the other day. There's some business we had to discuss. While I was there, we connected."

"Oh Lord, you had sex with her?" she whispered, as if someone was in the room with them and she didn't want them to hear her.

Frowning, he asked her why she'd chosen to whisper. "No one is here."

"What if Ariane is outside the door?"

Andrew barked out a laugh. "There is never a dull moment with you, Mom."

"I'm just sayin'. Is this serious?"

"I do have feelings for her," he confessed. "I want to help her, protect her."

"You've done that her entire career."

He thought about his mother's words. From the beginning, he'd appointed himself Paige's protector and pretended it was because Jax had asked him to take her on as a personal favor to him. He'd helped her build an impressive career, but she'd helped him, too. Representing her had opened many doors for him in the industry. Despite their friendship, they'd maintained a great working relationship. Could he risk that for romance?

"I'm just wondering if it's wise to change things between us," he said.

"I'm not worried about that," his mother told him. "I am worried about the fact that she's just out of a bad marriage."

"That, too," he agreed.

"It seems so soon. According to the magazine I read, the divorce was just finalized."

"Yes, but they've been separated for a while."

"I know that. But I'm still concerned. I don't want you to get hurt. I can tell you from my own experience that sometimes we think we're okay to move forward. But we're not."

His mother had never remarried after their father left her. Andrew had never even seen her go on a date or bring a man home. "Is that why you never had a male companion after dad left?"

She flashed a sad smile. "Sometimes hurt is so big, it's scary to risk feeling it again. I'm not saying that's where Paige is. But I know how it feels to be betrayed in the worst way by someone you love. Jumping into another romantic relationship might not be the best thing."

His mother hadn't said anything that he hadn't thought of himself. Julius had taken Paige through the proverbial wringer. Andrew wouldn't have been surprised if she'd told him she never wanted to date again after the hell she'd been through. Yet she'd been open to *him*. And it felt genuine, real. But maybe his mother was right? Maybe they needed to slow things down. Because he already knew she had the power to burn everything in his life to the ground if this didn't work out, and he wasn't sure he wanted to hand her the match and the lighter fluid just yet.

"Was your mom nervous to go into surgery?" Paige peered down at her iPad. She'd been waiting for Andrew's video call for an hour. They'd talked last night for a few hours and he'd explained the surgical process and recovery.

Andrew nodded. "She was. But she tried to act like she wasn't."

"Where are you?" She perched her tablet on her belly. "In the waiting room?"

"Yeah. My brothers went down to the cafeteria to grab food, but I'm not hungry right now."

During their chat last night, Connor and Damon had her cracking up as they told her a story about how Andrew nearly lost his cool when a male nurse kept talking over their mother. That part wasn't funny, but the way his brothers had mocked him was hilarious.

She sighed. "You need to eat, Drew."

"I'm eating," he said.

"Something other than sliders from White Castle."

Laughing, he said, "Don't hate. I have to get my fix every time I come to Detroit for an extended stay."

Paige rolled her eyes. Since she'd known him, he'd been trying to lure her over to the dark side. But she hated White Castle with a passion. The food never came like she ordered it and it always made her stomach hurt.

"Whatever," she grumbled. "Anyway, you have to eat green, leafy vegetables."

She was better at giving advice than taking it. Because she was currently eating the last slice of apple pie and she'd yet to touch the pot of collard greens that she'd made yesterday.

"How's that pie?" he asked, with a wink.

"Good," she mumbled around her food. "But we're not talking about me."

"We are now," he retorted.

Paige giggled. "You're silly. So, how are *you*?"

When she talked to Andrew, she wanted to be sure he knew that she cared about how *he* was doing. She knew he had a close relationship with Connie, so she imagined it couldn't be easy to watch her go into surgery. Even though it was an ankle injury, it was still an operation.

"I'm alright. I'm worried about her pain level. I don't want her to suffer, but it's a bad injury."

According to Andrew, Connie had a severe fracture and the surgeon wasn't sure what he'd find when they went in. But they were hopeful they'd be able to repair it in one surgery.

"Have you talked to her again about therapy?" she asked.

"No, she's not listening. She doesn't want in-residence therapy, so we've come up with a plan to hire a nurse that can see her during the day. Mrs. Fulton agreed to stay at night."

"That's good news. I know you were worried."

"Yeah." They talked for a few more minutes about their plan for his mother. "What have you been up to?" he asked.

Grinning, she said, "Wouldn't you like to know?"

"I would."

Paige stared at his beautiful face—his chiseled jaw, the deep dimple on his cheek, his brown eyes. He'd only been gone two days and she already missed him. They hadn't discussed the kiss or their relationship since he'd left and she wondered if they ever would. Either way, she didn't think the time was right to bring it up. He already had so much on his mind.

"I'm getting ready to go for a run on the beach," she told him. "Then I plan to do some yoga."

"Yoga?"

"Yep. I finished a good book this morning. Stayed up all night reading and I'm in love. I wanted to talk to you about it, maybe do another option."

Andrew nodded. "Whenever you're ready."

Paige smiled. She loved that he had no problem moving at her pace. He still hadn't broached the subject of work, and she knew he was getting bombarded with inquiries about her status.

"I'm coming back around to business," she admitted. "I've been thinking about some things."

"That's cool. Did you call Skye?"

She shook her head. "No. You know Skye. She has tunnel vision when it comes to work. She'll be on the first plane to Michigan to talk me back to Cali."

"You're probably right."

"If she calls you, though, you can give her the house phone number. I don't want her to be calling you right now for me. Your focus should be on your mother."

"If you're sure?"

"I'm sure." There was a knock on her door and she sat up. Frowning, she said, "That's strange. I'm not expecting anyone."

"Did you purchase something else online?"

"No." She stood and walked toward the door. "Oh no," she grumbled when she peered out the glass door.

"Who is it?" he asked.

"It's trouble. I'll call you later."

"Wait. You have to at least tell me who it is before you hang up on me."

"Don't worry. It's my mother."

He laughed. "Uh-oh. Talk to you later."

She ended the call and opened the front door. "Mom?"

Tina held out her arms. "Paige!" Her mother pulled her into a tight hug. "I had to come lay eyes on you since you haven't returned my calls since I gave Andrew the address."

Paige looked outside and noticed her mother's body-guard, Hugh, was standing near a town car. "Mom, what are you doing here?"

Her mother brushed past her and walked into the house. Spinning around, she removed her hat and sunglasses.

"Nice. Your uncle did a good job with this place." She pointed at a painting. "Except for that. I hate boat prints."

"Mother." Paige folded her arms over her chest. "What are you doing here?"

"I told you, I'm here to check on you. You obviously made Andrew leave, and he hasn't answered my calls, so I came to check on you myself."

Groaning, Paige closed the door and walked to the kitchen. Her mother was close behind her talking about everything that didn't matter to Paige—from concerts and recording sessions to the latest drama with her management team.

"I swear, baby, people don't understand how busy I am." Tina took a seat at the kitchen table. "Can you pour me a glass?"

Sighing, Paige pulled two wineglasses from the cabinet and poured them each some cabernet. She joined her mother at the table, setting one of the glasses in front of her. "Again, Mom, what are you doing here? You can't come to town with Hugh, in a limo, without attracting attention to me. You know dad's family is here in town. And you're easy to recognize."

Tina took a sip of wine. "I'm not worried about your father and his trifling family. I'm concerned about you. Besides, it's not a limo. I rented a town car to blend in."

"You can never blend in, Mom."

"Don't worry, babe. I'll be gone in a few hours. I'm headed to Paris for a show."

Paige leaned forward, resting her elbows on the table. "That sounds fun. Your favorite place."

"Girl, I'm tired of Paris. I'm ready to relax." She crossed her legs. "What happened with Andrew?"

It wasn't like her mother to talk around something, so

Paige wasn't surprised she'd veered the subject back to Andrew. "Nothing."

Tina watched her with narrowed eyes. "You didn't send him away, did you?"

Taking a big gulp from her glass, she shook her head. "I didn't."

"Okay?" Her mother leaned forward. "Spill."

"No," she said simply. Her mother had always been a little too interested in her love life.

"Really? You've always been able to share personal things with me."

Growing up, Tina had acted more like a big sister at times, preferring to bond with Paige over gossip and trivial stuff. She'd spent a huge chunk of her childhood on the road, until she'd begged to go to regular school. Then she'd ended up in the care of nannies while her mother continued to tour.

When her mother was around, though, they rarely spent mother-daughter time together. Tina had encouraged Paige to consider her a friend. At one point, her mother had even asked her to call her by her first name, which Paige didn't like. Instead of serious talks about her teenage struggles, they'd conversed about pop culture and boys. Instead of confiding in her mother about her issues with self-esteem, she'd allowed her mother to give makeup and hair lessons.

Paige loved her mother, but sometimes she wished Tina would just be her mom. Sometimes Paige needed a mother's comfort, a warm hug, a listening ear.

Eyeing her mother over the rim of her glass, she said, "There's nothing to share."

"I don't believe you."

"Why not?"

Tina tapped a finger against the table. "For one, you're blushing. And two, you look like you did something wrong."

Paige dropped her head on the table. "Oh God, why?"

"I could always tell when you were guilty of something. You get so defensive. I also could tell when you liked someone, because you can't stop blushing."

Lifting her eyes, Paige said, "If I tell you what happened, will you stop talking?"

Tina laughed. "You know I can't promise that."

"Fine." Paige finished her glass and stood. "I need more wine for this." After she refilled her glass, she rejoined her mother. "Okay, Andrew and I reconnected when he came here."

"That's it?" Tina asked flatly.

"No. Can I finish?"

Tina gestured her on with the flip of her hand. "Go ahead."

Paige gave her mother a quick summary of Andrew's time at the house, leaving out much of the details, but including the kiss. "Then he had to go see about his mother."

Frowning, Tina asked, "What's wrong with Connie?"

"She fractured her ankle," Paige explained. "She's in surgery right now."

"Oh no." Tina pulled out her phone. "I'll have Elaine send her a basket or something." She tapped the screen, presumably sending a text to her assistant.

Elaine Sutherland had worked for Paige's mother for decades. The woman had been a surrogate mother to her as well, standing in the gap for Tina often.

"That's nice," Paige said. "I'm sure Connie will like that."

Setting the phone down, Tina turned her attention

back to Paige. "Done. So, what are you going to do about Andrew?"

Shrugging, Paige said, "I don't know. What should I do?"

"Babe, Andrew's a good guy. He cares so much about you. But are you sure you're ready to date someone?"

"I haven't really thought about dating," she admitted.

"Oh, so it's a sex thing," Tina chirped. "In that case, I say go for it."

Paige's mouth fell open. "Mom, really?"

"What?" Tina batted her eyelashes. "No sense in being celibate forever."

"But don't you think we should talk about this before we take another step?"

Things had been hot and heavy between them the last time she'd seen Andrew. But she hoped they could come together and actually have a conversation about everything. She would hate to start something they couldn't finish and then negatively impact their working relationship. His friendship was important to her, yes, but so was his role as her agent.

"I mean, sex always complicates things," Paige continued. "What if we have sex and it's bad. How am I supposed to look at him?" Although, she doubted it would be terrible after the way he'd kissed her. Shit, she'd dreamed about his talented mouth.

"You'll never know until you try him." Tina sipped her wine. "But you two have chemistry in spades. I doubt you'll have that problem."

"You think we have chemistry?"

"Baby, please. Of course you do. You've been working together for years. That counts for something. Plus, I've seen the way he looks at you. You forget, he came to my house asking me to help him find you. And I've noticed the way you look at him."

"What about Julius?"

"What about that asshole?" Tina murmured, with a hard roll of her eyes. "He doesn't deserve any more of your time and energy. Leave him where he is—with that nasty-ass Catherine Davis."

Paige laughed. "Mom, you're too much."

"That's what they tell me. Listen, if you like Andrew—and you're ready to date again—go for it. If you just want to have sex, go for that, too. As long as you have a conversation about expectations first. That's the most important thing."

Tina stood and walked over to the refrigerator. "I'm hungry. Let's eat something before I leave."

Paige and her mother spent the afternoon together. They made lunch, chatted more about Andrew, and Tina's next show. Tina had encouraged Paige to follow her heart, but don't ignore her mind. Even though her mother had dropped in unannounced, Paige was happy she'd come. In her own way, Tina had provided much needed clarity. Paige couldn't wait to see Andrew again so they could talk—or do more than talk.

Chapter Ten

PAIGE MILLS'S SECRET LIFE—
DRINKING, PARTYING, AND MEN.
WHAT THE STAR DOESN'T WANT YOU TO KNOW.

Paige muttered a curse as she read the headline a second time. It was the second trash story about her she'd come across today. The first one was all about her plastic surgery nightmare. The world had seemingly jumped on the "Where is Paige?" bandwagon. People were speculating on her whereabouts, posting about potential baes and hideaways.

Reading bogus headlines had been a part of her life forever it seemed, partly because of her mother. There was always a "friend" or "close acquaintance" who leaked information on the condition of anonymity. The rise of social media had made it exponentially worse, because vloggers and bloggers made a lot of money to go on YouTube and pretend they had "reliable" sources. She'd watched one lady lie to her viewers about knowing the secretary of the doctor who'd performed the botched surgery on Paige's ass. That same vlogger swore Paige was hiding out because she had to have her butt implants removed.

Normally, it wouldn't bother Paige. It was the nature of the job. But this headline, the secret life one, hit differently. Because it felt like a personal attack. It felt like something Julius would do.

Paige wasn't an alcoholic and she rarely partied. She could count on one hand the amount of random flings she'd had in her thirty-six years. She'd tried to keep her romantic relationships private because she'd seen how the media could destroy them. Watching her mother deal with the reality of marriage in the public eye had shied Paige away from dating publicly—until Julius. *Worse. Mistake. Ever.*

Grabbing her phone, Paige placed a long overdue call. When Skye answered, Paige said, "Hey."

"Oh my God, it's about time you called me," Skye said. "Where are you?"

Paige noticed Skye hadn't said her name and thanked God for her discreet publicist. "I'm fine."

"Hold on." She heard the buzz of activity in the background, and wondered where her publicist was. The tap of heels against a floor signaled Skye was moving. Soon, there was silence. "Okay," Skye said. "Had to get the hell out of that room. Where are you?"

"Skye, please. I can't tell you where I am." She wasn't ready for her safe haven to be breached. Not yet. "But I'm safe and hidden."

"You do realize there's a shitstorm brewing right now. People coming out of the woodwork with Nefarious Paige stories. We need to come up with a plan."

"Which is why I'm calling you now."

Skye sighed. "Fine. I just need to know one thing."

"What?"

"You didn't really have ass implants, did you? Because

then I'll have to craft a sympathetic plastic surgery horror story, and I don't want to do that."

Paige laughed. "You're crazy. No, my ass is God given."

"Good. No parties or drinking?"

"Just wine and the occasional mixed drink," Paige replied.

"What about men? Any affairs I should know about?"

Paige hesitated. She'd never been a cheater. Torrid affairs weren't her thing. She didn't date multiple men at the same time or run around with married men. But . . . *Andrew*. Although she hadn't done anything wrong, full disclosure was the only way Skye could do an effective job as Paige's publicist.

"Paige?" Skye called. "Please tell me you're not hiding away with someone's boo."

There was no judgment in Skye's tone, but Paige didn't like the insinuation. "No," she snapped. "I'm not *that* woman."

"I had to ask. If you are sneaking around with someone, I'm not judging you. There's no way I can help if I don't know everything."

"I'm not in a relationship with anyone—yet."

"Oh God," Skye grumbled. "Do I need a drink for this? In the middle of the day. I don't have to tell you how bad the timing is, right?"

"I know."

"Okay, hit me with it. Who is he?"

"Before I go any further, nothing has really happened between us. I'm only telling you this for full disclosure."

"Got it."

"And I haven't even talked to him about this." Paige wondered if she should walk her admission back until she could speak to Andrew. What if he didn't want anyone to know? He had a professional reputation to uphold as well.

"Well, I don't know him. So how would he know that I know."

"You do know him," Paige admitted softly.

"Wait a minute . . . Paige if you took Julius back after everything that muthafucka put you through, I'm—"

"Hell no. I didn't take him back."

Skye let out a heavy sigh. "Woo, chile. I knew you weren't stupid, but I couldn't think of anyone . . . else." She gasped, and Paige knew her publicist had figured it out. "No."

"Nothing happened," Paige rushed on. "Not much anyway," she added.

"Oh no, Paige! What? Why?"

"Because, it just . . . I can't stop wanting him."

"Oh boy," Skye grumbled. "He works for you. You're not supposed to date your employees."

"Technically, Andrew works for Pure Talent."

"Semantics."

Paige was well aware of the many reasons she shouldn't date—or sex—Andrew. But there were many reasons why she should. The first one on the top of the pro list was that he knew her. She was comfortable sharing herself with him.

"Skye, you told me that you gave Garrett another chance because you knew him and he knew you. You knew he would never do anything to hurt you."

"I call foul. You can't throw my words back at me. And, *news flash*, Andrew did hurt you."

"And you hurt Garrett," Paige tossed back. "But he forgave you. Why can't I forgive Andrew? Aside from the last several months, he's never done anything to hurt me."

"You told me you couldn't trust him."

Paige remembered the conversation she'd had with Skye only a few weeks ago. "I was angry. I didn't mean it." Despite the small, wary voice in her head telling her to be careful, Paige did trust Andrew. She trusted him with her career and with her life.

"This isn't a good idea," Skye said. "There are certain things that need to be separate. Work and love."

"Xavier works with Zara," Paige argued. "They're happy."

"Damn, damn, damn." Skye grumbled another string of curses before she said, "I still think there's a difference."

"How? Zara works for X. Just like Andrew works for me—kind of."

"How serious is it?"

"We're just talking." Not really talking about a relationship, though. They'd talked every day since he'd left, but not about making anything official between them. Maybe time apart had effectively doused the flame he had for her? Which would be a shame since every time she heard his voice, her heartbeat kicked up a notch. *Am I skipping ahead to something he doesn't even want?*

"No sex?" Skye asked.

"You don't need to know that."

"You're right. But I'm nosey."

Paige bit down on her bottom lip, torn between sharing more and keeping her love life to herself. In the end, she decided she needed some girl talk. "No sex."

"Okay, so you're taking things slow? That's better."

"Mostly . . . slow."

"What the hell does that even mean, Paige? Either you're doing it or you're not."

"We almost did," Paige confessed. "I wanted to. I still want to."

"Again, I have to warn you against this. Even before this started, you were so hurt that he hadn't been around. What happens if you do explore this and it doesn't work out. Then you're out an agent—and a friend."

Standing up, Paige paced the floor. One of the things she appreciated about Skye was that the other woman had no problems telling her the truth. A lot of the people who worked with Paige were "yes" people, often only telling her what they thought she wanted to hear. Skye had never been that way. It was the reason she'd hired her. Andrew was the same way, which was why they'd worked so well together through the years.

"What if I can't go back to how things were before?" Paige asked.

"That would suck, because Andrew is one hell of an agent."

Skye didn't have to tell her that. Paige knew Andrew had worked hard for her, protected her from many things that could have derailed her career. He'd gone to bat for her time and time again.

"I know you were mad at him for stepping back and letting Vonda handle the day-to-day," Skye continued, "but if you think Vonda did anything without his approval, you're wrong."

Paige hadn't considered that. "Did he tell you that?"

"He didn't have to," Skye said. "Despite my initial reaction, I'm not that surprised this is happening between you two. Y'all have been close for a long time, closer than most agent-client relationships. I believe that your obligations and his job have kept certain feelings at bay. But they've been there. They're not new."

Paige sighed. "Facts."

"Thanks for admitting that and not feeding me a line of bullshit that I would've been forced to call you out on."

Laughing, Paige said, "You're crazy."

"I'm real," Skye countered. "Anyway, I'm just going to say this. If you're not sure if things can go back to the way they were, I would encourage you to have a frank discussion with Andrew about expectations. And if you decide to do this, three words: Keep. It. Quiet. At least until you're back at work and this whole divorce thing blows over."

Swallowing, Paige nodded. Her mother had told her the same thing about managing expectations earlier. And their relationship was nowhere near the public outing stage, so she didn't have a problem with that request. "Okay, got it."

"Good. The last thing you need is more headlines. Trust me, they'll find a way to spin this negatively."

"I know."

"Now, is this your number? Can I call you if I need you?"

Paige giggled. "Yes. Please call me if there's something you think I should know."

"I'm not going to bother you unless I have to," Skye assured her. "Now that I know you're okay, I'll continue to handle things on my end. Are you checking your email?"

"I am."

"I've already sent you several press releases. I'm assuming they're okay."

"Of course," Paige said. "I know you're on top of it."

Over the next few minutes, Skye caught Paige up on several things. When they hung up, Paige contacted Tanya and Chastity to let them know she was alright. Business done, Paige stepped out on the patio. The weatherman had forecasted another severe thunderstorm, so she'd already

ordered groceries and prepared for a potential power
outage. She stared out over the lake. As peaceful as she
felt out there, she knew she couldn't hide out forever. It
was time to start living her life again. If that included
Andrew at her side as more than her agent, she had to be
ready for everything that entailed.

It was late. But Andrew couldn't let another night pass
without talking to Paige—in person. It had been five days
since they'd seen each other. Phone conversations and
video chats were good and all, but they had things to discuss that shouldn't be discussed over the phone. So after
he'd visited his mother in the hospital, he'd hopped in his
rental and made the drive back to South Haven.

The storm was already underway when he pulled into
the long driveway. The house was dark, though, and he
wondered if she'd lost power. He ran up to the front door
and let himself in with the spare key she'd given him.
Dropping his bag near the front door, he kicked his shoes
off and walked through the house, noting the dim light in
the kitchen and the soft jazz playing. *Power's still on.*

He spotted a bottle of wine on the counter and the iPad
on the kitchen table, and went to search for her. After
checking upstairs, he headed back to the kitchen. Lightning
lit up the sky, followed closely by a loud crash of thunder.
The rain picked up, pounding the house. He approached
the window, peering out at the lake. That's when he spotted
her, sitting in her chaise under the awning, watching the
storm. A glass of wine dangled from her fingers as she
bounced her bare feet. There was no way she could hear

the music in the house with the storm raging outside, but he knew she liked to sing—badly—to the tunes in her head.

Andrew took his socks off and stepped out onto the patio. As he neared her, he was struck by the sight in front of him. He'd expected her to have on her signature sweats and T-shirt, but she had on a long, sheer nightgown. *Shit, I'm in trouble.*

He circled the chaise and stood in front of her, not even caring that the rain fell on his head. She didn't care either because she was soaked. He took her in, his gaze traveling from her feet to her legs to the low-cut vee in her gown. *Perfect.* Her eyes were closed and she had a soft smile on her full lips.

"Hey?" he called.

As if she wasn't even surprised he was there, she glanced up at him. Her smile lit the area around them. "Andrew?" She jumped up and hugged him. "You're here."

He wrapped his arms around her. "How are you?"

"I'm good now." She leaned back. "How's your mom?"

His mother had a few tough days. The doctor had a difficult time managing her pain, and as a result, she'd had to stay in the hospital a little longer. "She's hanging in there. Being bossy, trying to hook us up with nurses."

She arched a brow. "Really? Nurses, huh?"

He searched her face, tucking a strand of hair behind her ear. "Yeah," he whispered.

"I'm trying to figure out how I feel about that," she admitted, her gaze dropping to his mouth.

"Jealous?" he asked.

"Maybe."

"But I'm here with you." He slid a finger down her

neck, enjoying the way her eyes fluttered closed. "Are you happy to see me?"

She exhaled. "Yes."

Leaning down, he brushed his lips over her ear and whispered, "Did you miss me?"

Paige nodded.

"I thought about you every day. Did you think about me?" He nipped her earlobe.

"All the time," she breathed.

Andrew drew in a deep breath, pulling her closer. "Don't worry."

"Worry about what?" she whispered.

"I don't want a nurse."

Paige leaned back, peered into his eyes. "Who do you want?"

He licked her bottom lip, enjoying her breathy gasp. His hands skimmed down her side and finally settled on her hips. Squeezing them, he lowered his face until the tip of his nose brushed against hers. "Do you have to ask?" he murmured.

"No."

Then he pressed his lips to hers. Over the last week, he'd tried to be okay with the distance, but he couldn't deny that he'd missed her. Having her in his arms, feeling her lips on his made the late-night drive through torrential rains worth it. Hearing her tell him she'd missed him was the icing on the cake.

Andrew had told himself that he was coming to talk to her, to ask her if she was really ready to do this. But he'd also come for this.

Finally pulling back, he rested his forehead on hers. Only for a second, though. He captured her lips with his again, kissing her with everything he had, pouring everything into it. The rain falling on them didn't matter, the storm passing overhead didn't matter. The only thing that mattered was this. Licking, nipping, biting . . . *Damn, I want her*.

A crack of lightning jolted her, and she stepped back. "Oh my," she whispered. "That was close. I think it hit one of the trees."

Andrew stalked toward her, tugging her flush against him. Pressing his lips against hers again, he ordered, "Go inside. I'll grab everything."

Nodding, she turned and went inside. Andrew gathered up her glass and a soaked blanket and joined her in the house.

"Power's out." Paige lit a candle, illuminating the room and giving him a full view of her nightgown—and the fact that she was naked underneath it. "I figured that might happen."

In the dim light, he could make out her puckered nipples, her flat stomach, and her . . . *Damn*.

Approaching her, he stopped right behind her. He swept her hair to the side and brushed his mouth over the back of her neck. "You're wet."

"Tell me about it," she whispered. "Everywhere."

He pulled her gown up slowly, pleased that she wasn't stopping him. "Everywhere, huh?"

"Yes." Her head fell back against his chest.

"You're so beautiful, Paige. I can't stop wanting you."

She groaned when his finger brushed against her clit.

"Drew." Her voice was a whispered plea. And he wanted to grant her every wish.

"So wet," he murmured, stroking her slowly.

She giggled. "I told you."

Andrew had never wanted another woman as much as

he wanted Paige. He burned with need for her. It was electric, dangerous. She shuddered against him.

He slid his free hand up her stomach, over her breasts and to her neck. Gripping her neck, he turned her mouth to his and kissed her. Slipping a finger in her heat, he closed his eyes as she rolled her hips taking him deeper. "Paige?"

"Yes?"

"I want you. And I need to know if you—"

"Yes." She kissed him. "Please. Don't make me wait."

And Andrew didn't, sliding another finger inside her. It didn't take long for her to fall over, and she did so with his name on her lips. It was the sweetest sound he'd ever heard. She slumped against him and he scooped her in his arms.

Her eyes popped open. "You don't have to take me upstairs."

He laughed. "Really?"

Shaking her head, she said, "I know you probably want to make it romantic and slow and hot, but I just want to be with you. Right now."

Taking the few steps to the sunroom, he lowered her to the couch. He trailed a line of kisses from her mouth to her cheek to her neck, then back to her mouth again.

Paige tugged his shirt off while he pushed his pants off. He slipped the strap of her gown down, dipped his head and took a nipple in his mouth. Groaning, he sucked greedily before turning his attention to the other one.

There were so many reasons to stop what was happening, but he wanted to give in to the feeling for once. He wanted to act first, think later. He wanted to get lost in her scent, her curves, her soft moans. As he nipped and sucked at her lips, he realized he could never get enough of her. With every stroke of her tongue against his, he dived deeper into her.

Reluctantly, he pulled back. "Are you sure?"

"Yes." She slipped her hand inside his underwear, gripped his erection in her tiny palms. "Yes."

He leaned over and pulled a condom out of his wallet. Sheathing himself quickly, he pressed the tip of his erection against her entrance. Andrew gripped her hips and entered her.

"Shit," he whispered.

Her eyes fluttered closed. "Right."

Paige wrapped her legs around him, taking him deeper and he moved—slow and deep, enjoying the feel of her around him. He wanted to revel in her, take his time with her, but the pull of her wouldn't let him be great. And the cute curse words coming from her mouth made it worse.

The urge to complete rushed over him, and he moved faster, harder, kissing her as he moved inside her. His heartbeat pounded in his ears as he got closer to his release. Paige shattered first, letting out a breathy gasp as she climaxed beneath him. Then he let go, coming so long and hard it felt like the pleasure had split him in two.

When he could breathe again, he looked down at Paige. A smile spread across her swollen lips, before she opened eyes as bright as the sun. Then she laughed.

"What?" Unable to resist her, he kissed her. "Why are you laughing?"

"You." She brushed her thumb over his brow. "See, I told you we didn't need the bed."

Chuckling, he dropped his head to her shoulder. "You're right. We didn't."

Paige smoothed her hand over his back. "But, I think we could try it out." His head snapped up. "Just for research purposes."

Andrew rolled off the couch. "Run."

Paige jumped up and bolted up the stairs. And Andrew had no choice but to follow her.

Chapter Eleven

Paige awoke to the smell of coffee and a thoroughly sexed body. After hours of lovemaking, she'd finally fallen asleep wrapped around Andrew's delicious body. Everything about last night had been perfect—the storm, the man, the couch, and the bed. She'd had no choice but to hold on for the ride, to get swept up in the whirlwind that was Andrew.

Moaning, she rolled over and cracked one eye open. She smiled. "You made coffee?"

From his position in the doorway, looking so good in his boxer briefs and nothing else, Andrew smirked. "I figured you'd need a cup."

She tossed what she hoped was a flirty, sexy grin his way. "Thank you." Sitting up, she leaned back against the headboard and took the offered mug. "What were you doing just standing there?"

He climbed on the bed and kissed her, before settling beside her. "Watching you."

"I probably look crazy." Sipping her coffee, she groaned. "So good. Your coffee skills have improved."

Andrew brushed a finger over a pebbled nipple, before

sucking it into his mouth. *Oh my*. Releasing it with a pop, he lifted his gaze to hers. "The wonders of K-Cups."

"Right?" Paige smirked. "I like that look in your eyes, though," she said.

"What's that?"

"Like you want more." She winked.

Andrew pried the mug out of her hands and set it on the bedside table. "I definitely do." He pulled her mouth to his. "I want so much more."

"Wait," she said. Reaching over to the table, she grabbed the mug of hot coffee and took another sip, then another, before setting it back down. When she met his gaze again, she shrugged, smoothing a finger over his furrowed brow. "It's coffee."

Leaning in, he wrapped his hand around the back of her neck. "I'm trying hard not to be offended that you chose coffee over me."

Paige laughed. "Don't be offended. Me and coffee go way back."

"Whatever," he murmured against her lips, before kissing her fully.

Then she was lost in him, consumed by his scent, his hard body against hers. Never before had a man loved her so thoroughly, completely. Andrew seemed to know exactly what she needed at every turn. It was sweet, but intense. And the way he kissed her—like she was the key to his survival—made her tremble with need.

Her back arched off the bed as he kissed his way down her body, placing gentle bites on her sensitive skin along the way. When she felt his breath on her core, she gasped. And when she felt his tongue on her clit, she purred. Andrew feasted on her, slipped two fingers inside her while he sucked on her bundle of nerves. An orgasm crested within her and, in a few moments, she let out a hoarse cry as waves of pleasure rolled through her.

When her heartbeat slowed, she collapsed onto the bed, burrowing into the mattress. But he wasn't done with her, because Andrew kissed his way back up her body.

"Paige?" She opened her eyes to find him staring down at her, a soft expression in his brown eyes. With his lips only a whisper away, he said, "More."

Wrapping her legs around his waist, she invited him in, rolling her hips into his hard length. "More," she repeated, biting down on his lip. She was so wet, so ready for him she fought the urge to beg him to come inside.

He sank deep inside of her, filling her so completely she wanted to weep at the sensation. She lifted her hips, pulling him in deeper.

"Damn, you feel good," he murmured.

Her eyes fluttered closed. "Please, Drew."

Andrew kissed both of her eyelids, then her nose and lips. Slowly, he moved in and out, out and in. Soon, slow and steady turned fast and frantic. He pounded into her hard as they moved together, meeting each other with equal force, equal desperation to complete. A crazed need for him seemed to take over and she clung to him, kissing him with everything she had.

Paige cried out first, gasping for air as she climaxed again. He followed soon after, groaning her name as he fell over the edge.

Rolling on his back, Andrew pulled her with him. She swept a hand over his stomach. "I'll take that any day over coffee." She felt the tremble of his laughter beneath her and smiled, propping herself up on her elbow. "With cream," she added. "And sugar."

Andrew barked out another laugh. "That's serious."

"Oh, it's definitely serious."

"I guess I should be proud of myself, huh?" He kissed the tip of her nose. "Beating coffee for the best thing about waking up."

Resting her head back on his chest, she giggled. "Absolutely. Hands down. No contest."

"Good to know."

Silence descended over the room for a few moments. "Drew?"

"Yes?"

"I'm really glad you came back."

"I was always coming back," he admitted, smoothing his hand down her back. "I just didn't expect to end up here."

"What did you expect?" she asked. "Things were pretty heated before you left."

"Yes, but I thought we'd talk about what happened."

Paige lifted her head, resting her chin on his chest so she could look at him. "What changed?"

"You in that damn nightgown." He smirked. "I couldn't keep my hands to myself."

Grinning, she told him, "I wasn't expecting company."

Frowning, he met her gaze. "You just walk around like that when no one's around?"

Paige shrugged. "Sometimes I like to feel sexy."

"Sexy? You nearly killed me."

She traced his jawline with her finger. "I'm glad. I've been thinking about us. There are so many reasons to not take this step."

Andrew tucked a strand of hair behind her ear. "And a lot of reasons *to* take the step."

"I thought about it while you were gone, every day. And

I kept coming back to the same thing over and over. We know each other, we care for each other, and—"

"And if we're honest with each other, this might work," he said, finishing her thought and proving that he *did* know her.

"Right. But I don't think we should make promises or commitments right now."

"Let's just see where it goes," he said, completing yet another thought she'd had.

Nodding, she kissed his chest and climbed on top of him, straddling his legs. "Exactly."

Andrew sat up and pulled her into a heated kiss, stealing her breath. The intense hum in her veins and his growing erection pretty much ensured that breakfast would be more like brunch. She lowered herself on him. "More," she whispered, biting down on his shoulder. "Then food."

"Try this." Paige held up a forkful of vegetable lasagna.

Andrew opened his mouth and she fed him. An explosion of garlic, cheese, and green pepper made him moan out loud. Nodding, he pointed at the pan as he chewed the rest of his food.

"Good?" she asked.

He took a sip of his beer. "Delicious."

They'd spent the last day exploring each other in various ways and Andrew couldn't stop falling for her more and more every second, every hour. He'd realized a while ago that he had feelings for her that went beyond an agent-client relationship, or even a platonic friendship. But he was sure he felt more than simple attraction, simple adoration for her, simple desire for her.

Paige cut him a big piece and set it on a plate. "I should

have made garlic bread." She added green salad to his plate. "Or some type of bread."

"It's fine," he assured her, carrying his full plate over to the table.

A moment later, she joined him. "I'm thinking I should have probably added more vegetables. It is a vegetable lasagna."

"I can't believe you waited until I got back to make it."

"Well, I was making it for you in the first place. It's your favorite. And I wanted to show you how much I improved."

"You've definitely improved. It's not juicy."

Paige laughed. "You got jokes. I'll never live that down."

Andrew remembered the first time Paige had made lasagna for him, as a reward for a contract he'd negotiated. It was early on in their friendship, about twelve years ago. At that time, Paige hadn't cooked much on her own, so it turned out soupy. It was so bad she'd tossed the entire pan out and ordered a pizza. Then she'd enrolled in a cooking class.

"Nah." He kissed her. "But you're pretty amazing now."

"Thank you."

They ate mostly in comfortable silence, each of them focused on their food. After a few minutes, she looked at him. "I've been thinking about something."

He eyed her silently, waiting for her to continue.

"I want to shift some things in my career a little," she said.

Raising a brow, he asked, "How so?"

"Maybe spend some time behind the camera."

He smiled. "Wow. I didn't know you were considering a change. You want to direct."

"Not really. I want to do more production work. I actually enjoyed the process and I think I've made some connections. What do you think?"

"I think you're amazing."

Paige eyed him skeptically. "Seriously?"

"Oh yeah. I can help you with that. Set up a few meetings, figure out what projects you might want to work on."

A shaky laugh burst from her lips. "I'd like that. Remember I told you about that book I read?" He nodded. "I really want to do something with it, if it's possible."

"We can try."

"I want you to read it." She beamed. "I think you'll like it. It's about a family of assassins, escaping into a lair five floors underground. Fast-paced. I loved it."

"I'll take a look," he offered. "Is it in your room?"

"Yep." She stood and ran up the stairs. A few moments later, she returned with the book and handed it to him. "I earmarked several passages that stuck out to me. What's awesome is the author is from Michigan. Isn't that cool?"

Andrew eyed the mysterious cover and read the blurb on the back of the book. "Looks interesting. We can definitely talk about this."

"I know you're on a leave now, but maybe we can touch base once you're back to work."

Andrew had taken family care leave when his mother fell and injured herself, but he'd done some things remotely. "We don't have to wait. I'm here with you."

"On a leave," she reiterated. "This can wait. But I'm glad I brought it up. I'm excited. Now, finish eating so we can have dessert."

"I hope dessert involves you naked with a slice of pie."

Since he'd missed the first apple pie, Paige had baked another one, so he could try it out. The scent of apples, brown sugar, and cinnamon filled the entire kitchen while she'd baked the pie that afternoon. And when she'd pulled it out of the oven, she'd warned him not to touch it until he ate his dinner.

"Dessert includes me, pie, and ice cream."

"Sounds like my kind of treat." He pulled her to him and planted a kiss on her mouth. "We can skip to that if you want."

"Not a chance." She cut into her lasagna. "I talked to Skye."

He paused, fork midair. "Really?"

"Yeah. I figured it was time to reboot communication."

Andrew was surprised at this turn of events. He didn't expect Paige to reach out to her publicist so soon. She was stubborn that way. But he was glad she did. "How did that go?" he asked.

"It went well. Skye is good people. I'd count her among my small group of friends. We didn't really talk about work, but I did give her a heads-up about us."

That's unexpected. Especially since they hadn't really established they were an "us." "Oh, okay."

"I know it seems weird, since we're not really together. Officially." Paige moved her fork around her plate. "But she's my publicist, so I figured . . ."

Andrew stared at her and waited for her to finish. But when she didn't say anything else, he asked, "Do you regret talking to her?"

She shrugged. "No. I kind of needed the ear."

"Paige, look at me." After a moment, she glanced at him. "What did you need the ear for?"

"To talk. I don't have many friends and I felt like I needed to get some things out."

Curious, he asked, "About what?"

"How I feel about you?"

The revelation that she'd voiced her feelings about him to someone *other* than him made him happy. "How is that exactly?"

"Are you really asking me that after . . . ?"

"Actually, I am." He leaned back in his chair and observed her. Andrew couldn't help but notice the way she avoided eye contact, staring at an unknown spot behind him or at her plate or anywhere but him. "You're nervous."

She met his gaze then and bit down on her bottom lip. Nodding, she sighed. "It's not like this isn't weird. We've known each other for a long time and now we're . . ."

"Getting to know each other differently," he said.

"Right. There are a lot of things to consider. It felt good to talk about some of it with Skye."

"I get it," he told her. "I'm not mad or anything. But don't you think *we* should talk about it?" Paige slumped forward, as if he'd pulled the pin out of her sail. And he laughed. Pulling her onto his lap, he kissed her. "I promise I won't bite."

Paige wrapped her arms around his neck. "Really? I kind of like the bites." She rested her head on his shoulder.

"I'll bite later," he joked.

She giggled. "I'm worried we might be moving too fast."

"Me too," he admitted.

"But I can't stop myself from wanting to be with you."

Paige continued talking, but he'd gotten stuck at that sentence. Of course, she had no idea how long he'd waited to hear her say that. Hell, *he* didn't even know until she'd said it.

"You know?" she asked.

He blinked. "Huh?"

She sat up, peered into his eyes. "Did you hear me?"

Andrew thought about lying, but he promised he wouldn't lie again. So, he told the truth. "I'm sorry. I didn't hear you after you told me you couldn't stop yourself from wanting me."

Paige frowned. "You don't think I want you?"

Shaking his head, he rushed to assure her. "No. It's not that. I just never thought I'd hear you say it."

"Is that . . . ?" She dropped her gaze, ran her finger over the top button of his shirt. "Are you okay with that?"

He gripped her chin gently and lifted her head up so that he could peer into her eyes. "I'm more than okay with that. I'm here, right?"

She smiled. "Does this mean that we're going to continue exploring each other?"

"I think that's what it means," he said, chuckling when she shoved him playfully. "Okay, I'm just messing with you." He kissed her jaw. "I want to explore everything with you."

"Me too." And Paige was looking forward to whatever that included.

Chapter Twelve

Andrew pulled the brim of Paige's hat over her eyes.
"You're sure about this?" he asked.

"I'm sure," Paige said, with a hard nod.

He smiled at her, so adorable in her hat and jogging suit.
He took her in, lingering on the curve of her mouth. "I'm
not," he said. "You still look like Paige Mills."

Lifting her chin up, she said, "I *am* Paige Mills."

"I'm just sayin'. This disguise isn't very good."

"I'm just going into your mother's house, Drew."

Andrew's mother had been released from the hospital.
When he'd told Paige he needed to go see her, she offered
to come with him. At first, he'd hesitated. He didn't want
to do anything to put her at risk. She'd done a good job of
remaining hidden. But Detroit was a big city full of Paige
Mills Fans. The probability of someone spotting her there
was pretty high.

"Come on," she said. "It'll be fine."

Sucking in a deep breath, he told her, "Okay. We're going
to go into the house. And, whatever you do, don't look at
Mrs. Fulton."

Her brows furrowed. "Who is Mrs. Fulton?"

Pointing toward the house to the right of his mother's he said, "She owns the house next door. I guarantee you she saw my car pull up. She'll probably come out and try and talk to us."

Paige shrugged. "Okay, but what's wrong with that?"

"If she recognizes you, the whole world will know you're here."

Laughing, Paige said, "You're joking, right?"

He shot her a blank stare. "Do I look like I'm joking?"

Paige's smile fell. Shaking her head, she said, "Okay. Got it."

Andrew got out of the car, jogged around to the passenger side, and pulled it open. Holding out his hand, he waited until she slipped her palm in his and helped her out. They hurried, hand in hand, to the front door. Right before they stepped onto the porch, he heard his name being called. *Shit.*

"Andrew?" Mrs. Fulton called again.

He felt Paige tense next to him. Giving her hand a comforting squeeze, he turned toward Mrs. Fulton and waved. "Hi, Mrs. Fulton."

With her hands on her hips, Mrs. Fulton said, "Hey! Is that your girlfriend?"

"Yes." The word came out before he could stop himself. Because he knew he'd opened himself up to more questions.

"That's so sweet. I need to come over there and meet her," Mrs. Fulton said. "I'm so happy to finally see you with someone. Maybe now your mother will get that grandbaby she's been dreaming about."

Paige giggled.

Andrew frowned.

Mrs. Fulton started the slow trek across the lawn toward

them, the whole time yapping away about the bad kids who keep kicking her trash cans.

"Here she comes," he grumbled.

Paige gripped his hand tightly. "Oh no," she whispered.

It took a moment, but Mrs. Fulton finally approached them. She gave him a hug. "It's so good to see you boys. Your mama is in hog heaven with you all here." She reached a hand out to Paige. "I'm Mrs. Fulton."

Paige gave the woman a quick hug, but kept her eyes low when she said, "I'm Pa . . . Perel."

Now it was Andrew's turn to laugh. *Where the hell did she come up with that name?*

Mrs. Fulton divided her gaze between him and *Perel*. "Aren't you a cute couple? Do you work together? Andrew has done us all proud here. I remember when he would be running around in his underwear. He used to flash everyone in the neighborhood."

Aw, man. He sighed. Mrs. Fulton told that story every time someone new came around. It didn't have to be anyone they knew, either. She'd tell it to the mailman if he gave her an ear.

"I tried to get him to keep his pants on," the older woman continued. "But he liked to be free." Lowering her voice, she added, "We used to say he would make some woman very happy one day."

What the . . . ?

Paige burst out in a fit of giggles, falling against him as she cracked up.

"Mrs. Fulton," he said. "We have to go inside and see Mom."

"Oh, I know. I'm glad to meet you, Per . . . What did you say your name is again, sweetheart?"

Clearing her throat, Paige said, "Perel."

"Alright, Perel. I better get back over to my house. My story is coming on any minute. That *All of Our Lives* is something else."

Paige choked, and he smoothed his hand over her back.

"Are you okay, baby?" Mrs. Fulton asked, concern in her eyes.

Nodding, Paige said, "Yes. I'm fine."

Mrs. Fulton tilted her head and stared at Paige. "You look so familiar to me. Did you go to Mt. Mary Baptist Church on the East Side?"

"She's not from Detroit," Andrew answered quickly. "We better get inside. Talk to you later."

He unlocked the front door with his key and ushered Paige inside. Once they closed the door, he leaned against it and let out a sigh. "That was close."

Pulling off her hat, Paige fanned herself. "This baseball cap is hot. I thought I was going to die out there."

"It might have been all that laughing you were doing, *Perel.* Where did you get that name?"

She shrugged. "I was thinking about how I forgot my hand sanitizer and that's the only thing that came to mind."

Andrew laughed, tugging her to him. He kissed her. "That's some quick thinking right there."

Paige dropped her forehead on his chest and wrapped her arm around his waist. "If you don't mention it to anyone, I promise not to tell another living soul about your stint as a stripper."

He squeezed her, until she laughed. "You think that's funny, huh?"

Peering up at him, she said, "It's hilarious. I'm wondering if you'll come out of retirement and give me a show." She winked. "I have dollars."

"I'll do it for you for free."

"Tonight," she said, rising on the tips of her toes to kiss him. "At the hotel."

Andrew had booked a room at a hotel about forty miles outside of Detroit, in case he didn't feel like making the three-hour drive back to South Haven. "That can be arranged," he said, nuzzling her neck with his nose.

"So, are y'all going to just stay in here all day or what?" His older brother, Connor, stepped farther into the room. "I mean, we've been waiting a good ten minutes for you."

Pulling away from Paige, Andrew embraced his brother. "What's up, bruh?"

"Nothing much." Connor hugged Paige. "You look beautiful as always, Ms. Mills."

Over the years, Paige had grown close with Andrew's family. She'd even attended a few functions as his guest. He wondered if his family would embrace this new change in their relationship.

"Hey, Connor," she said. "How are you?"

"I'm well. Why don't y'all come into the family room. Mom has been asking for you all day."

Paige slipped her hand in Andrew's again and let him lead her to the family room. His mother was on the couch watching the end of her favorite game show. To his left, his younger brother, Damon, was sitting at the desk typing furiously on his laptop.

"Hey, family," Andrew said.

Mom's eyes lit up when she saw him. "Drew, you're finally here." She gasped. "Paige! You're here, too."

Damon stood. "What's up, Drew?" He walked over to them and gave them each a quick hug.

They made their way to the couch. Andrew leaned down and kissed his mother's cheek. "I told you I was coming."

"Hi, Connie." Paige hugged his mother. "You look beautiful as always."

"Thank you. I'm so glad you're here."

"Me too," Paige said. "How are you feeling?"

"In some pain," his mom answered. "But right now, it's subsided a little. So I'm grateful for that."

"Is there anything I can do for you?" Paige asked.

Mom waved her off. "Yes, have a seat. I've been wanting to talk to you about that last movie you starred in. I'm so glad she didn't choose that other brother. He was crazy. Bipolar *and* an alcoholic. Goodness, I wanted to kill him."

Paige laughed, taking a seat on the adjacent sofa. "You're not the only one. People have been tweeting about him nonstop."

Andrew stared at Paige as she chatted with his mom about movies and game shows. Even though she was nervous to meet Mrs. Fulton, Paige had hugged her anyway. She was everything people believed about her and more. *She's amazing*.

Connor walked over to him and handed him a beer. "When did this happen?" his brother asked.

Eyeing him, Andrew said, "None of your business."

"You brought her home, man."

Andrew popped the top off his beer and took a long pull. "It's not like she hasn't been here before."

"Never as your girlfriend," Connor said.

His attention drifted back to Paige, who was now showing his mother something on her phone. Seeing the two women he cared most about enjoying each other's company did something for him and made him want to have more moments like this. Forever.

Damon approached them. "Paige is still fine as hell."

He stared at Drew out of the corner of his eye. "Think she'll finally give a brotha a chance?"

"You might want to stand down, Dame." Connor snickered, shooting Andrew an amused stare. Taking a sip of his beer, Connor added, "Unless you're ready for a beatdown."

Andrew pinned his younger brother with an unamused stare. "Don't even think about it."

"Told you." Connor shrugged.

Laughing, Damon said, "I had to try."

Paige stood and walked over to them. "I told your mother I'd make lunch," she said to Andrew. "But I'll need some things from the store. Do you mind running out?"

Andrew shook his head. "No. Just give me a list and I'll go get it."

"Thanks." She kissed him, then went back to the couch to join his mother.

Andrew didn't miss the way his brothers exchanged knowing looks with each other before they turned back to him. He glanced at Connor, then Damon, and then back at Connor again. "We're taking it slow," he admitted.

Connor clasped Andrew's back. "Keep telling yourself that, bruh."

Later, they all had lunch in the family room while watching a Marvel movie. Paige had made homemade pizza, which his mother couldn't stop raving about. Mom rarely ate other people's cooking, so it had shocked him and his brothers that she'd been so complimentary.

"Can I borrow your phone?" Paige asked, drawing his attention from the movie. She set her iPad down.

He frowned. "Is everything okay?"

She nodded, but he suspected it was only because other people were in the room. Because everything was definitely *not* okay. Without questioning her further, he unlocked his phone and handed it to her. When she went into the adjoining living room, he turned to his mother, who was watching him with a curious look in her eyes.

"I like you with her," his mom said. "And don't tell me nothing is going on because I see it."

"I wasn't going to say that," he told her.

"Good."

Andrew heard a gasp from the other room, and hurried to Paige. They locked gazes for a moment, before she turned away from him. With one arm folded across her chest, she told whoever was on the phone, "I don't care what you have to do. Fix it."

She tapped the screen of his phone—hard—and handed it to him. "Thanks," she said, her voice shaky.

"What happened?" He squeezed her shoulder. "Tell me."

"I can't believe this," she said. He couldn't figure out if she was talking to him, or to herself. But when she looked at him, she said, "That sorry asshole filed a lawsuit against me for breach of contract."

Paige sucked in the cold October air. It felt good to be outside, to breathe in fresh air. She'd almost had a panic attack after she'd talked to her personal attorney, Michelle Lars, on the phone. Andrew had promptly whisked her out of the house, and away from his family, so she could calm down.

As they strolled down his mother's block, she couldn't help but feel a bit hopeless. The little slice of happiness she'd had today—being with Andrew and his family—had been eclipsed by her ex-husband's behavior.

Filing the lawsuit was just the latest behavior in a string of spiteful moves by Julius. It seemed as though her ex-husband had started a new full-time job as a rep for Let's Fuck With Paige, Inc.

"I can't believe he's doing this," she murmured.

"I can." Andrew shrugged. "He's desperate. He needs your money."

Paige knew that, but it still didn't make her feel better. She'd worked hard for her money. She saved, she invested, and she gave back. If she had to fork over a large sum to Julius because of a judge's order, she'd be livid.

"But I didn't breach any contract. In his motion, he said that it was a verbal agreement between us that I would star in his last movie."

The filing stated that because Paige didn't follow the agreement, he couldn't find a studio to back the film. As a result, the movie was dead in the water, with no hope of getting made.

Andrew shoved his hands in his pockets, but Paige wished she could just hold his hand. She wished that she could draw some strength from him. "What did Michelle say?" he asked.

"She told me not to panic, but I . . ." *How the hell am I supposed to not panic*? "It's just one thing after another with him."

"I'll contact Michelle when we get back to the house. We can work together on this."

"No." She stopped and turned to him. "We're here to spend time with your mother. I already feel bad enough that we're out here when you should be with your family."

"They'll be fine. We're just taking a walk." They started their slow stroll again. "See that over there?" He pointed to the tree on the right side of the street.

She nodded. "Yeah, it's a tree."

"It's not just any tree. It's *my* tree."

Confused, Paige stared at the large tree. The branches were huge, long and thick. In elementary school, she'd learned about the different types of trees, but she didn't remember a damn thing. The only word dancing in her brain was *oak*.

"Back in the day, I spent hours up in that tree, hiding," he explained. "I'd take a book with me and sit up there until the streetlights came on."

Paige smiled, imagining Andrew as a kid running home so he wouldn't get in trouble. "Did you ever not make it home in time?"

"All the time. And I paid for it, believe me."

"Did you have a lot of friends in the neighborhood?" she asked.

Shaking his head, he said, "Not really. I had some. But I was kind of a loner. I still am."

Paige was a loner, too. She'd thrived in solitude, practicing Shakespeare and reciting poetry in front of her bedroom mirror.

They started their walk again. He showed her the path he and his brothers would take to the corner store and the huge rock they used to draw on in the summer.

"In the summer, we'd run through the sprinklers to 'get wet.'" He chuckled softly. "Mom couldn't swim, and she was scared of deep water, so she didn't let us go to the pool when we were small."

She frowned. "Wait, who taught you to swim, then?" They'd been to the beach several times, and Andrew was an excellent swimmer.

"I took a class at the community rec in high school, paid for it with money that I'd saved up mowing lawns and shoveling snow."

"Wow," she said. "Impressive. You were a hard worker, even as a teenager."

"That was nothing but my mom. She worked so hard, all the time. We had no choice but to do the same. She'd always say, 'If you want to eat, you have to work.'"

Andrew pointed out another house—the candy house. He shared a story about how he'd saved up money to buy the little Fun Dip candy. But when he got to the candy house, some of the neighborhood kids jumped him for his money.

"Oh no," Paige said.

"Connor beat the shit out of them. Then he took me to Old Man Hennessey's house to learn how to box."

Paige enjoyed hearing him talk about his youth. She enjoyed hearing him talk at all. He was so strong and pensive. Hearing him share a piece of his childhood with her made her feel special, like he was giving her another piece of himself.

"Did you always want to leave Detroit?"

"Not always. The block was a safe haven for us. It was a community here, family. Everyone looked out for each other. It was different in the city back then," he said.

Although Paige's mother had grown up in Detroit, Paige had never lived in "The D." She'd visited sometimes, but hadn't had the chance to really explore the area. She hoped to be able to do that someday, because it was a part of her history.

To her right, she heard a young girl on her phone, talking about boy drama. She watched the girl as she rambled on about a Halloween costume and an upcoming dance at school.

She met the girl's gaze for a brief moment and smiled at her.

The girl gasped. "Oh my God."

Oh my God is right. Because Paige had just been recognized.

The girl ran up to her. "Oh my God," she repeated. "You're Paige Mills."

Paige glanced at Andrew, then back at the girl. She placed a finger over her own lips, silently telling the girl to keep it quiet. Then she nodded.

The girl squealed, then smacked a hand over her mouth. "Oops. I'm sorry. My name is Paige, too. We're twinsies!"

"Right?" Paige laughed.

"I love you. I use your hair products." Young Paige shook her curls. "I've been following you on Instagram. You're so beautiful in person—and on screen."

Paige's heart melted and she smiled. "Thank you. You're lovely yourself."

The girl ducked her head, a shy grin on her face. "Oh my God," she whispered again. "I heard your TED talk. It inspired me to want to do more community work. I just started applying to colleges. I want to go to USC."

"That's cool. You should totally come to Cali. You'd love it there."

"It's my main goal in life right now." They chatted for a few more minutes. Then the girl asked, "Can I take a picture with you?"

Paige bit her lip. This was a teenage girl. If she took a pic with her, there was no way that girl wouldn't post it on her social media. But while Paige didn't want to be seen, there was no way she could tell the intelligent young lady in front of her no.

Nodding, she agreed to take a pic. Andrew snapped the pics with the Young Paige's phone and his own phone—probably because he knew she'd want a memento.

When he handed the girl her phone back, she peered at the screen and squealed again. "Thank you."

Paige hugged the girl. "You're welcome. It was good to meet you, Paige."

"You too." Then Young Paige took off, running toward her house.

She felt Andrew's eyes on her and turned to look at him. "What?"

"You're amazing."

Bumping his shoulder, she said, "Oh, stop."

"No, I'm serious. So when you start to feel hopeless, remember how much of an impact you had on that girl." He stepped closer to her, but they didn't touch. "You're going to be alright."

"I will," she said. "Thank you for this. Thank you for getting me out of the house. And thank you for taking me on this little tour of your old neighborhood. I loved every minute of it."

"Wait until I show you the haunted house of the neighborhood."

Paige's eyes widened, excited because she loved spooky stuff. "Oh, I need to see that."

They finished the tour and returned to Connie's house. They played cards, ate popcorn, and laughed so much her sides hurt. Sometime during the evening, Paige realized she could never go back to the way things were before with Andrew. Because the more time she spent with him, the more she knew she'd never be satisfied with less of him. She wanted more.

Chapter Thirteen

"*Shit.*"

"What is it?" Paige asked from behind him. "Did you forget something in Detroit?"

Andrew blinked, surprised that he'd spoken out loud. Because he'd been thinking it, thinking about how life was about to change for them. All because of a grainy snapshot.

Paige poked him. "Drew? What's wrong?" she asked again.

His gaze fell to his phone and the text he'd received moments ago from Skye. There were three words below an image of him and Skye hugging while taking a stroll in his mother's neighborhood: You fucked up!

Andrew wanted to choke the incognito photographer for snapping a pic of an innocent moment between them and turning it into a salacious headline. He clicked on the link and scanned the article. *Shit.*

PAIGE MILLS'S SECRET EXPOSED. YEARS OF
UNBRIDLED PASSION ERUPT IN HER SECRET HIDEAWAY
WITH LOVER AND AGENT

The subtitle was even worse: JULIUS REEVES SPEAKS OUT

Paige stepped in front of him, a frown on her face. "Drew? What happened?"

Without a word, he showed her the article and watched as the color drained from her face. She met his gaze again, horror in her eyes.

He squeezed her shoulders. "I'll fix this. Don't worry."

"Don't worry?" she shouted. "This is bullshit. One picture and they're painting me as the villain. Forget that he covered up a whole baby and an affair. Forget that his ass was arrested for sexual assault." She whirled around and stormed out of the room. And he was right behind her. "I hate him." Paige unlocked the patio door and pushed it open, stepping outside. Again, he followed her. "First, he sues me for breach of contract for a movie I never even agreed to make. And now this? It feels like I'll never be free of him. And I need to be done with him."

Andrew pulled her into his arms. He understood her anger was about more than a tabloid article. Julius had continued to antagonize her, after he'd put her through so much in their short marriage.

"Baby, it's okay." He kissed the top of her head. "I'm going to fix this."

Paige looked at him, her eyes swimming with unshed tears. "You can't fix this, Andrew. You can't protect me from everything."

"I can try," he told her.

"You don't get it."

"Probably not. But as far as this article is concerned, you know how it is with the press. They'll talk about it for a while, then it'll die down."

She dropped her head. "Did you read what Julius said?"

Andrew had read every word. But as angry as he was, he knew someone had to remain calm. "It doesn't matter."

"To you. You know how they paint black women in the media. They're harder on us than anyone. People have been waiting for me to be the damn slut, the damn homewrecker, the damn adulterer. They won't let this go."

Everything she'd said was the truth. He'd seen celebrities destroyed because of perception. And it always started with an article. Most people in the industry shook it off, but Paige actually cared about her reputation. She was very aware of her image and she'd been diligent in protecting her privacy and avoiding scandals. But all of that changed when she'd married Julius Reeves. Since then, she'd been fodder for all types of blogs and gossip television shows—and now she was a target for baseless lawsuits.

"You should be mad, too," she said. "You're affected by this. I'm surprised your phone isn't blowing up right now."

Just then, his phone buzzed. *His mother*. Andrew didn't answer, though. He needed to think, he needed a plan. A moment later, his phone went off again. *Connor*.

Andrew could have believed that his mother had called because she wanted to know if they'd made it back to South Haven safely. But since his brother had now called two times in a row, he knew they'd seen something. Maybe they'd read an article in one of his mother's grocery store magazines.

"See?" Paige said, raising her brow. "You should probably call your family back."

"Not right now. Let's take a minute," he said. "I need to—" Andrew peered down at his buzzing phone. *Xavier*. Turning his phone off, he sighed. "Listen, we're fine. There's nothing to see. We've been careful."

The photographer hadn't caught them in an embrace or

even while kissing. They were walking down the street, nothing more. The captioned photo could be explained away easily. Andrew had been her agent for years. They'd attended galas, premieres, award shows, and other events together. They'd been photographed out to dinner, at parties, and even at the park before.

Andrew framed her face with his hands. "You trust me?"

"Of course I trust you. I don't trust Julius. This is just the thing he needs to make my life more miserable."

"Paige, that's never going to happen. Everything will be alright." He kissed her. "It's cold out here. You said you wanted a shower. Why don't you go do that while I make some calls?"

Once Paige disappeared up the stairs, Andrew pulled out his laptop. After he sent several emails, he called his mother back.

"Andrew?" Mom answered. "Where are you? Are you with Paige still? There are men with cameras here and they won't leave. Connor almost choked one of them for peeking in my windows."

Grumbling a curse, he asked his mother how many photographers were outside. She estimated there were approximately five. "I'm sorry, Ma. It's because of me and Paige that they're there."

"What? Why?"

"They're looking for a story, and we gave them one when we went out for a walk yesterday."

Andrew had put the pieces together, and guessed Young Paige had posted a pic to her social media, and the gossip mill went from there. He didn't blame the teenager. It wasn't every day that a star of Paige's caliber walked down a random Detroit street.

"Oh no, son. I'm sorry. If you hadn't been here looking after me, then—"

"Don't. I was there because I wouldn't be anywhere else. You're my mother."

"But Paige . . . she's probably so upset."

"She'll be okay." He sighed. "I'm coming back to Detroit, though."

"No," his mother said. "You don't need to be here. You have to stay with Paige. Connor is here, and he's not leaving any time soon."

"Ma, if you need anything, let me know. I'll send security there for a while."

"You don't have to do that. I have Ms. Betty here, right under my mattress." Ms. Betty was the name of his mother's three-eighty-caliber gun. She'd purchased it a couple of years ago when she went to firearms training to get her Concealed Pistol License.

"I know you have Ms. Betty, but you can't go pulling that out on the paparazzi."

"I know what I'm doing, boy."

"Yeah, but you can barely walk right now. Just let me send someone to watch over you. That's it. Connor can't be there every hour of the day."

She reluctantly agreed and, before he hung up, made him promise to call often. He placed another call seconds later.

Vonda answered immediately. "Andrew? What the hell is going on?"

"Nothing."

"Have you seen social media? You're trending. They even have a mash-up for you and Paige—*Prew*."

"What?" He shook his head. "Never mind. Listen, I

need security posted at my mother's house. Jax has relationships with several security firms. I think Hill Security is located out of Detroit." Andrew instructed Vonda to hire the company and send them to his mother's house. He gave them Connor's number as a contact.

"What else?" she said.

"I'm going to be here for a little while longer, so I trust that you have everything under control client-wise."

"Oh, you're good on that front."

"I had no doubt."

"I did receive a call from the studio. They're still waiting on that contract, threatening to hire Heather Franklin for that role. Also, the producer has been hounding me over the reshoots."

Andrew nodded. "I'll call Robert, and I'll talk to Paige about the contract."

"Then I'll wait to hear from you."

He ended the call and sent Connor a text message about security. Then sent a text to Skye letting her know that he'd handle everything.

Her reply came through a minute later: Yeah, right.

"Drew?"

Paige's voice stopped him from sending a terse response to Skye. Instead, he put his phone down and stood. "Hey."

She approached him, dressed in a short lace nightgown. His gaze raked over her, lingering on the outline of her breasts under the lace. Stepping between his legs, she wrapped her arms around his shoulder. "Hi."

He smoothed his hands up her back, pulling her closer. "You're so damn tempting."

With raised brows, she climbed on his lap, straddling him. "And you're so damn dressed."

Laughing, he kissed her, picked her up in his arms, and lowered her down on the glass table. He took his clothes off quickly and pulled her to the edge of the table. Seconds later, he was inside her, inside her warmth. He took her hard and fast as she writhed under him. It didn't take her long to climax, and this time they fell over together, lips fused and bodies pressed against each other.

"Oh," she moaned. "You're so good at this."

Andrew met her gaze, searched her face. "We're good at this."

A slow smile spread over her face. "Now I have to take another shower." She brushed her mouth over his. "Want to join me?"

He picked her up, laughing at her surprised yelp. "Definitely."

Paige awoke to a loud knock at the door. She glanced over at Andrew, who was still sleeping. Grumbling a curse, she slid out of the bed and put on a robe. She jogged down the stairs and paused. She recognized the person on the other side of the door. And she wasn't ready.

Clearing her throat, she walked to the door and opened it. "Skye, what are you doing here?"

"My job." Skye brushed past her, walking into the house.

"Come in," Paige muttered sarcastically, slamming the door.

Skye breezed through the house like she owned it. "We need to talk."

"How did you know I was here?" Paige glanced up the stairs, hoping Andrew didn't come down naked and ready for another round. "Did my mother tell you?"

"Yes." Skye folded her arms across her chest. "Because she knows you need me."

"I already know about the article. You didn't have to come here. I was going to call you today."

"Well, it's good that I'm here then." Skye pulled out a chair and sat down, crossing her legs. "What were you going to call me about?"

Paige leaned against the counter. "You already know the answer to that."

"But I want *you* to tell me why you completely ignored my advice to keep things quiet between you and Andrew."

I need coffee. Sighing heavily, Paige went to the sink and filled the Keurig up with water and popped a K-Cup inside. She pulled a mug out of the cabinet, placed it on the drip tray, and pushed the button.

Turning to face Skye again, Paige rested her elbows on the island countertop. "I thought it would be okay to go to Detroit with him to see his mother."

"Why would you think that?"

"Because! We're friends."

Skye arched a brow. "Are you really going to stand there and tell me you're just friends with Andrew?"

"No. You already know we're not *just* friends. But we *are* friends, nonetheless. There's nothing wrong with going to see my *friend's* mother after she had surgery."

"Except that's not exactly what happened."

"We didn't do anything wrong," Paige argued. "We were walking down the street—talking. For goodness' sake, he was giving me a tour of his old neighborhood. We weren't 'getting it on' in the middle of the street. We barely touched each other."

"It doesn't matter, Paige. You know this. It's all about perception."

"There's nothing to perceive. Even if we were hugged up, kissing, fondling, or whatever, we're both single. Am I supposed to never date anyone?"

Paige knew the photo leak wasn't a good thing, but it wasn't a bad thing either. The thing that had bothered her the most about the article is that Julius had weighed in on it, insinuating that she'd been having an affair with Drew for years.

Skye stood and approached her. She pulled out her phone, tapped the screen a few times, and showed it to her.

Paige's mouth fell open. "Where did you get this?" She eyed the picture of Julius's latest cover article—all about *his* heartbreak, about *his* failed marriage.

"A friend of mine gave me a heads-up. The article is scheduled to publish next week. There's something else." Skye showed her another screenshot—it was a motion to reopen the divorce. Julius had accused Paige of hiding assets and wanted alimony. "He filed it yesterday after the pictures leaked. A blogger got ahold of this and did a video about it."

Paige didn't have it in her to react. Court motions were public record. There was nothing she could do about it being posted. Until she talked to Demi, who was out of the country on vacation, she couldn't worry about it. She had to prioritize her issues, and her main concern right now was dealing with Andrew.

The Keurig beeped, and Paige pulled her mug off the tray. She poured a small shot of hazelnut creamer into the mug and dumped a tablespoon of sugar inside.

"Coffee?" Paige asked.

"No, I'm okay." Skye tilted her head to get her attention. "It's not about the pictures, Paige. It's not about who you're dating. The problem is you've been hiding out here for weeks while Julius is painting this damning narrative about you in public. You didn't do any interviews after the divorce. You didn't speak out after his many arrests. It's time for you to get ahead of this."

Paige lifted her head. "You're right." She'd become comfortable in hiding, away from the prying eyes of the paparazzi, away from the reminders of the huge mistake she'd made by marrying Julius. It was time for her to take control of her life.

"I know he hurt you." Skye squeezed Paige's hand. "I know you needed this time to gather your thoughts and rest. But we need to get back in the game. Let's turn the tables on that asshole."

Paige hugged Skye. "Thanks. I appreciate you."

"Girl, you know I've got you. Demi will handle that dumbass divorce filing when she gets back, Michelle and/or Andrew will tackle that breach of contract shit, and I got you on this faux scandal."

Having a team that had her back meant everything to Paige. She was grateful for their persistence and their dedication. When this was over, she planned to do something nice for all of them.

"Another thing." Skye tapped her chin. "We need to talk about Andrew. Where is he?"

Paige glanced at the stairs. "In the bedroom."

"Hm. So I take it you've graduated from lustful thoughts to real life fu—"

"Shh!" Paige held up a finger up. "Don't say it. He might be able to hear you."

Shrugging, Skye said, "What?"

Paige scratched the back of her neck. "I just . . . want you to be quiet."

Skye barked out a laugh before covering her own mouth. "I'm sorry. Forgot you were hiding me downstairs."

Swatting her friend with a towel, Paige smiled. "You're a nut. What were you going to say about Andrew?"

"What about me?" Andrew walked down the stairs—fully dressed. He approached them. "Skye."

"Andrew," Skye tossed back. "I figured I'd just show up. Because Lord knows if I'd called, you wouldn't have answered."

"That's not true." He pulled a mug from the cabinet and started himself a cup of coffee. "I was planning to contact you today."

"Really?" Skye narrowed her eyes on him. "What about?"

"We've already been through this," Paige cut in. Turning to Andrew, she told him about their conversation. "And I'm going to go back to L.A. so we can handle this."

Andrew ran his thumb over her chin. "Are you sure?"

Nodding, Paige said, "Yes."

"Which brings me to my next agenda item," Skye quipped. "I'm going to need you two to cool it."

Paige's eyes flashed to Skye. "What?"

"It's best that you're not seen together until we're able to get your side of the story out there."

"Seriously? Why?" Paige asked incredulously. "We went over this already. We're both single."

"I know that, but the goal is to get you some positive press. Although you're not doing anything wrong, it's best not to give him more ammunition to play the sympathy card."

Andrew pressed a comforting hand to Paige's back. "As much as I hate to agree with Skye, she's right."

Paige massaged her temples. "You're still my agent."

"Yes, but I think we need to concentrate on your career for the time being."

"What does that mean? So we're not going to see each other at all?" Paige asked.

"Right," Skye chirped.

"Wrong." Andrew glared at Skye before turning his attention back to Paige. "We'll just have to be careful."

"You mean like you were being careful in Detroit," Skye pointed out.

"Can you give us a minute?" he asked.

"Whatever. I'll give myself a tour of this fabulous house." Skye stalked off, muttering something about arrogant men who think they know everything.

Andrew rested his forehead on Paige's. "It's not forever," he said. "Just until Skye can schedule some positive publicity. In the meantime, I need you to concentrate on you."

"I do need to shift my focus right now. I just don't want to—"

He pulled her into a searing kiss. When he finally pulled away, he met her gaze. "We're fine. I'm going to be there with you. I'll be pulling the strings in the background."

Paige closed her eyes as relief washed over her. "Good, because I need you with me."

"I'm always going to be there."

She wrapped her arms around his neck. "Promise?"

"I promise."

Paige let him hold her for a minute before calling Skye back into the kitchen. It was time to hit Julius where it hurt. And she would gladly rise to the occasion.

Chapter Fourteen

Andrew walked into the Pure Talent Los Angeles office on a mission—to get in without answering any questions. Yet, from the moment he'd stepped into the lobby, he'd been bombarded with weird "hellos" and different looks.

Greeting his colleagues with quick head nods, he didn't stop until he was behind his closed office door. He dropped his bag on the sofa in his office and walked over to his desk. The desk was just as he'd left it a few weeks ago, bare except for the file he'd requested Vonda leave on it this morning.

Taking a seat, he scanned the document in front of him—a copy of Paige's contract for her last movie. He had a meeting scheduled with Robert Wilkes to discuss reshoots. Before he'd left Michigan, she'd agreed to fulfill her contract, but he wanted to request specific provisions for her return to set.

A knock on the door drew his attention away from the contract. "Come in."

Vonda poked her head inside. "Hey, Andrew." She entered the office and approached the desk. "How are you?"

Andrew nodded his greeting and focused on the contract.

"I'd like you to come to the meeting with Robert today. It'll be good practice for future clients."

"I had planned on it." She sat on one of the leather chairs in front of his desk. "I also gathered the information about the author you emailed me about yesterday."

He lifted his gaze to her. "Good. We can get started on that as well. I need to set up a meeting with Xavier to discuss my thoughts on a packaging deal."

Andrew had read the opening chapters of the book Paige gave him, and wanted to find out a little more about the author. He'd done a preliminary search himself, but figured it might be a good idea to reach out to the author's literary agent.

"How is everything else?" he asked Vonda. "Any fires that need dousing?"

She shook her head. "No. But are we going to talk around the elephant in the room like it's not there?"

Chuckling, he let out a heavy sigh. "No."

"I'm not trying to get in your business or anything, but if I can help in any way, I'd love to assist you."

"You are helping, by going with me to this meeting today."

"Right, but I know there's a lot going on between you and Paige. I also know that she's been dealing with some very personal things. If you need to keep your distance, I'm more than willing to step in."

Andrew swallowed. Leaving Paige last night had been the hardest thing he'd ever done. Although they'd talked, he felt like there was more that needed to be said. He felt like he owed her his truth, but the timing didn't seem right after everything that went down in Detroit, then at the lake house.

"I appreciate that," he said. "And I'll let you know if I need you."

"Well?"

He stared at the capable junior agent. "What?"

"Are the rumors true?"

Frowning, he considered the question. Skye had suggested a generic response to anyone who asked, but he didn't want to lie to Vonda, so he simply said, "Maybe."

"Wow."

"Listen, Vonda, I know you're just trying to help but I don't really want to talk about it."

She nodded. "That's fair. How's your mother?"

"She's well. Bossy."

Before he left Michigan, he'd stopped by his mom's house to make sure she was alright. She'd made good progress since she'd started physical therapy, but had a long road ahead of her. Of course, she'd grilled him about Paige and the news. And he'd given her the safe answer—that he had everything under control. Normally, he would have been confident in his answer. This time he wasn't so sure. There were many variables that couldn't be controlled, like his feelings for Paige. He'd fallen for her—hard and fast.

"Did the security work out?" Vonda asked.

"Yes, thank you."

Vonda ran down a list of client tasks she had to complete for the day. He gave her a few pointers on how to tackle them, and she left him alone.

Losing himself in work, he answered several emails, made a few calls, and reviewed three new contracts. Before he knew it, it was lunchtime. Andrew stared at his phone. Although he was tempted to call Paige, he didn't because he knew she was traveling today. They'd had a heated discussion about security going forward. She'd agreed to travel with two bodyguards, so he'd contacted her security team to arrange it. Two of her favorite guards had flown to Michigan so they could travel with her, which made him feel better. She'd also chosen to charter a plane so she could avoid the paps.

According to her itinerary, she'd be in the air within the hour. He decided to send her a quick text: **Miss you.**

Seconds later her reply came through: **More.**

Andrew smiled, and fired off a response: **Maybe I'll sneak into your bedroom tonight and give you more.**

His phone buzzed a moment later.

Paige: **I'll be waiting. Miss you, too.**

Andrew's hand hovered over the keyboard, tempted to tell her more. But the first time he told he loved her would be in person. Because, yep, he was definitely in love with Paige Mills. He'd probably always been a little in love with her. And it was time he confessed.

He stood and walked over to the window. Peering out at Wilshire Boulevard, he pondered his next move. The biggest question he'd asked himself was would he be able to continue working for Paige as her agent. It had been done before, no doubt. He'd known several agents who'd dated their clients, and it had never worked out well.

Although he'd never dated one of his clients before Paige, he'd gone out with several actresses and learned early on that it was never a good idea. It was a lesson he'd told every mentee he worked with—stay away from the industry people. And he'd learned that after several crazy personal experiences. Inevitably, those relationships had ended in hurt feelings and hard feelings.

Paige made him want to throw out all of his rules to be

with her. She'd always had that effect on him, from their first meeting to last night. He'd denied the connection for a long time. Yet, when she'd married Julius, his jealousy had gotten the best of him and he couldn't take it. Andrew's asshole-ish behavior had almost destroyed their working and personal relationship. But he'd never regret his decision to drop everything and go to her.

A knock on the door pulled him from his thoughts. Andrew called for the person to come in. Bishop Lang entered the office.

"What's up, bruh?" Bishop gave him a dap. "How long have you been back?"

Bishop worked in the legal department for the agency. He'd been instrumental in the development of Pure Talent Audio. He was also a close friend.

"Got back last night." Andrew grabbed a bottle of water from the fridge he kept in his office. He offered Bishop one, then tossed a bottle toward him. "Been busy trying to catch up on work."

"How's Mama Connie?"

Andrew told his friend about the accident and subsequent surgery. "She told me to tell you that she wants to see some honorary grandkids soon."

Bishop chuckled. "She's hilarious." A few years ago, Bishop had met and married Paityn Young, who was Jax's goddaughter. "Tell her we're trying."

"You know Mom. She's always talking about babies."

"Trust me, my mother is the same way. Can't stop buying baby shit, like Paityn is already pregnant."

Andrew barked out a laugh. "Now that's hilarious."

Bishop took a long gulp of water. "So, what's up, bruh? I've read the headlines, seen the pic. You finally made a move on Paige, huh?"

Frowning, he asked, "What do you mean 'finally'?"

"You should probably stop denying that shit." Bishop set his bottle on the table. "It's been obvious for years."

Andrew waived a dismissive hand at his friend. "Man . . . shut the hell up."

"Seriously, we had bets on it."

"What?" Andrew asked.

Bishop laughed. "I told X you would make your move after her divorce. He said you'd never step over the line."

Shaking his head, Andrew grumbled a curse. X was right, though. If they hadn't been in close proximity, he would have never stepped over the line. He told Bishop as much.

"Good thing I don't have to give X that money," Bishop said. "You did step to her after the divorce."

"Whatever, bruh."

Bishop sighed. "Well? Is this a thing now? Should I tell Paityn so she can invite you and Paige over for dinner?"

Chuckling, Andrew said, "I don't know when we'll be able to go to dinner parties together. We have to keep a low profile for the next month or so."

"I don't see that happening."

"It has to." Truth be told, Andrew wasn't confident he could stay away from her either. They'd have to get very creative about time spent together. "I don't want to do anything that will make it harder for her to emerge from this latest scandal with her reputation intact."

Bishop glanced at his watch. "Shit, I need to go home. Paityn has me on a strict regime of scheduled sex. Gotta get her pregnant."

Laughing, Andrew walked Bishop to the door. "Let's get a meeting on the schedule. I want to go over the spreadsheets you sent for Audio."

"I'll set something up."

Andrew shoved his hands in his pockets. "Tell Paityn I said what's up."

"Will do. Tell Paige we'll invite you both to dinner when you stop hiding."

"Get the hell out of here, man."

As Bishop walked out of his office, laughing at himself, Andrew couldn't help but wonder if dinner parties and babies were in *his* immediate future. And he found himself looking forward to the possibilities.

Paige opened her front door for Demi. "Come in."

"Hey." Demi walked into the house. "How are ya?"

"I'm good. Thanks for dropping by so late. I appreciate it." The plane had landed less than an hour ago, and Paige had immediately contacted her attorney to set up a meeting to discuss the latest motion to reopen the divorce case. "I just felt like I needed to get an understanding of our next steps."

"Not a problem."

Paige led Demi into her den. "Wine? Coffee?"

"No, thanks." Demi sat down on the love seat and set her briefcase on the coffee table. "I have late dinner plans."

Smiling, Paige asked, "Date?"

"No," Demi grumbled. "I wish. It's been a long and lonely couple of years."

During one of their earlier meetings, Demi had shared that she'd been celibate for several years, and not by choice. Paige suspected Demi was holding out for someone, but she'd never asked for details.

"Aw." Paige sipped her coffee. "I've been there. It's not fun."

Demi eyed her curiously.

"I know what you're going to ask," Paige said. "You've seen the article?"

Smirking, Demi nodded. "I did. And you totally don't have to tell me what's going on between you and Andrew."

"I . . ." Paige smoothed a hand over her ponytail. "It's kind of complicated right now."

"Well, it's not complicated because of the divorce. It's final."

"Let's hope it stays that way."

"I'm not worried, and you shouldn't be either. Your ex is an asshole. He's doing what he knows will get to you. You can't let him. So what else makes this complicated?"

"The havoc Julius is wreaking with his publicity tour and the frivolous lawsuit."

"Have you spoken with your personal attorney?" Demi asked.

Paige nodded. "We're meeting tomorrow morning."

"Good. As far as the alimony motion is concerned, I got you on that. I already filed a motion to dismiss it this morning."

"Thank God," Paige breathed. "Hopefully, the judge does the right thing. It's not my responsibility to pay for Julius's criminal case."

"Speaking of criminal cases . . . A friend of mine works in the prosecutor's office in Atlanta. Don't be surprised if his defense team calls you to testify at his upcoming criminal hearing."

Her mouth fell open. "What? I don't want to do that."

Julius had been indicted in both L.A. and Atlanta. Since then, more women had come forward. But knowing Julius, he planned to draw out the matter by filing crazy motions.

It wouldn't surprise Paige if the actual trial didn't take place for a couple of years.

"You might want to talk to your attorney about that as well."

Paige leaned forward, resting her elbows on her knees. "What if we countersue? For defamation."

Demi raised a brow. "Is that something you really want to do?"

Paige didn't want to have another court date. But she needed to send a strong message to Julius that his behavior would not be tolerated. "I don't know, but I want to keep that in my back pocket in case I need to take that step."

"As your divorce attorney, I'm willing to do what you want me to do. As a woman who's been there before, I wouldn't do it. Fight and move on. I'm pretty sure the judge will dismiss the motion. Julius and his attorneys submitted no viable proof that you're hiding assets. They mentioned you own property in Michigan but didn't provide an address or anything else to support the claim. So I think you're good there, but I'll keep you posted."

"Did you get the paperwork from my uncle?"

Demi nodded. "I did. But I'll only submit it if I need to."

Paige nodded. "Thanks, Demi. And thanks for coming again."

They talked for a few more minutes about a few things related to the original divorce. Once they finished, Demi stood. "I better get going. Have to be in Santa Monica in an hour."

"Oh yeah. You better hit the road now." L.A. traffic wasn't for the weak at heart. Paige had found herself driving while livid on more than one occasion. She walked Demi to the door. "I'll call you soon."

"Yes, keep me posted about the other lawsuit. Let me know if I can help."

Paige nodded and waved as Demi left her house.

Half an hour after Demi left, Paige heard her doorbell ring. She hurried to the door, grinning when she realized who it was. Swinging the door open, she jumped into Andrew's arms and kissed him.

Lifting her off the ground, he carried her inside never breaking the kiss. She'd missed him. *Oh, God, I miss this.* It hadn't even been forty-eight hours since she'd seen him last, but it felt like a lifetime.

Andrew pulled back, held her gaze. "Where do you want to go?"

She pointed to the living room couch. "Over there is good."

The low rumble of his laughter settled something inside her. The nervous churning she'd felt talking to Demi about court and the apprehension about possibly testifying at the criminal trial seemed to melt away under his touch, under his warm lips and hands.

He took her to the couch, setting her down on her feet and turning her around so that her back was against him.

She groaned when she felt his tongue against her neck. Slowly, he slid her shirt up and off and removed her bra. Paige purred when she felt his knuckles against the small of her back, she trembled in anticipation when she heard him pull the zipper on her skirt. The fabric fell at her feet and she stepped out of it.

Andrew groaned, ripping her panties off with one motion. *Oh my God.* Paige needed his mouth on hers. Turning in his arms, she pulled him down to her for another kiss and removed his shirt, tossing it behind them. She brushed her lips against his chest, unbuckled his pants, and pushed them down. Shoving him onto the couch, she rolled a condom over his thick erection and climbed on top of him.

"You feel so good." He held her against him, pushing his tip against her entrance. Smacking her ass, he said, "Come on. Don't make me wait."

Smirking, she lowered herself on him, closing her eyes as sensations overloaded her. His fingers tightened on her hips as he thrust into her, drawing a low groan from her mouth. They moved to a rhythm all their own, enjoying the connection, taking their time. Paige loved hard and fast, but this . . . she *loved* slow and tender, eyes on eyes, skin to skin. She loved him.

"Drew," she moaned. *I love you.*

Paige loved his spirit, his dry sense of humor, his wit, his dedication, his sensibility, his face, his body . . . everything about him. She didn't think she could ever have enough of him. He made her feel dizzy and powerful, treasured and respected. She wanted more with every passing minute. She wanted him. Only him.

A wave of pleasure spread over her, and she arched her head back as she came, still moving, still riding him through her orgasm until he followed her over. Collapsing against him, she burrowed into his chest when he wrapped his arms around her. "I missed you," she confessed breathily. She felt him chuckle beneath her and lifted her head to meet his gaze. "What are you laughing at?"

"I can definitely tell."

Paige laughed. "I'm glad you came."

Andrew blessed her with his beautiful dimpled smile. "Me too." She felt him hardening again inside her. "I think I'm ready to come again."

Chapter Fifteen

Paige couldn't believe how much her life had changed in a matter of weeks. Instead of feeling suffocated, she felt free. The weight of her anxiety had lifted, and she could breathe again. She had been back in L.A. for a week and she'd actually gone out in public. She'd even returned to her boutique gym and had a cup of coffee with Skye outside.

The paparazzi had hounded her, but she'd made a decision to keep moving, to keep pushing, to keep living. Paige credited many people with this transformation. Skye had refused to let her sulk for an extended period of time. Her mother checked on her daily just to see if she felt okay—and to give her makeup advice. Chastity hadn't missed a beat, working diligently and effectively on her behalf. Tanya had continued to send her potential opportunities. Demi had successfully handled Julius and that bogus motion without breaking a sweat.

Paige even had to give credit to herself, for making an effort to break free from the shackles of depression, to take control of her own life so that she could be better. She'd wasted too much time on Julius. And she was ready to move forward—with the shirtless man currently sitting across from her, brows furrowed with concentration as he tried to figure out where the puzzle piece in his hand should go.

Andrew had played an important role in her transformation, too. He'd held her, he'd comforted her, he'd pushed her, he'd laughed with her, and he loved her. They hadn't said the words yet, but Paige could feel his love in every part of her. It had filled empty spaces that she thought would never be filled again and it had healed her broken heart. And she wanted to tell him how much he meant to her, she wanted him to know how hard she'd fallen for him.

Picking up a piece of the thousand-piece puzzle they were working on together, she stared at him. "How was work?"

He lifted his gaze a minute, before dropping it again. "Long." He stretched his neck and placed the single piece in its place. "What made you get this puzzle?"

Paige smiled. "I liked it."

Once complete, she'd hang the puzzle of a black woman holding the world in her hands. She'd already identified the perfect place for it—on her office wall.

"You hate it?" she asked.

Andrew shook his head, his attention on the scattered pieces. "No, it's nice. But you know this is going to bother me until it's done, right?"

Giggling, she said, "You don't have to put it together for me, baby. I bought it so that I could do it."

When he'd arrived at her house late that night—as he'd done for the past week—they'd eaten pizza to celebrate the judge's ruling and the pending deal to option the book she'd told him about. And she thought they'd cap the night off with hot, toe-curling sex. Which was why she'd worn the blue satin nightie she had on, fully expecting the same reaction he'd had back at the lake house. She'd even shaved her legs for him.

It had started promising, frantic kisses up to her bedroom, hands moving over her body, teeth nipping at her skin. She'd managed to get his shirt off and unbutton his pants, but then . . .

Andrew had spotted the puzzle on the table and got to work. *How the hell was I supposed to know he was a puzzle fanatic?* It wasn't something they'd ever talked about. Ever. But she learned today. And her horny body was paying the price for that lesson. While his singular focus was endearing, it was also annoying. Because *she* was ready to go to bed, to make love to him, to fall asleep in his arms.

"I also thought it was going to be an ongoing project," she continued, raising her brow when he met her gaze again. "For me."

Sighing, he stood and pulled her to him. He brushed his mouth over hers. "I get the hint."

"Good."

He wrapped his arms around her and walked her backward toward the bed. "You have all of my attention now."

"Lovely." She pushed the straps of her gown off and let it fall to the floor. "Now, get naked and do me."

Early the next morning—after he'd made it up to her *two* times—she emerged from the shower to find him already dressed.

"I hate that you have to leave so early," she told him.

Since they were lying low, he'd always arrived late and left before the sun came up. He also parked in her garage in case someone was lurking outside her house.

Andrew tugged her to him and traced her lips, before

placing a sweet kiss on her mouth. "I know. But it won't be forever."

He'd told her the same thing back in South Haven. But there was no telling when they'd be able to stop the pretense and live their lives. Skye had scheduled so many interviews with trade magazines and talk shows. She'd even secured an invitation to *The Opal Winfield Show*, all in an attempt to spin the narrative.

Paige wrapped her arms around his waist and snuggled into him. "I'll be glad when it's over." Although she knew Opal, she still hated the idea of going on a show to *clear* her name when she'd done nothing wrong—in her marriage or with Andrew. "I still don't get why I have to clear my name for anything."

"It's not clearing your name. You didn't commit a crime."

She glanced up at him. "Exactly."

"So let's not call it that anymore. You're just telling your story."

The big interview was next month. Until then, she'd do everything that Skye had requested, including pretending Andrew was nothing more than her agent. In public.

"Did you get the invite to Jax's retirement party?" she asked.

Andrew nodded. "I did. It's finally sinking in that it's real."

"Mom is distraught." Jax Starks had been her mother's agent for over thirty years. Paige understood why her mother was flipping out at the prospect of working with another agent, because she'd probably feel the same way if Andrew left the business.

"I'm sure X will do just as well with her career."

She scrunched her nose. "I actually think she's going to ask you to represent her."

Frowning, he asked, "Why?"

Paige shrugged. "She likes you. And it has nothing to do with me."

"That would be weird, don't you think?"

"Yes, that's why you have to turn her down and let X do it. Me and my mother can't have the same agent. It just won't work."

Andrew agreed with her. "Either way, we don't know what she's going to do." He grabbed her hand and pulled her toward the door. Bending down, he put on those ugly work shoes he always wore.

When he looked up at her, he frowned, standing up. "What's wrong?"

I really have to control my facial expressions around him. "What are you talking about?"

Andrew tapped her nose. "Your nose is all scrunched up right now. Are you okay?"

Letting out an exaggerated sigh, she warred with herself over whether the truth would really set her free. But since they'd promised to be honest, she knew she had to go with the truth. "I sort of have a confession to make."

With a frown on his face, he led her over to the living room couch and pulled her down on his lap. Brushing her hair out of her face, he kissed her brow. "What is it?"

For a moment, Paige almost felt bad for what she was about to tell him. Almost. But she knew it was for the greater good, so she let it rip. "I'm sorry, but I hate those brown loafers you insist on wearing to work."

Andrew blinked, shooting her a confused stare. "What?"

"I keep wondering why you don't buy another pair. Do they ever get worn out?" When he didn't respond she babbled on, "Ugh, I feel so bad. You obviously love those shoes, but gosh, they are hideous. Like you should wear them at a church barbecue or a Motown dinner cruise. You're too young and too fine to be walking around here looking like someone's grandpa." Paige held his face in her hands. "Consider this an intervention."

He stared at her with wide eyes. Then he laughed. And she let out a sigh of relief, dropping her head to his shoulders and laughing with him. When she pulled back, she had tears streaming down her face. Andrew wiped them away and kissed her gently.

"You had me thinking something was seriously wrong," he said, a wide smile on his face. "I was bracing myself for some hard truth."

"I'm sorry. You were putting them on, and I couldn't take it anymore."

Chuckling, he traced her bottom lip. "I hope you know," he said, "those are my good luck shoes."

She raised a questioning brow. "I have no idea why. They are so old and ugly. When did you buy them? 1999?"

"They're not old. I just bought a pair last month."

Paige smacked a hand over her forehead. "Don't tell me you just keep purchasing the same shoes over and over again? Oh my God, where did you buy them?"

Andrew scratched the back of his head. "Famous Footwear," he mumbled.

She gaped at him. "Seriously?"

He nodded. "That BOGO sale is the best. I can get two pairs at a time."

Paige shook her head. "It's worse than I thought. You need help."

"My shoes are comfortable."

"Comfortable and ugly. I need you to do better. I need

your shoe game to be great. When we finally walk out in public together?" She jabbed a finger into his chest. "You better not have on those shoes."

"Why don't you buy me a pair then?"

"You ain't said nothing but a word."

He barked out another laugh. "Whatever you do, I don't like hard soles because they're too slippery. I like to be prepared to run if I have to."

"Got it." She nodded. "I'll make sure you have fashionable rubber sole shoes. If they even exist," she added under her breath.

"You got jokes, huh?"

He squeezed her tight and she broke out in a fit of giggles. When she settled down, she ran her fingers through his hair. "I'm sorry. That's my confession. So what's yours?"

"I love you. And I'm not sorry."

Paige held her breath, covering her mouth with her hand. "What?"

"This is my confession."

"Oh my goodness. Andrew?"

He framed her face in his massive hands. "I can't think of anything that has ever felt so right to me."

This time, Paige's eyes filled with tears of joy. The first tear fell, and he kissed her cheek where it landed. "Drew, you love me?"

"I don't *just* love you. Paige, I'm so in love with you I can't even think straight."

In this moment, Paige felt like she would burst open with the love she felt for him. And she couldn't let him take this step alone. "I love you, too," she whispered.

Andrew pulled her closer, wrapping her in his warm embrace. "Music to my ears."

They stayed like that for a while, holding each other.

Then Paige slid off his lap and grasped his hands, tugging him to stand. "I hope you know you can't go to work today, not after that."

He arched a brow. "Oh?" Then he yanked her to him. "Where am I going then?"

Paige pulled him into a deep kiss, moaning when his tongue met hers. She unbuttoned his shirt, pushing it off his broad shoulders. Breaking the kiss, she leaned back. "I think we need to go back upstairs—or wherever."

Andrew nipped her bottom lip before sucking it into his mouth. When he pulled back, he met her gaze. "I think the kitchen counter is perfect."

Paige's body hummed with anticipation. "I like the way you think."

They both took off toward the kitchen and started their day with more lovemaking. And Paige had never been happier.

"Connor?" Andrew shifted his phone to his right ear and slid into his driver's seat. "Hold on." After he started his car, the Bluetooth connected. "Okay, what's up?"

"Calling to give you an update about Mom," his brother said.

Connor gave him the details about his mother's follow-up appointment. The ankle wasn't healing properly, and the doctors warned they might need to do another surgery in a few months.

"When will we know for sure?" Andrew asked, merging onto the expressway.

"Maybe next week," Connor replied. "Mom is climbing the walls. She wants to go out with her friends and do more than sit down all day."

Andrew wasn't surprised his mother was having a hard time with the recovery. Prior to the injury, she was looking forward to retirement, excited about traveling, hanging out with her friends, and tackling home improvement projects. Now, she'd have to push everything back.

"Did the docs say she would be cleared to go to Vegas at Christmas?" Andrew hoped she'd get the okay. She'd been looking forward to the trip.

"Even if they don't have to do the second surgery, she may have to sit this one out."

Damn. "How is she emotionally?"

"She's Mom. Putting on a brave face and bossing every-one around. Are you still good to come back in a couple of weeks?"

Andrew sighed. "I'm working on it." He had several irons in the fire at work and wasn't sure he could take another full week off so soon, especially with Jax's retire-ment right around the corner.

After a company-wide meeting in Atlanta yesterday, he'd learned that Jax had tapped him to take on several of his agency clients. Which was an honor, but it meant that he'd have to spend more time in Atlanta training with his mentor.

"You don't sound too confident," his brother said.

"There's a lot going on."

"With Paige?" Connor asked.

Paige was the least of his problems right now. As her agent, he'd ensured she had no repercussions from any shoots she'd missed. He'd also negotiated her newest con-tract and facilitated the book option for the project she wanted to produce. As her lover, they were closer than ever. They'd continued to see each other—in private—and he'd fallen more in love with each passing day. And the more he fell, though, the more he wondered if it could be real.

Andrew blew his horn at a car who'd tried to cut him off. "She's good."

"That's it?" Connor asked. "I'm your big brother. I can hear it in your voice."

Pulling off I-10, he turned toward Malibu. He hadn't seen Paige in a few days, and he was anxious to get to her.

"Bruh," Connor called. "You still there?"

"I'm here."

"Well?" his brother prodded.

"We're good. Not taking it as slow as I'd said initially."

Connor chuckled. "I knew that wasn't going to happen. I could see it when you brought her to Detroit with you. I will say that you actually looked happy. And I haven't seen you happy in a long time."

Happiness had always seemed to elude Andrew. He hadn't had the best luck in relationships. Which was why he didn't enter into them lightly. But he'd jumped headfirst into this one. "I am happy."

"But?"

Obviously, his brother wasn't going to let this go. Growing up, Connor had taken on the role of man of the house when their father left, even though he wasn't that much older than Andrew. He'd fought the bullies on the block, helped with homework, and made sure they had food when they got home from school in the afternoons. Connor had taught Andrew how to drive, how to repair a faucet, and how to build a computer.

It wasn't that Andrew couldn't talk to Connor. He just didn't know if he wanted to give voice to the small doubts in his head about Paige. Still, he needed to talk to someone.

"Things are good," Andrew repeated. "But I can't help but feel conflicted."

"Conflicted about what? How you feel?"

"I know how I feel." When he told Paige he loved her, he meant every word. *Did she?* "But I'd be lying if I said I wasn't concerned I might be a rebound for her."

"Ah, I get it now," Connor said, with a chuckle. "You love her."

Frowning, Andrew said, "I didn't say that."

"You didn't have to. You're in love and now you're searching for reasons to protect yourself."

Andrew sighed, focusing on the road ahead. Connor's words resonated with him, though. He was dangerously in love with Paige. Which was nice, but along with that, came the revelation that he'd basically given her the means to wreck him.

"I do think it's a valid concern," Connor continued. "Because it does seem sudden."

In Andrew's mind, it didn't feel sudden. It just felt different, like they were speeding down a winding road in the dark, with no map. "It's not sudden, though."

"Maybe not on your part, but she was married."

"And now she's divorced," Andrew said.

"Exactly. She's getting out of something real ugly. Listen, you've always had good instincts. If you're feeling conflicted, it might not be a bad idea to slow things down a little. Tread lightly."

His phone beeped and he glanced at the screen. "Hold on, bruh." Andrew answered the second line. "What's up, baby?"

"Drew?" Paige called, her voice shaky.

Andrew didn't like the sound of her voice. "What's wrong?"

"You won't believe what happened to me today. Where are you?"

"On my way to you. What happened?"

"I got subpoenaed—to testify before a grand jury in Houston."

New claims of sexual harassment and assault had dogged Julius over the last few days. Up until now, Paige hadn't been required to appear at any criminal proceedings, even though her attorney had warned her there was a chance she'd have to testify.

"Did you talk to Michelle?" Andrew asked.

"I did. Apparently, the woman who accused him stated that he assaulted her several times within the last few years. The defense wants me to testify on his behalf because I was with him during one of the alleged incidents."

Andrew hated the fact that she'd married that mutha-fucka, but he didn't say that. Instead, he told her he'd be there in twenty minutes. When Paige hung up, he swapped to the other line. "Bruh?"

"I was about to hang up on yo ass."

"Sorry. It was Paige. There's a situation involving Julius."

"Hm. And she's *still* in something real ugly."

Squeezing his steering wheel tightly, he grumbled a curse. "Listen, I need to go."

"Drew, I'm not trying to piss you off. I just don't want you to get hurt."

Andrew knew Connor was coming from a good place. His brother was recently divorced himself, ending a twelve-year marriage after his wife cheated on him. "I get it."

"I think Paige is a beautiful woman—kind, intelligent. She definitely doesn't want your money. She's a catch. I don't believe she'd ever hurt you intentionally. But she's still dealing with her ex and all the baggage that he left her. I'm not telling you to let her go. I just want you to remember what I said. Tread. Lightly."

"Thanks, bruh. I'll call to check on Mom tomorrow." Ending the call, Andrew thought about everything Connor had said. Paige had told him she loved him many times since he'd said it—*first*. And she'd never lied to him. Yet, despite his desire to move forward with her, he couldn't let the doubt go. Because maybe it really *was* too soon, too fast.

Chapter Sixteen

Paige paced the private room at the Harris County Justice Courthouse. Grand juries were typically conducted in secret, so she'd managed to get to the courthouse without being spotted by paparazzi. After prepping her for a few minutes, her attorney left her alone to gather her thoughts.

It was a struggle getting on the plane to Houston, knowing what she was coming to do. Learning her husband was a sexual predator, on top of being an adulterer and a liar, had been a difficult pill to swallow. It had only highlighted just how oblivious she'd been before and during their marriage.

Nervous, she bit down on her thumbnail as her mind replayed every trip she'd made to Houston with Julius. They hadn't traveled to Texas often, but they'd attended a couple events there during their marriage—the wedding of one of his friends and a birthday party for one of her colleagues. But she couldn't remember anything specific about either of those visits, so she wondered what the prosecutors planned to ask her.

The fact that her attorney couldn't actually go into the

room with her heightened her anxiety. Andrew had done his best to calm her nerves before she left for the airport that morning, but he wasn't able to come to Texas with her because of work. Her only solace was that Julius wouldn't be in the room either, and neither would his attorneys.

Paige pulled her cell phone out of her purse. She still had another half an hour or so before she'd be called into the room. She needed to focus on something else. Namely, her job.

Last night, she'd received a script for a new thriller and wanted to read it over. The director of the film had specifically requested her for the role, but the studio wanted another actress for the part. Andrew had set up a meeting with the director and the producer for next week, and she wanted to be familiar with the project before they met.

Opening the document, she started reading. Seconds later, a text came through.

Andrew: **Miss you. How are you?**

Smiling, she thought about the going-away present he'd given her that morning before he left her house like a thief in the night. After her second orgasm against his tongue, he'd taken her hard against the wall. She loved that they didn't need a bed to get freaky. Over the past month, they'd christened every room in her house, and almost every surface. And she'd loved every minute of it.

She typed out a response: **Miss you more. I'm nervous. Waiting for them to call me.**

A moment later his reply came: **You got this.**

Andrew had always made her feel like she could do anything. She'd signed with him because he was genuine and knowledgeable. But more importantly, he believed in her. That meant the world to her.

Replying, she said: **You always say that.**

Andrew: **Because it's true.**

Paige smiled. She wanted to live up to his belief, she wanted to be the woman he believed she was. She replied: **Thank you. Love you.**

Andrew: **I'll be waiting for your call afterward. Love you, too.**

Paige stared at the text. He'd typed a full sentence, but her mind was stuck on those two words. He loved her. And it wasn't just words for him. Andrew showed her every day how much she meant to him by the way he treated her—with respect. He accepted her for who she was, and he never made her feel bad about her choices. He didn't insult her or blame her for his faults. Yet it was still hard to trust it at times. Because she'd been disrespected, she'd been hurt, she'd been lied to, and she'd been manipulated.

Even though she'd tried not to, she found herself anticipating the moment the other shoe would drop. In the back of her mind, she assumed he would disappoint her eventually. It wasn't fair to him, but she couldn't help it.

Sighing, she sent him a response: **Talk to you soon.**

A few minutes later, her attorney let her know they were ready for her. She walked into the room. Gratefully, there weren't many people there, aside from the grand jury and the prosecutorial team. Once they swore her in, they asked her several questions about the nature of her relationship with Julius.

Knowing the history and saying it out loud to a bunch of strangers made her want to run out of there screaming. But she held her head up high and answered each question as best she could.

The line of questioning veered toward one night in particular—her colleague's birthday party. As the prosecutor launched into a series of questions about the party, the guests, and Julius's behavior, she realized that the alleged assault had taken place there.

She was distraught when the prosecutor asked her what they'd done after the party. Embarrassed and a little ashamed, she had to admit that they'd been intimate that night. She also had to recount to twelve strangers about the argument they'd had afterward, the same fight that had resulted in her husband disappearing for the rest of the night. Paige hadn't seen him again until the next morning.

By the time they'd finished questioning her, she was shaking. The implication that he'd had sex with her and then assaulted another woman made her blood run cold. Once they dismissed her, she rushed out of the courtroom and called her driver. When he'd confirmed he was pulling up in front of the building, she headed toward the doors.

As soon as stepped outside, she saw movement out of the corner of her eye and steeled herself for a photographer to jump out. But it wasn't a pap. It was Andrew. Without thinking, she ran into his waiting arms.

"You're here," she whispered, basking in his comforting hold on her. "I'm so glad you're here."

"I wouldn't be anywhere else," he murmured against her neck.

They stood like that for a moment before reality set in—that she was standing out in the open hugging the same man she was supposed to be avoiding. She jerked back, stumbling a bit. He gripped her hips to steady her.

Paige eased out of his grasp and smoothed a hand over her head. "I'm sorry."

"What for?"

"I'm not supposed to be hugging you like this." But she needed him, she wanted his arms around her.

Andrew glanced around, probably to make sure there

were no paps waiting in the wings with a camera. Paige scanned the immediate area herself. She didn't see anything, but that didn't mean they weren't there—waiting, watching.

Paige took a healthy step back. "I didn't know you were coming."

"I couldn't let you be here alone. Soon as I got out of my meeting I hopped on a plane."

Smiling, she nodded. "Thank you."

Andrew looked back one more time. He pointed at the car. "Is that your driver?"

"Yes."

He gestured toward the car. "Let's go."

Paige hurried to the car and slid inside. A few seconds later, he was with her, instructing the driver to circle the block. The car pulled off and Paige turned to him. Unable to help herself, she ran her finger over his chin.

"I can't believe you're here," she murmured.

Andrew glanced at the driver and told him to stop at the parking garage on their right. When the driver pulled in front of the garage, Andrew slid the man a large tip and told him he was no longer needed.

Confused, Paige looked to Andrew for answers, but he didn't speak. He climbed out of the car and held his hand out to her. She placed her hand in his, got out of the car, and followed Andrew into the parking garage.

He led her to a dark SUV. The lights flashed and he opened the passenger door for her. Paige hopped in and waited for him to climb in on the driver's side. Again, Andrew held his hand out for her. When she slipped her hand in his, he pulled her over the middle console and into his lap. Kissing her knuckles, he said, "I couldn't let you do this alone. Even if I couldn't be in the room with you, I wanted you to know I was there."

Paige kissed him then. "I love you, Andrew." She rested her head against his shoulder. The fact that he'd risked being spotted to support her made her feel warm inside. "I was on the verge of a panic attack leaving the courthouse. I didn't even go back and talk to Michelle." Speaking of her attorney . . . "I should probably let her know I left, huh?"

Andrew laughed, pressing his lips to her temple. "That would be a good idea."

She snuggled into him again. "We should probably get out of here."

"Probably," he agreed.

"A few more minutes?" she asked, biting her lip. "I just need you to hold me."

He tightened his hold on her, enveloping him in his warm embrace. "Anything you need."

They sat there for a few moments in silence. "The prosecutor asked very hard questions." She gave Andrew a brief explanation of her time in the room. "The thought of him being with me and . . ." She swallowed past a lump in her throat. "What the hell? The more I discover, the angrier I get—at Julius and at myself. I was his wife. How did I not know he was a damn predator?"

With his thumb, Andrew brushed a tear she didn't know had fallen away. "He's been doing this a long time, baby. It's not your fault you didn't know. He's had practice concealing his activities."

She didn't watch TV often, but when she did, Paige loved to watch true crime. Paige had seen many stories about women who had no idea their husbands were serial rapists *or* serial killers. When watching, she'd often thought to herself how naïve those women were. The notion that she'd be in that same category was foreign to her, because she'd always been sure she was smarter than that. Now she didn't know what to believe.

"Hey." Andrew tipped her chin up to peer into her eyes. "It's not your fault," he repeated. "You're his victim, too. Just not in the same way."

"I can't get that night out of my head—what we did, the things he said, how he'd acted. I should have known something was off with him. I *did* know something was off. I just didn't want to admit it to myself."

Andrew brushed his lips over hers. "The thing to focus on is that you did leave. You divorced him."

"I should've never married him."

"You can't change that now. You just have to move forward."

Nodding, she sighed. "I hope the paps didn't see us." The last thing she wanted to add to this day was another headline.

"Hopefully, they didn't."

"I hate sneaking around. It kind of makes this feel illicit."

He eyed her, a frown on his forehead. "But we're not."

"I know we're not. Nothing about us is forbidden. Which is what makes this harder. Hiding how I feel about you from the world sucks. Because we're not doing anything wrong here."

"No, but we have a plan. You've worked too hard for your career, your image, to let him continue to paint you with his brush. The Opal interview is coming up. And Skye has done a phenomenal job of infusing positive press in the midst of this shitshow Julius has started."

Julius's "heartbreak" article had been released days ago

and, of course, he'd done everything in his power to make her the baddie in their relationship. But Skye had already set things in motion to mitigate any brewing scandals. Paige had been everywhere, on television, on podcasts. She'd even appeared on a cooking show.

"Did I tell you Skye booked me on Wendell Wilson?"

The Wendell Wilson Show had been calling for months to get her on, but Paige had resisted. Paige didn't care for Wendell. The "hot topics" television show host had constantly bad-mouthed her on his daytime show, even before she'd married Julius. The loud host had a penchant for railroading his guests with inappropriate questions and stirring the pot to create the illusion of brewing drama.

"Yeah, you did."

"Admittedly, I'm nervous. Not looking forward to it at all."

"You'll be fine."

She laced her fingers in his. "Wish you could be there."

"Who says I can't?"

Chuckling, Paige said, "That would give the gossips something to talk about."

"I'm still your agent."

She met his gaze, searched his eyes. Having Andrew there would certainly help. He had a way of centering her. He didn't even have to say anything, just his presence alone calmed her nerves. Today, she'd been on the verge of a breakdown as she left the courthouse. Then he was there, and she'd immediately felt at ease.

"You'd do that for me?" she asked.

He kissed her. "I'd do anything for you, Paige."

Paige's heart cracked open a little more with his whispered confession. God, she loved this man, with everything in her. And she looked forward to the day she could stop pretending he was *just* her agent.

"I don't think it's a good idea," Andrew said, scrubbing his face with his hands.

"Why?" Paige asked.

"The deal is trash," he told her.

It was one o'clock in the morning in Detroit and he'd been on a video conference with Paige and her manager for hours, discussing a passion project that she'd seemingly pulled out of the air.

Maybe it was the fact that his mother had to have another surgery? Or maybe it was the fact that he hadn't slept in twenty-four hours? But Andrew was irritated. Although he had a good working relationship with Paige's manager, Tanya, he didn't like that the woman always seemed to champion the opposite of what he thought was best for her.

"Drew, I think it's something that will transform my career," Paige told him.

"I think you should strongly consider the NetPix drama," he said. "The offer is solid, the shooting schedule is reasonable, and there's a potential for the show to continue for multiple seasons. They're also willing to give you a producer credit, which is what I thought you wanted."

And Andrew had worked hard to get her that deal. The fact that Tanya had swooped in and convinced Paige that it would be better to do an independent film pissed him the fuck off.

"She wants to do something different," Tanya argued. "The movie will open the door for more dramatic roles."

"But streaming is booming right now. Isn't it better to have consistent work?" The market had shifted lately as more and more people cut the cord on cable television and switched to streaming platforms. NetPix had built a strong portfolio of popular original series that had transformed careers in ways people had never dreamed of. And the schedule allowed actors and actresses to do other things.

"Paige is a film actress," Tanya said. "This movie is a game changer. It will allow her the opportunity to sink her teeth into a meatier role, something different from the cute innocent heroine or torn lover roles she's taken in the past. You know this will be good for her."

Andrew didn't know that. The only thing he knew was that Tanya was getting on his nerves. "Why is it better for Paige to turn down guaranteed money and exposure for a film by a director with a history of failed box office receipts?"

"Oh." Tanya snickered. "I get it. It's about the bottom line for you."

"Don't play me," Andrew warned, his patience dangling on a thin thread. "I've never done anything for Paige because of money. I've always encouraged her to do what's best for her career."

"You mean your career," Tanya muttered.

"I don't care what you think, Tanya. My main concern is Paige. I'm not going to pretend this is a good deal. And I'm certainly not going to encourage her to sign a bad contract for a movie because you're dating the damn director."

"Okay, that's enough," Paige said. "I can't do this right now. I have to meet with Michelle tomorrow."

Andrew shook his head, his frustration at a tipping point. Yesterday, Julius filed another lawsuit against Paige for defamation of character, after her interview with the

ladies of *The Chat*. He'd had to console Paige via video
chat, and he hated it.

"I'm hopping off," Tanya grumbled before disconnect-
ing from the video conference.

After a tense moment, Paige called his name. "What's
wrong?"

"I'm just frustrated right now. Mom is still in a lot of pain
and I can't help her. Work is busy as hell, and I'm tired."

They'd both had rough weeks. Between his mother and
her ex, his job and her publicity schedule, they needed to
decompress—away from everything and everyone.

"I'm sorry, baby," she said. "I wish I was there with you
so I could hug you right now."

He smiled. "I wish you were here, too. How are you?"

"Nerves bad. I'm thinking about canceling the Wendell
Wilson interview this week. I don't want to open myself
to more gossip, more scrutiny. This lawsuit has prompted
a new wave of press that I don't need right now."

"I'm sure Skye is on it."

"She is, but I'm tired. Now I see why some women
never get into another relationship after divorce."

"You'll be fine."

"And you'll still be there?" she asked.

"Yes. My flight leaves tomorrow night. I'll come to
your place when I get back."

"Thank you. I'll feel better if you're here."

"I promise I'll be there."

"I just want this to be over. I thought the divorce would
give me my life back, but unfortunately I married an asshole." She let out a frustrated sigh, shaking her hands in
the air like he imagined she wanted to shake Julius.
"Anyway, enough about me. You mentioned Connie is still

in a lot of pain. What are the doctors saying? Is she at least improving a little?"

He nodded. "She is. But it's a slow process. They told her today she couldn't go to Vegas at Christmas."

"Oh no! I know she was looking forward to it."

"She was. We're going to come here for Thanksgiving and Christmas, to sit with her."

"That's a good idea. Maybe I'll join you for one of those holidays."

He raised a brow. "You'd come to Michigan in December? You told me you're allergic to snow."

Paige laughed. "I am. But I'd rock a pair of snow pants for you."

Chuckling, he said, "Now, I'd pay to see that."

"Who knows? Maybe I'll do a clothing line with a variety of sexy snow pants. Think I could pull it off?"

Andrew stared at Paige. "I think you make everything sexy."

She groaned. "When you say stuff like that, I just want to do you."

"Well . . ." He unbuckled his pants. "There's magic in video chats. Take your clothes off."

Chapter Seventeen

Andrew stared at his mother, lying on the hospital bed. She was finally asleep now, but it hadn't been easy to get her to rest. They'd rushed her back to the hospital that morning. He'd never seen his mother so emotional, and it tore him up to hear her cry out in pain.

Connor approached him, squeezing his shoulder. "She's going to be okay."

Nodding, he swallowed. Tears burned the back of his throat as he recalled her piercing scream. His mother had tried to get up and walk herself to the bathroom and hurt herself—again.

"She's too stubborn, man," Andrew said. "What if we weren't there?"

In fact, *he* almost wasn't there. He'd decided to take an earlier flight back to Cali, so that he could see Paige. Andrew was getting ready to leave for the airport when his mother injured herself.

"But we were there, bruh." Connor brushed a hand over their mother's arm. "Can't think about what-ifs."

That what-if nearly took him out. He couldn't imagine his life without his mother. The thought of something happening to her while he was gone . . . Closing his eyes, he drew in a slow breath. He cut a glance at his older brother. "She's alone here. None of us are close enough to get to her if she needs us."

Since the first surgery, they'd been alternating weeks, flying in to stay with her. Connor had stayed the bulk of the time since he could basically do his job remotely. But Andrew didn't know how long they could sustain the arrangement.

"How long can we do this?" he whispered.

"As long as it takes. She's strong, bruh. You know that."

Despite knowing that she'd survived worse, he couldn't help the overwhelming worry that he felt when he thought about her alone in that house, depending on Mrs. Fulton to hear her if she cried out.

"I know that," Andrew said. "But you didn't hear her. You didn't hear her beg me not to leave her." Connor had run out of the room to get towels for the blood, leaving Andrew alone with his mom. "The fear in her voice . . ." He shuddered as the sound of her loud wails replayed in his mind. "She was so scared."

Connor peered at him, tears in his eyes. "I know. I've seen it. I saw it when Dad left, and she would cry at night from the heartbreak. I saw it when she worked so long and so hard that she could barely walk in the door. I saw it when Damon graduated from high school and she knew she would be alone. So, yes, I get it."

Averting his gaze, Andrew wiped a tear that had fallen from his eyes. He knew Connor had experienced more than his childhood brain could comprehend. His brother had never really talked much about those years, though.

"The thing about Mom, though?" Connor said. "She

survived. Yes, she cried. Yes, she hurt. But she still got out there and did the best she could for us. Even when she was in pain, she got up and went to work. Even when she saw Dad out in the streets with that woman, she held her head high and kept it moving. That's what she raised us to do. I know you're worried. I am, too. But Connie Weathers is not going to let an ankle fracture take her out. She's ready to enjoy her life, after working all those years."

"I hear you." Andrew traced his mother's brow with his thumb. "I just love her, man."

Connor chuckled. "Don't we all."

His mom's eyes fluttered open. "Hey, my babies," she said, her voice scratchy.

Andrew bent down and kissed her cheek. "You gave us a scare."

"I don't know how many times we have to tell you to sit yo ass down somewhere," Connor said.

Mom cracked a smile. "I don't know how many times I have to tell *you* that you are not my daddy."

Andrew barked out a laugh, grateful that his mother still knew how to cut a brotha. "Seriously, Mom, you need to be careful. You're doing too much."

"When Damon moved out, I didn't know what to do with myself," Connie said. "So I worked. Every day I worked hard, never calling off, always on time. That work got me through the loneliness." A tear fell from her eye, and Andrew dabbed it with a tissue. "I built my life around you boys. And I'll never regret it because you're all my greatest accomplishments. You're living lives that I've never even dreamed of living.

"Connor, you spend your days building wealth for people." Mom grasped Andrew's hand, smiling through her tears. "And Drew, your regular day's work is talking to people I watch on TV like it's no big deal. Damon manages an entire IT department for a Fortune Five Hundred company. I have nothing to regret when I look at the three of you. I'm so proud of you."

"Mom, don't cry," Connor grumbled. "Please."

"Oh, shut up." Mom swatted Connor's hand away when he tried to straighten her blanket. "I'm talking now."

Connor raised his hands. "Okay. Your turn."

Andrew chuckled. "But he does have a point. We don't like to see you cry."

"Like Bobby Brown says, it's my prerogative." They all laughed. "Listen." She held out her other hand for Connor. "You want to know why I really retired?"

"I thought you were just tired of the plant," Connor said.

"I was," she continued. "But one day I was sitting out on the deck alone, and it suddenly dawned on me that *I* wanted some of that life y'all are living. I've worked hard, now it's time for me to play hard."

"That's fine, Ma," Connor said. "That's what we want for you."

"We just want you to be careful," Andrew added. "And again, stop doing too much."

"If I promise to be careful, you two have to make me a promise, too."

"What is it?" Andrew asked.

"For goodness' sake, bring me some damn grand-babies!"

Connor clasped Andrew's shoulder. "I think she's talking to you."

Glaring at his brother, Andrew said, "Whatever. Don't

you think I should have a wife or a public girlfriend before I bring a kid in here?"

"Is this you admitting that Paige is your girlfriend?" Connor raised a challenging brow. "I mean, as far as we know she's still your *friend*."

"Right?" Mom agreed.

"I think you both know she's not just my friend," Andrew confirmed. "I do love her."

His mother gasped. "Oh, yes. Finally, you admit it. Now, I have another question."

"Don't ask about babies." Andrew shook his head. "It's not the time."

"I wasn't going to ask about babies," she said. "I was going to ask why you're still here. Don't you have a plane to catch?"

Andrew laughed. "I did. But I'm not leaving you. I need to hear what the doc says, make sure you get home okay, call—"

"All things Connor can handle," she insisted.

"We'll see," Andrew said. "Let's give it a few hours."

His mother let out a heavy sigh, finally releasing their hands and burrowing back into the mattress. Her eyes drifted closed. "Fine. But I reserve the right to wake up and yell at you if you're still here."

Bending down, he hugged her gently. "I can take it."

A few seconds later, his mother drifted off to sleep. Andrew picked up his phone and stared at the text he'd already typed letting Paige know that he wouldn't make it home in time for the taping. Sighing, he deleted it. While he wasn't sure he'd make back to L.A. by tomorrow, he also wasn't ready to leave his mother yet. And Paige would have to understand that if they ever had a chance of making it.

* * *

After countless weather delays, Andrew had finally landed at LAX early the next morning. He immediately drove to the office, arriving just in time for his nine o'clock meeting with one of his clients.

The meeting didn't go as planned, though. Hours of going back and forth with his fifty-five-year-old client about why he shouldn't audition for the role of a twenty-five-year-old hip-hop artist had worsened his mood.

"That was crazy," Vonda said, plopping down on a chair after the client left. "I don't get it. Why would he even think this was plausible?"

Andrew sat down at his desk and typed a few notes to himself for his next meeting. "Some people are just not ready to play someone's daddy or grandfather on screen."

"But some people need a reality check," she said with a shrug.

"That's our job."

He glanced at his phone and noticed he'd missed several calls from Paige. They hadn't talked much since yesterday morning, before his mother went to the hospital. They'd exchanged a few texts, but nothing substantive. He hadn't even told Paige about his mother's latest injury, because he didn't want her to worry while she was on set filming most of the day. Every time he meant to call her or text her, something had happened to distract him.

As much as his mother tried to convince them that she was okay, it was clear that she wasn't. It had been hard to leave her, but true to his mother's word, she'd yelled at him until he reluctantly agreed to rebook a later flight. Mom had called it "Operation: Grandchild."

Andrew sent Paige a quick text: In a meeting. I'll see you at the studio.

Forcing his attention back on his assistant, he said. "Give me an update. Anything hot right now?"

Vonda shook her head. "Not at the moment."

"Good news." Andrew leaned forward, clasping his hands together. "As you know, my responsibilities at the agency have shifted."

Nodding, she crossed her legs and folded her hands in her lap. "Yes. Will you have to move to Atlanta?"

The thought had never crossed Andrew's mind. Moving to Atlanta wasn't something he wanted to do. *Maybe a conversation with X about logistics is long overdue.* "No," he answered. "I plan to stay in Los Angeles."

Vonda sighed. "Woo, that's good. I didn't particularly want to move to Atlanta. And I don't want to work for another agent."

"Which leads me to my next act."

Shifting in her seat, Vonda asked, "Is everything okay? I thought I was doing a good job as a junior agent."

Andrew held up a hand. "Whoa, calm down. You're doing an excellent job. Not many agents can handle the things that I've given you. I'm pleased by your progress. I've spoken with X and he agreed with me that it's time to promote you."

Vonda flinched. With wide eyes, she leaned forward. "You're promoting me?"

"If you want the job," he said.

"If I want the job!" She smiled widely. "Of course I want the job." She stood and did a little dance, then she held up a hand. He high-fived her. "I can't believe it."

"You've worked hard. You deserve it."

He spent a few minutes giving her an overview of the

promotion process. "I'd like you to start next week. Does that work for you?"

"Yes."

"Put something on my calendar. We can discuss clientele. You've been working with several of my clients. All of them have expressed their gratitude for you. Some of them are willing to let you handle everything for them."

"Oh my God. This is a dream come true," she said, a wistful look in her eyes. "Thank you for believing in me. Can you tell me which clients?"

Andrew rattled off a few names. "I'm sure there are more. But we can talk about that later."

"Does that include Paige?" Vonda asked.

Representing Paige would no doubt get more and more complicated with each passing day. Andrew was a successful agent because he'd mastered the art of compartmentalizing. He knew how to keep his business and his personal life separate. Yet Paige had always been an outlier for him, she'd always been different from everyone else.

Xavier had called him on it a while ago, but he'd balked at his friend's observation. It was true, though. Andrew *was* different with Paige. She had always blurred his professional and personal lines. Every deal he'd negotiated for her was personal. He didn't just *want* her to succeed, he *needed* her to succeed. Because her happiness meant something to him. And he couldn't let her go as a client. Not now.

Even though it would probably be best if Vonda represented Paige going forward, he answered, "No."

"Okay," Vonda said. "How is she? I know she's probably distraught over the new lawsuit."

Sighing, he dropped his gaze to his phone again. Paige hadn't called him again, and he felt bad that he hadn't been able to call her back. *I need to call her.* "I'll see her in a little bit," he said.

"Right, she has that interview with Wendell Wilson today. That should be interesting. I hate that man. He's a dick."

Andrew chuckled. "Tell me how you really feel."

She covered her mouth. "I'm so sorry."

He waved her off. "Don't worry about it. For your next step, think about the type of assistant you want, because you'll need to hire one."

Vonda pressed a hand to her chest. "I get my own assistant?"

"You do. And treat them well. They'll save you one day. Just like you've saved me."

"I'm not going to cry at work." She sniffed. "I'm not. I promise."

He eyed her and the tears forming in her eyes. "Are you sure about that?"

Vonda laughed. "I'm sure," she said, shakily.

His office door swung open and Skye marched inside. Smacking a piece of paper on his desk, she said, "What the hell is this?"

His gaze dropped down to the paper. The headline: PAIGE MILLS COZIES UP TO HER LOVER IN A HOUSTON PARKING GARAGE.

Andrew skimmed the article before meeting Skye's gaze. He opened his mouth to respond to her, but nothing came out. Because there was nothing really to say. The article wasn't anything deep or libelous. The writer just mentioned they were spotted kissing in a dark SUV. Which was the truth.

Skye glared at him, snatching the paper from the desk

and shoving it in her purse. "What part of keep it quiet don't you get?"

Vonda jumped up. "Um, I think it's time for me to go. Let me know you if you need anything."

Andrew waited for Vonda to leave the office *and* counted to ten. Because he was going to lose it.

"Damn, it's like talking to toddlers." Skye stalked to the other side of the office, stopped abruptly, then whirled around to face him. "I tell you to stop, but you do it anyway."

"But I'm not your damn kid, though," he growled. "I'm a grown-ass man, and I can do whatever the hell I want."

"Even if what you want is affecting Paige?"

Andrew stood abruptly, tipping his chair over. But he made no move to pick it up. "Skye, I'm not in the mood for this. You need to leave."

He crammed the things on his desk into a drawer. The taping of *The Wendell Wilson Show* would start in a few hours, and he'd promised Paige he'd be there.

"Where are you going?" Skye walked over to him and picked up his chair. "I know you're not going to the taping."

Ignoring her, he packed up his laptop and mouse and stuffed a couple of file folders into his bag.

"Andrew?" Skye called.

"I'm minding my business, Skye," he said through clenched teeth. "Maybe you should mind yours."

"Paige *is* my business. Her career is my business." She pointed her manicured finger at him. "*You* should know better. Of all people, you know how important it is to make a plan and stick with it. The plan was for you and Paige to stay away from each other for now—at least in public. But, no . . . You couldn't do that. Now, I have another headline on my hands, right before she goes on *The Wendell Wilson*

Show. So, no, you're not going. You need to stay the hell away from that studio."

He turned away from her and turned off his monitor.

Skye sighed heavily. "Andrew, I get it."

Pausing, he glanced at her. "Get what?"

"You love her. That much is obvious."

He straightened to his full height. "Is it now?"

"Of course." Skye sighed, leaning on the edge of the desk. "I noticed at the lake house. Hell, I noticed *before* the lake house. I think it's great. I hope you two will be happy together. Eventually. Not today."

"It's an interview," he argued. "I'm her agent. It's not out of the realm of possibility that I would show up."

"You're also the agent that everyone thinks she's having a long-term affair with."

"We didn't have an affair."

"I know that," Skye said. "That's not the point."

Andrew wasn't going to apologize for being there for Paige, not when she needed him. "We didn't do anything wrong."

"I never said you were wrong, Andrew. That's not why we're doing this. If you were thinking with your brain and not your heart, you would know I'm right. It's not a good idea for you to go to the studio. Especially, after that article."

"Shit," he grumbled.

"We've known each other a long time. I'm inviting you to my wedding. Do you know what that means?"

He raised a questioning brow, not certain how her wedding guest list had anything to do with this. "No, but I'm sure you're going to tell me."

"It means that I consider you a friend. I'm not trying to piss you off. But right now I'm Paige's publicist. Her well-being is number one for me. You trust me to do my job, right?"

Is this a trick question? Because as annoying as Skye was, she was a damn good publicist—so good that Jax had invested in her private firm when she left Pure Talent.

"Yes," he answered. "What does that have to do with anything?"

"If you trust me, let me do my damn job. You know it's not a good look for you to come. Tanya will be there. I will be there. *You* don't need to be there. You can see her when it's over."

Andrew hated when Skye was right. Unfortunately for him, the publicist was often right *and* extremely annoying about it. But . . . "I promised her I'd be there, Skye." He dropped his head, ran a hand over the back of his neck. "She asked me to come."

"After this?" She held up the crumpled piece of paper again. "You need to stay away."

Placing his palms flat against his desk, he leaned forward, dropping his head. "Tell me something?" He shot her a sideways glance. "If this was Garrett, and he asked you to be there for him, wouldn't you be there?"

Skye's eyes softened. "Hell. Yeah."

"So tell me again why I shouldn't be there."

"The difference is that even though I'd try my damnedest to show up for him, I have friends who will lock my ass in a room if they thought my presence would hurt him."

Skye didn't need to say anything else to convince him he shouldn't go to Paige, because he knew it was a bad idea. At the same time, he was willing to risk it to make sure she knew he was there for her.

"We both work to protect Paige's career," he said. "But I need to protect Paige. She's already anxious. She even told me she wanted to cancel the damn interview. Add in the fact that I don't have a good feeling about Wendell." It was no secret that Wendell had ties to Julius. The two had worked together years ago in radio.

"That's why I'll be there," Skye said. "And I promise you, if he pulls a fast one, I will skewer him over hot coals."

A heaviness settled in his chest as he contemplated his next move. He had a sinking feeling that this would not end well for him. Still, he found himself agreeing. "I won't go. But I want to send Vonda."

Skye shrugged. "Okay."

"Make sure you tell Paige why I'm not there," he told her.

"I promise to tell her—when the interview is over." He opened his mouth to argue, but she rushed on, "Because if I tell her beforehand, she'll be upset. I need her on her game."

Andrew picked up his phone. "I'll call her myself," he grumbled.

"No." Skye snatched his phone. "Don't call her. Don't text her. Let her concentrate on this interview. If she goes out there distracted, he'll pounce."

He grabbed his phone. "Fine. Go. I won't show up."

Skye offered him a sad smile. "Don't worry. I'll be the baddie. I'll let her know that I told you it wouldn't be a good idea for you to show up." She glanced at her watch. "Shit, I gotta go. I'll be in touch." She rushed out of the office.

For a few minutes, he warred with himself about it. He knew Skye was right. And if Paige was any other client, he would have championed Skye's plan. But, personally? He knew he was wrong to not be there. And he couldn't help but regret his decision.

Chapter Eighteen

After staring at the latest headline for twenty minutes, Paige closed the internet browser on her phone. Once again, her personal life had been displayed for all the world to see. Once again, she'd given the public the perfect conversation starter. Paige didn't bother to check her social media pages, because she knew what she'd find—judgment, hurtful memes using her worst photos and GIFs, and commentary from people who thought they knew her but had no idea who she really was.

Yet, when she'd looked at the image of her in Andrew's arms inside the SUV, she'd seen two lovers who were resolute in their adoration of each other. She'd seen a man who had dropped everything to be there for the woman he loved and a woman who'd desperately needed comfort after being so humiliated in front of a group of strangers. Instead of celebrating black love, the writer had turned something beautiful, something pure, into a twisted ugly mess.

Paige dialed Andrew again. *Straight to voicemail*. It had been that way all day. Her calling. Him not answering. He'd texted earlier and said he'd be at the studio, but he wasn't there. *Where the hell is he?* She wondered if he'd seen the article, if he'd blamed himself for it . . . *Did he blame me?*

She fired off another text: **Are you okay? Call me.**

Her stomach rolled as she waited for a reply, as dread filled her, as doubt threatened to tilt everything on its head. It wasn't like him to not answer her calls.

Wasn't it, though? That niggling thought grew louder with every passing minute. Because he'd done it before.

She tried not to let her mind skip ahead to all the negative reasons he could be avoiding her. After all, he had a lot going on with his mother. The last time they'd talked, he sounded so stressed out, so tired. Yet he'd promised her that he would be there.

Yet, another voice filtered through her mind—her mother's. "*The only person you can depend on is yourself.*"

At the time, her mom had just come out of her third bitter divorce and had taken the day to drown her sorrows. Paige still remembered the smell of the liquor and the song playing on the speakers. Bobby Womack's "If You Think You're Lonely Now." She also recalled the way she'd felt, watching her strong, unstoppable mother collapse under the weight of her heartbreak.

Her mother had never married again.

But Paige continued to move forward. She'd kept her mind and her heart open to love, even though she'd been hurt herself many times. She could have closed herself off, vowed to never love again. Maybe she'd even voiced that thought after the debacle that was her marriage to Julius. Then . . . *Andrew.*

Despite her recent divorce, she'd fallen—heart first—into a relationship with a man who made her feel treasured and loved. Trusting someone after hurt was hard. But they'd agreed to be honest with each other, they'd agreed to try. So she would try—to be open, to tamp down her doubts, to not jump to conclusions about his absence, and to believe that he would keep his word.

"Hey, Paige." Skye hurried into the greenroom at the studio. Giving her a quick hug, she dropped her large purse on a chair. "I thought I wouldn't make it. Traffic is a nightmare."

"It's always a nightmare," Paige agreed. She cleared her throat.

Paige felt sick, like she was coming down with something. Her throat hurt, her head pounded, and her stomach was queasy. Maybe she was just extremely anxious? Or maybe she was just tired?

Skye typed something on her phone. "How are you?"

Her gaze shifted to the doorway again, hoping Andrew would round the corner and be there. "I'm not feeling well," Paige admitted. "Maybe we should reschedule?"

Skye rubbed her hands down Paige's arms and gave them a friendly squeeze. "Oh no. Is it a stomach bug? I can get you some ginger ale?"

Shaking her head, Paige told her, "No, I'll be okay."

"Sure?" Skye tilted her head to meet Paige's gaze. "Because I don't want you to go out there if you're not feeling your best."

Gripping her throat, Paige said, "I'll be fine." *I hope.* "Tanya is running a little late. She should be here any minute."

Paige looked at the door again. Despite her earlier pep talk, she couldn't shake the feeling that Andrew wasn't coming. She tried to think of a reason why. *Is his mother okay?*

Connie had been having a hard time healing from her ankle fracture, and Paige knew he was worried about his mother. *Is he still in Detroit*? If he was, why wouldn't he call her? Being there for Connie was way more important than this interview.

"What are you looking for?" Skye asked, concern on her face.

"Andrew said he'd be here." Paige flattened a hand over her belly. "I've tried to call him, but he won't answer."

Skye's phone buzzed, and she held up her forefinger, silently asking Paige to give her a minute. Stepping off to the side, Skye answered her call.

A few minutes later, the door opened. A wave of relief washed over Paige—until Tanya breezed through the doorway. Her manager approached her. "Hey, Paige. Sorry I'm late."

Paige gave her a tight smile. She loved Tanya, she loved how invested the top manager was in her career, but Tanya was always late. And Paige *hated* to be late.

"There's an accident on the 405," Tanya explained. "It was hell getting here." She dropped her keys into her purse and flipped her hair out of her face. "Remind me not to get bangs again. This shit is whack." She ran her fingers through her hair. "You good?"

Smiling at her, Paige said, "Yes. Just ready to get this over."

"It's only a short time out of your life. Then you'll do the *Opal Show* and have a good cry."

Opal Winfield had a knack for getting people to cry on her show. The questions were always thought provoking and she was extremely sincere, almost like a favorite auntie. Every single time Paige had visited the talk show, she'd cried.

"Did you get my email?" Tanya asked, staring at her phone. "I talked to James. He still wants you."

Paige shook her head. Tanya had been trying to get her to sign on for her boyfriend James's film. Initially, Paige thought it would be good for her career. But after Andrew had given his opinion, she'd taken more time to think about whether it was the best move. In the end, she knew he was right. The NetPix deal was better, by far. And she would have creative input, which would align with her plan to segue into more production projects.

"We'll talk about it," Paige said absently, glancing down at her phone again. Still no calls from Andrew.

Skye approached them again. "Okay, they're ready for you."

After one last look toward the door, she followed Skye to the set.

Twenty minutes later, Paige stormed off the set, fury lacing through her veins. She scanned the area, looking for Andrew. *No Andrew*. Checking her phone, she realized he hadn't called either. Maybe he was off fixing things, pulling strings like he'd done so well throughout her career?

At the far end of the room, Tanya was yelling at one of the producers. Off in the corner, Skye was barking orders at someone on the phone. Paige couldn't make out every-thing her publicist was saying, but the words *fuck* and *you* resonated with her, even though Skye hadn't actually said them together. Paige wanted to say them, though—to Wendell Fuckin' Wilson.

Despite the measures they'd put in place prior to the interview, despite the agreed-upon discussion points, Wendell had followed his own plan. And, once again, Paige was the one who suffered.

The interview had started out well enough. Questions about upcoming projects, compliments on her latest per-formance *and* her shoes. But things took a sudden and dangerous turn, especially when Wendell blindsided her with a series of questions about her relationship with Andrew. Things got even worse when that damn asshole interrogated her about her "secret life."

But the worst thing that had happened? *She'd* stumbled. Instead of eloquent and measured responses, she'd paused, she'd stammered, and then she'd shut down. In front of the studio audience. Everything that she'd rehearsed flew out the window as Wendell hammered her with a recap of her tumultuous marriage, the contentious divorce, and her alleged bad behavior and fake ways. *Dammit*.

The door opened, and once again, she thought it might be Andrew. Only to be disappointed when one of the production assistants she'd met earlier rushed inside. She glanced at her publicist and her manager again. Everyone was there, except for the one person she expected to be there—the one person who'd promised to be there.

Tanya fired off one last threat to the producer and headed toward Paige. She opened her mouth to speak, but Paige said, "Not now, Tanya."

"We're going to light him up," Tanya said. "We got you."

Paige knew her manager and her publicist would do everything they could to help her. But sometimes, even the best efforts didn't cut it. Paige had learned that people could not be controlled, that people did what they wanted to do, that *people* broke promises. But she didn't want to hear about their plans. She needed to get out of there. Now.

The door swung open one more time, and Vonda stepped through the door, phone in hand. *What the hell?* Vonda's presence meant only one thing—Andrew had sent her. After everything they'd gone through to get back right, he'd turned around and done the same damn thing. Instead of calling her, he'd sent Vonda. Instead of being there, he'd sent Vonda.

Fuming, she asked Tanya, "When did Vonda get here?"

Tanya glanced back at Vonda, who was now talking to Skye, then turned back to Paige. "Oh. She got here while you were on set," Tanya said. "I guess Andrew couldn't make it?"

First, Andrew didn't answer her many calls. Now, he was back to sending Vonda to handle her. With her thoughts spinning—about Andrew, about Wendell, about Julius—she snatched her purse off the chair. Her eyes filled with tears, and she willed herself not to let a single one fall. Paige was done crying. *I'm so fuckin' done with everything*. Then, without another word, Paige left.

An hour later, Paige pulled into her driveway. She looked down at her buzzing phone. Skye again. Her publicist had called her numerous times since she'd left the studio, and Paige hadn't answered a single call. What she needed right now was to be alone.

Tanya had called, too. So did Chastity. Everyone had called except *him*. Just like everyone was there but him. When her phone rang again, she sent the call to voicemail and sent out a group text to her team: **Stop calling. I'm not going back to Michigan.**

Paige wasn't planning on pulling another "South Haven," as Skye had called it. But she was going to make a few key changes. It was time she stopped depending on everyone else to handle her business. No more running. Paige wasn't a victim. She was a victor. And she knew what she had to do.

She'd only been in the house long enough to pour a glass of wine when there was a knock at the door. Jogging to the front of the house, she paused when she recognized the outline of her visitor through the glass. *Andrew*.

Taking a deep breath, she continued to the door and swung it open. He stood on the other side, hands in his pockets and a soft smile on his lips. He looked like temptation bathed in chocolate. His shirt was unbuttoned at the neck and his beard was freshly shaven. He smelled like spices and leather and grapefruit. Yesterday, that look would have gotten him sexed thoroughly as soon as he'd crossed the threshold. But today? *Not happening*.

"Hey," he said, his voice low.

"What are you doing here?" she asked, skipping the pleasantries. Because she felt anything but pleasant right now.

"Came to check on you."

"Really? Why?"

He frowned. "Why wouldn't I?"

Is he really going to act like he didn't basically ignore me the entire day? Counting to ten, Paige said, "I'm busy."

"Vonda told me about the interview," he said. "What happened?"

"What happened?" she asked incredulously. "Where the hell have you been, Andrew?"

He blinked. "What do you mean? Did you talk to Skye?"

"What does Skye have to do with this?" she yelled. "You know what? Just go. You obviously have better things to do than be here with me."

"Paige, what—?"

She held up a hand. "Stop." Snickering, she rushed on, "That interview was terrible. But what was worse? You weren't there. I don't know why I'm so upset. It's not like you haven't done this before."

Paige had stupidly let her guard down. *Again*. She'd trusted a man, she'd trusted Andrew, to do right by her.

Again. And now she was forced to pick up the pieces of her broken heart. *Again.*

"I don't know why I thought things would be different. My fault for trusting you. I won't make the same mistake anymore. I'm not going to let *any* man hurt me like this again. And I'm never going to give another person the chance to break a promise to me."

"Oh, okay." Andrew sighed. "So you're just not going to let me talk to you, to explain what happened?"

"The only thing I need to know is that you weren't there, after you promised me you would be there."

"What if I had an emergency?" he asked. "You're not the only one that's going through shit, Paige."

Paige wavered a bit, because she did know that he'd been dealing with his mother. *Is Connie okay?* "Did you have an emergency? Is it your mother?" she asked, trying not to pay attention to the hope that fluttered in her chest at the thought that he *did* have a good reason to be absent.

"She's okay."

"Good. I'm so happy to hear that." She let out a sigh of relief. "Were you still in Detroit? Is that why you weren't here?"

He dropped his head. "No, but—"

That slight hope faded away with his admission, and anger took over again. "Okay, then. It doesn't matter anymore, anyway."

"Paige, can I come in so we can talk about this? Obviously, there's been a misunderstanding."

"No, I understand completely." She took a deep breath. "We *could've* talked about it had you called me back, texted me . . . anything. But you didn't. And I'm done."

"Is this where we're at now?" He met her gaze again.

"Me begging you to let me in—literally and figuratively—and you slamming the door in my face again."

"Oh, I haven't slammed the door in your face yet," she said. "I have one more thing to say to you. You're fired."

Then she slammed the door—in his face.

"Thanks for answering the door," Skye said, grinning at Paige. "I thought you were going to just let me stand out here looking stupid."

Paige stared at her publicist. "Honestly, I wasn't going to answer it." She held the door open and let Skye in.

Skye smiled at her as she entered the house. "What made you change your mind?"

"I figured I should tell you that I fired Andrew."

With wide eyes, Skye said, "What?"

"I. Fired. Andrew," Paige repeated.

The second time didn't feel any better than the first. In fact, she hadn't felt good since she'd slammed the door in Andrew's face. At first, it felt like the answer to her prayers. It felt final, like she'd finally put the period at the end of a long run-on sentence. Then it felt tragic. And *she* felt empty.

"Why would you do that?" Skye asked, a furrowed brow on her face. "And why didn't you call me back earlier?"

"I needed time."

"Time to make a mistake?"

"Who said it was a mistake?" Paige tossed back, trying to add some bravado to her voice. Because she couldn't bring herself to admit that it might have been a mistake. "Besides, I didn't want to talk about that interview. Not today."

"If you had just answered the phone," Skye said, through

clenched teeth. "I didn't call you about the interview. I called because I had something to tell you."

Paige's heart pounded. *Did something else happen?* "What do you have to tell me?" She didn't think she could take much more tonight. Maybe tomorrow, but not tonight.

"I know you were looking for Andrew to be there. I wanted to tell you that he wasn't there because *I* asked him not to come."

Paige's stomach fell.

"Before you say anything, let me explain." Skye let out a frustrated curse. "After the article, I thought it was best that he didn't show up to the studio. I didn't want to give Wendell any more ammunition against you. Andrew didn't want to stay away, though. It took some doing to get him to stand down. He even yelled at me."

Tears burned the back of Paige's throat, but she couldn't talk, she couldn't even think about anything except for the look on Andrew's face when she fired him. Panic rose inside her when she pictured the hurt in his eyes, the disappointment . . . *What the hell have I done*?

"Maybe I was wrong?" Skye continued. "But after what Wendell pulled today, I don't think I am. It was best for everyone that Andrew wasn't there to see what happened. The last thing we needed was for him to beat the shit out of Wendell. Which would have been a strong possibility since *I* was seconds away from knocking that asshole the hell out."

"Why didn't you just tell me?" she shouted. "Why didn't *he* just tell me?"

Skye raised her hand. "Me again. I told him not to answer your calls and not to return your texts. I snatched his phone away when he tried to call you. Like I said, he wasn't trying to hear anything I said."

Paige paced the floor, shaking her hands in the air. "Why?"

"Because all it would have taken was for him to hear your voice, and he would have been there." Skye shrugged. "And because if you knew he wasn't coming, you would have been even more distracted than you already were."

Exhaling slowly, Paige closed her eyes against the torrent of emotions she felt in that moment. She plopped down on the couch and her shoulders fell. There were so many things running through her mind, she didn't know where to start.

After a moment, though, she said, "I think what bothers me the most—and it's probably my fault because I've been a *lot* emotional lately—but y'all are out here acting like I'm just weak. That I can't take anything. Not even a phone call," she added. "You act like I would've fallen apart if you'd told me your reasoning then. I would have been sad, but I would have been okay. Instead, I thought he was ignoring because . . ." Paige ran shaky fingers through her hair. "I don't even know now. Because everything that I thought made sense at the time doesn't anymore."

Skye sat next to her. "It's my natural inclination to protect you because that's my job—and because you're my friend. In this case, I might have been wrong, and I apologize." She squeezed Paige's leg. "You're not weak, though. You're one of the strongest women I know."

The tears fell then, but Paige made no move to wipe them.

"I don't know many women who could deal with Julius and his trifling ass and still come out standing," Skye said. "Even when you thought you were at your weakest, none of us did. And that's the truth."

Paige rested her head on Skye's shoulder. "Thank you."

Skye hugged her. "One more thing." Lifting her gaze, Paige peered at her friend. "Don't punish Andrew for this. He really does love you."

Nodding, Paige said, "You didn't see the way I hurt him."

"It's not too late to make it right," Skye said. "Like I always tell my friends . . . fix that shit." Standing, Skye picked up her purse. "I hate to leave you, but X is in town and we have business."

Paige stood and walked Skye to the door. "Thanks for coming by."

"I had to set the record straight. I promised Andrew I would tell you why he didn't show up. I feel bad that I didn't tell you before . . ." Skye shook her head. "It's okay because you're going to handle this. Right?"

"Right," Paige said, her own voice sounding foreign to her ears.

"Talk to you later. I'll be in touch."

Paige watched Skye leave. She'd made a lot of mistakes in her life, most she recovered from. But this . . . Skye had said it was never too late, but this might be another thing her publicist was wrong about. Because Paige wondered if she could really fix it.

Chapter Nineteen

"Tequila, huh?"

Andrew glared at X, who'd seemingly appeared out of nowhere. Or maybe that fifth shot had made him appear? Either way, he didn't want to talk to anyone—real or imagined. He turned back to the line of shots he'd ordered at his favorite sports bar.

When he'd arrived a little over an hour ago, he'd ordered six shots of Patrón. One for every hour since he'd seen Paige. And he planned to make the most out of this last one. Picking it up, he tossed it back enjoying the burn as the liquor worked its way down his throat and settled in his gut.

Maybe he'd be numb after this one, maybe he'd be able to forget about the way Paige had slammed the door in his face again.

"Drew?" Real—*or faux*—X called. "Bruh?"

Andrew glanced at his friend. He decided he wasn't so drunk that he'd conjured up X. Because if he could materialize anyone, it wouldn't be Xavier Starks. It would Paige. "What are doing here?"

"Skye sent me."

Grumbling a curse, he waved the bartender over. "I don't even want to think about how Skye knows where I am right now." The publicist to the stars always seemed to know where everyone was.

"Well, she didn't. She just told me you might need company. And since I know you, and I know this is your favorite spot, I came here." X slid onto the barstool across from Andrew and ordered a drink.

"No tequila?" Andrew asked.

X shook his head. "Nah, man. If I come home with that Patrón in me, Zara will kick my ass out—*after* she kicks my ass."

"Knowing Zara, she would beat you down," Andrew said with a chuckle.

"It's all love, though. Even before we got together, she would always tell me like it is."

Andrew sighed. Although his relationship with Paige was technically new, he thought they'd passed the point of no return, the point where he'd started to think about forever.

The fact that Paige had fired him—as her agent *and* her boyfriend—still stung. She'd just let him go, without letting him explain, without even asking him why he didn't come. Paige had come up with reasons in her head that seemed legitimate enough to cut him out of her life completely.

Tread lightly. Connor's words were stuck on repeat in his head. His brother had warned him about rushing this, about moving too fast. And her reaction had proven him right.

"What happened, bruh?" Xavier said, pulling him from his thoughts.

Shaking his head, Andrew thought about how to answer

that question. Because he didn't know what happened. He suspected, but all he really knew was she was done with him. Even still, he told X the facts, starting from his mother reinjuring herself and ending with the slammed door in his face.

"Damn," X said, taking a sip of his drink. "This probably won't make you feel better, but Skye was right. You shouldn't have been there."

Andrew snorted. "Yeah, well . . . there's that."

Skye *was* right. She did what any publicist would have done in the same situation—protect her client from negative press. Ultimately, that's why Andrew didn't go to the studio. And after Vonda told him what had happened on set, he knew beyond the shadow of a doubt that he would be in jail if he'd been there, charged with assault on Wendell Wilson.

Yet, even though Skye had been right about that, she was wrong about her assertion that he shouldn't contact Paige until after the taping. Andrew shouldn't have listened to her. He *should* have called Paige, despite what Skye had said.

Andrew imagined Paige looking for him, he imagined her mind running wild with theories about where he was, trying to figure out why he wasn't there. He hated that he'd gone against his instinct to call her, to at least tell her why he couldn't be with her at the studio.

"If I had just called her, this might not have happened," Andrew said. "Because all she knew was that I wasn't returning her calls or her texts. All she knew was that I broke a promise to her. She didn't even know about Mom."

"Paige has been in the business for a long time, Drew." X finished his drink. "She knows how it works."

"And normally, I'd agree with you. But earlier this year,

I did the same thing to her. She felt abandoned, because I made her feel that way. I didn't want to see her with Julius, I didn't want to watch her hurting over that sorry-ass muthafucka. I stepped back because it was easier for *me*."

"Glad to see you're finally admitting that shit," X muttered, finishing his drink.

"And I take responsibility for that," Andrew continued, ignoring his friend's comment. "I know I fucked up, but she forgave me and we moved forward. I should have called her yesterday, because I knew what it would mean if I didn't."

That's really what it boiled down to. Andrew knew better. He knew that their recent history would color their present. And because he didn't follow his own instincts, he'd failed her—professionally and personally. If they hadn't been in a relationship, he would have called her and told her he couldn't make it. If he hadn't been her agent, he would have been there. Plain and simple.

"I've always admired you, bruh," X said. "You took me under your wing, taught me things that I would've struggled to learn by myself. I'm going to return the favor since I'm older than you—in relationship years, that is."

Andrew glared at X. "Shut the hell up, man."

"Hey, I had to clarify that you're still older than me in real years." X barked out a laugh. "Anyway, what happened between you and Paige doesn't have to be the end of the relationship. It was an argument, a misunderstanding. Shit happens—often."

"She fired me," Andrew pointed out.

X shrugged. "So? She was pissed. People say and do things in the heat of the moment all the time. Hell, I do."

"You didn't see her, man."

"I don't need to see her. I've seen Zara when I've lashed out and said things I immediately regretted. Like I said, it happens. Paige is reeling from everything that happened in that interview and with Julius."

"Meaning I am the rebound guy," Andrew said.

"I wouldn't say that. Think about it, she got subpoenaed, sued, and then hammered in a public interview. And the reason why all of this is happening is because of Julius. I don't think it has anything to do with you being a rebound. You're reading too much into it."

Andrew gulped down the glass of water the waiter had left with him earlier. "I hear you, but it hasn't been that long since she divorced him."

"Technically. Paige is recently divorced, yes. But that marriage was over a long time ago."

Andrew recalled a conversation he'd had with Paige. She'd told him she didn't love Julius anymore. At the time, his only goal had been to comfort her, to make sure she knew she wasn't wrong to feel that way. In hindsight, he realized her admission was her way of telling him that she'd moved on from her ex-husband, that she wasn't pining away for him and longing for the love they'd once had. Paige had already given him the answer to his question. She'd basically told him that he wasn't a rebound even before they'd taken the next step.

"If you're worried about being the rebound, don't," X continued. "It's like me and Zara. There was already a connection between us before we got together. Naomi doing what she did just kicked the door open to explore it."

Before X and Zara got together, Xavier had planned to propose to then-girlfriend Naomi Murphy. But Naomi cheated on him and got engaged to another man while they were together.

"True," Andrew said.

"That's how you have to think about her relationship with Julius. If there was no him, there would be no '*Prew.*'" X cracked up at Andrew's expense.

"Man, get out of here with that shit."

"Sorry, man. I couldn't resist. When Zara told me about that mashup name, I couldn't even breathe I was laughing so hard."

Andrew shook his head. "It's dumb as hell. Who comes up with that shit?"

"That *shit* is funny."

"Whatever."

"Okay, I'm done. Are we finished with this sappy conversation?"

Chuckling, Andrew said, "Yeah. This needs to be over."

"Well, well, well." Julius rounded the corner, approached their table. "I was wondering when I'd run into you."

Andrew narrowed his eyes on Julius. "Walk away," he threatened. "Now."

As if Andrew hadn't warned him, Julius continued, "I always knew you wanted my wife."

"Ex-wife," Andrew corrected, clenching his fists together. The thought of pummeling that cocky bastard had settled in his gut. After all, he wasn't her agent anymore. He might be able to get away with one uppercut—*maybe two*.

"You can have her," Julius taunted. "She's a fuckin' bitch anyway. How does it feel to have my sloppy seconds?"

Before he knew it, Andrew had Julius's neck in his hand and his head pressed against the table. The shot glasses he'd lined up perfectly were now shattered on the floor and water was dripping over the edge of the table. For good measure, he lifted Julius's head and slammed it against the table again.

"Don't think I won't fuck you up in front of this entire bar," Andrew growled. "If I ever hear you disrespect her again, I will come for you. Do yourself a favor. Get the hell out of here and stay away from her." Without another word, he shoved the director toward the door. Hard.

And just like Andrew expected . . . That sorry bastard hightailed it out of the bar without looking back, and so did the man who was with him. After a moment, he grabbed several napkins off an adjacent table and started cleaning up.

Glancing at X, he said, "Don't say one word."

Xavier raised a questioning brow. "Is this what we're doing now? Losing our temper in public?"

"I know you're not talking. Weren't you the one that threw Ethan Porter into a buffet table?"

X waved him off. "Yeah, I know. Another drink?"

Andrew laughed. "Sounds good to me."

Xavier waved the waitress over. "By the way, it was a dessert table."

"Same thing," Andrew muttered.

"Not really, but whatever."

The waitress came over and took their drink order. For the first time since he'd been fired, he felt better. Because he had hope that this wasn't the end for them, that this would be just another storm they'd weather—*together*.

Paige awoke with a start, her heart pounding and her head hurting. Glancing around the room, she screamed when she spotted a figure in the doorway, watching her intently.

"Mom?" Paige took a few deep breaths in an attempt to calm her nerves. "Oh my God, you scared me." She fell back on her pillow.

"You need to be scared," Tina retorted.

Paige's eyes popped open. "What?" Her gaze followed her mother's movement around the bedroom, watching as she inspected perfume bottles, read the back of a book, and even picked up her bra and tossed it in her hamper.

Turning to face her, her mother narrowed her eyes. "You heard me."

Rolling over, Paige said, "Mom, I'm sleepy. Can we talk later?"

"Do you always sleep in full clothes?"

Paige groaned. "Yes." *No.* But the alcohol she'd consumed last night had made it impossible to do anything but fall across the bed. *No more dark liquor.*

After Skye had left, Paige had poured out her wine and pulled out the bourbon. She wasn't really a hard liquor person, but it started to taste good—after the second glass. *Or was it the third?*

"Get up, babe?" Tina yanked the thin sheet from her and gasped. "Oh Lord. Look at that hair. Just went to bed without a bonnet or a scarf. Good luck with those tangles."

"Mom!" Paige shouted into the pillow. "You're making my head hurt. I love you, but I need to sleep."

"You can sleep when you fix your mess."

Sighing, Paige sat up. "Who told you I made a mess?" She pushed her hair off her face. "Jax?"

After Andrew had left yesterday—before Paige had wilted under the pressure of the day and the ramifications of her hasty actions—she had sent a terse email to Pure Talent indicating that she'd fired Andrew.

"Jax did contact me, yes," Tina admitted.

Groaning, Paige asked, "What happened to confidentiality?"

"He called because he was concerned about you—and because you wouldn't answer his call."

Oh. Paige had turned her phone off last night after Skye left.

"And confidentiality flew out the window when you fired your agent," Tina continued. "Now, get up and get dressed. Let's talk."

Before Paige could object, her mother walked toward the door. "Ten minutes, Paige. And do something with that hair," she yelled as she exited.

Twenty minutes later, Paige entered the kitchen, where her mother was buttering a piece of toast. Tina lifted her gaze and pointed Paige to the barstool in front of her. Sliding onto the seat, Paige waited for her mother to say something.

Tina spread a thin layer of jelly on the toast, set it on a plate, and slid it over to Paige. "Eat that. You need something in your system."

"I hate toast," she murmured. A long time ago, one of her nannies had made her wheat toast for breakfast. It had been so hard and so burnt, it had scraped the roof of Paige's mouth and effectively ruined it for her.

"Eat," Tina ordered, pouring a glass of orange juice and setting it in front of Paige.

Paige bit into the toast. To her surprise, it wasn't hard. And it was good. *Or I could just be hungry*? She stared at the bread, then back at her mother. "Did you do something different with this toast?"

"I put it in the oven, not the toaster. That's the trick."

"Hm . . ." Paige devoured the toast and gulped down the orange juice. When she finished, she looked at her mom, who was watching her with wide eyes. "What?"

"Hungry, much?"

Paige ducked her head. "I haven't eaten in a while," she murmured lamely.

"Oh, so you didn't add food to your liquor diet?"

Shrugging, Paige explained that she'd eaten an early dinner before she'd started drinking. "But you don't have to worry. I won't be doing this again anytime soon."

Leaning forward, Tina rested her arms on the counter. "I know you won't. Now tell me what happened."

Paige ran her thumb over a small ridge in the counter. "I thought you knew," she whispered, keeping her eyes trained on the counter. Not her mother.

"I want *you* to tell me," Tina insisted.

Sighing, Paige told her mother everything, even the parts she'd been afraid to admit out loud. Like how she realized how wrong she'd been and that she'd called him last night only to get his voicemail again. This time, she didn't blame him for avoiding her. She'd acted like a crazed, spoiled brat.

"I agree with Skye. Andrew wasn't there because he *shouldn't* have been there. I know you wanted him with you, but he made the right decision. This was about protecting your brand."

"I know that now."

With a heavy sigh, Tina said, "You would have known that last night if you'd given him a chance to talk."

"I know," she repeated. One the hardest things about last night was the realization that their entire encounter could have been avoided if she'd just used her words and not her heightened emotions to do the talking for her. "I still don't know why he didn't just call me."

"I'm sure he wanted to, but he's had a lot going on. I talked to Connie yesterday. She called because she received the basket of smutty romance novels I sent to her. She told me that she'd reinjured herself."

Paige's head snapped up. "What?"

Nodding, Tina continued her story. "They rushed her to the hospital. She's doing fine now, but Andrew stayed with her the entire day—until she finally convinced him to go home."

Slumping forward, Paige rested her forehead on the counter. Before she'd felt like an ass. Now she felt like an asshole. It couldn't have been easy for him, watching his mother suffer only to come home and deal with her.

A moment later, she felt fingers running through her curls. Shifting, Paige wrapped her arms around her mother's waist and hugged her. "I messed up, Mom. I really messed up. I love Drew. I don't want it to be over."

Up until now, Paige thought her biggest mistake was marrying Julius. But losing Andrew . . . She'd pulled out the liquor last night to numb herself. Because every part of her ached for him.

Tina smoothed a comforting hand over Paige's back. "It's not over, Paige." She kissed the top of Paige's head. "You can make it right."

After a few minutes, Paige sat up and wiped her eyes. It felt good to talk to her mother like this, like she'd always imagined a mother-daughter duo would talk, complete with comforting hugs and tears. "What do you think I should do?"

"I think you should stop making decisions based on emotion."

Paige frowned. The warm fuzzies she'd experienced only a minute ago evaporated. It was just the type of thing her mother would say, and it didn't help anything. "I'm asking you what to do about Andrew."

"The answer is the same," Tina said. "You've been through a lot this year. And I've watched you handle things with grace. I've also watched you hide away. You were going to sign this house away to that fool. When Andrew came to see about you, you slammed the door in his face. You have to stop being foolish."

For some reason, her mother's words angered her more than they calmed her. It felt like an impossible expectation, one that she'd never be able to meet. She stood, pushing the chair back. "I'm a human being, Mom. I'm not perfect. But I'm me. I had to deal with things how *I* felt they needed to be dealt with. If that meant going away, that's what I did."

"Paige, stop."

"No, you stop," she said. "I'm emotional. I wear my feelings on my sleeve. I react without thinking. I do all those things, sometimes in the same conversation. And that's okay! You might think I'm weak, but I'm not. If anything, it proves that I'm strong, that I can feel the gamut of emotions and still work, play, and live. I can get hurt and still fall so head over heels in love that I can't imagine life before that feeling." Paige sucked in a deep breath. "You told me not to depend on anyone else. But having a strong support system is not a bad thing, it's not a crutch. It's freedom."

Paige adored her team. They fought for her, valued

her, and encouraged her. It meant everything to her. They allowed her to be great, allowed her to concentrate on acting. They were the difference between Paige the Great and Paige the Has-Been. And that team leader had always been Andrew.

"I agree with you." Tina approached Paige, framing Paige's face in her hands. "Paige, I don't think you're weak. I don't know where you got that from. I actually admire *you*. You rise to every occasion, good or bad. I feel extremely proud that you're my daughter."

Tears spilled onto Paige's cheeks and a sob burst free. "Really?"

"I watched you work your way to the top the hard way, without my help. The main reason you're Black America's Sweetheart is because you're strong, determined, and talented. You're everything I taught you to be and more."

"You did help me," Paige said finally. "You had Jax send Andrew."

Tina smiled. "Yeah, but you made that work. Not me. When I told you to stop making decisions based off emotion, I said that because I don't want you to end up like me. I've been so hurt that I fear I'll never be able to love a man again. I left Hunter because I thought he cheated on me. He didn't, but I didn't give him a chance to explain. I reacted off of pure emotion and kicked his ass out."

It was the first time her mother had mentioned her third husband's name in years. Hunter had been one of Paige's favorite people the world. He'd loved her mother so fiercely, and he loved Paige. When he left, Paige had mourned the loss of that relationship for years.

"Why didn't you tell me that?" Paige asked.

"Because it hurt too much to talk about it. It's hard shining the negative light on yourself."

"Why didn't you go after him?"

"I was a fool," Tina admitted. "I've regretted that decision every day. When I heard what you did, my immediate fear was that you'd close yourself off like I did. I don't want you to make the same mistakes." Tears fell from Tina's eyes. "And you're right . . . Your ability to love *is* a strength."

"Mom, I—"

"I've made so many mistakes, Paige. But having you was the best thing I could have ever done. And I know you missed a lot of time with me because of my career, but I hope you know that I thought of you every hour of every day. I wasn't at home baking cookies, I couldn't sign up to be your scout leader, but—"

"No, Mom. Don't say that. Because I didn't need you to do those things."

"But I should've," Tina said. "I should have been there more with you. You needed a mother, not a friend."

"I needed a mother *and* a friend," Paige corrected.

Tina kissed Paige's cheek and pulled her into another hug. "I love you, baby."

"Love you, too, Mom."

"Now." Tina pulled back, squeezing Paige's arms. "You really need to do something with that hair if you're going to see Andrew."

Paige laughed. "Okay, Mom. Will you help me with my makeup?"

Tina's eyes lit up. "And your hair?"

"And my hair." Paige grabbed her phone and sent one text: Do you have time to see me today?

The reply came seconds later: Yes.

After she'd been primped, prodded, and then primped some more by her mother, Paige stared at herself in the full-length mirror in the hallway leading to the front of the house. Her mother had finally left, after giving Paige strict instructions to call as soon as she talked to Andrew. Paige agreed to send some kind of update to her mother, but she couldn't promise to call. Her ability to call depended on whether things went her way or not. If it didn't go according to plan, she would call. If it did go her way, she'd text—because if he forgave her, she hoped to be naked in a matter of minutes.

Either way, Paige had a plan. She didn't know what would happen when she saw Andrew again. But she did know two things—she'd never willingly walk away from him again and she loved him more than she thought she could love anyone. And she'd do her best to convince him of that.

Okay, Paige. You got this. Taking a deep breath, she walked the distance to the front door and opened it. Smiling, she said, "Xavier, thanks for coming." She held the door open for him.

Xavier stepped over the threshold and gave her a quick hug. "Of course."

They took a seat in the small sitting room near the kitchen. "I appreciate you coming on such short notice," she said, crossing her legs. "I won't keep you long, because I know you're here on business. Can I get you anything? Water? Coffee?"

"No, thanks," Xavier said. "And it's no trouble."

She cleared her throat. "Before I get started, I wanted to apologize."

Frowning, Xavier asked, "What are you apologizing for?"

"For that email I sent yesterday. I acted hastily, and I'd like to discuss my plans with you personally."

"No need to apologize," Xavier assured her. "Trust me, I know all about hasty decisions."

Clapping her hands together, Paige drew in a deep breath. "Thanks. Here's what I'm thinking. I'm sure you know about the personal nature of my relationship with Andrew." When he nodded, she rushed on, "But I've realized that if we stand a chance, I have to end my professional relationship with him."

Xavier stared at her intently. "So you *did* mean to fire him?" he asked with a raised brow.

"Yes." She laughed nervously. "I mean, no. I fired him because I was angry. But then this morning, I realized he needed to stay fired. Andrew can't be my agent, because I need him to be my forever."

Chapter Twenty

Andrew was surprised to see Paige on his doorstep, with a pie pan in her hands and a nervous smile on her lips. His gaze roamed over her, starting from her deep curls to her low-cut black dress to her *fuck-me* high heels. *Stunning.*

Paige swayed on her feet. "Hi," she breathed.

"Hi," he replied, allowing himself one last, slow perusal.

Andrew couldn't figure out if it was the tequila he'd imbibed last night, the sight of her, or the simultaneous regret and arousal coursing through him that made him feel little unhinged. But he knew he needed to say something.

Clearing his throat, he said, "Come in."

Paige stepped into the house, brushing past him. Leaning forward, he took in the scent of her hair. He wanted to touch her, but he resisted the urge to pull her into his arms. Everything about her called to him, made him want to lose himself in her again. It had been a long time since they'd been this close to each other.

She turned to him, shifting her weight from one foot to the other. "I made you an apple pie. I figured we could have a piece? And talk?"

Nodding, he led her to the kitchen. Andrew handed her a knife and pulled out two saucers. As she sliced the pie, he watched her. Having her there had been the answer to his prayers. He'd already planned to reach out to her, but he appreciated that she'd come to him.

A moment later, he tasted the pie. Just like her, it was delicious. Absently, he wondered how it would taste on her stomach. He cleared his throat. "This is the bomb."

"I know," she said, a soft smirk on her face. "I really put my foot into this one."

Andrew chuckled. It felt good to be with her like this, to laugh, to just sit and enjoy each other's company. He wished he could bottle the moment for safekeeping, simply because he didn't know what she wanted to talk about. Although he hoped he was eating "make up" pie, he could very well be eating "break up" pie.

"Drew?"

Meeting her gaze, he peered into her beautiful eyes. "Yes?"

"I'm sorry."

He released a breath he didn't realize he'd been holding. "What for?"

"For not giving you a chance to talk. For being an overly emotional, crazed, and selfish bitch to you. You didn't deserve it." Standing, she paced the room. "I'm sorry for jumping to conclusions. And I'm sorry for slamming the door in your face again." She froze, and her shoulders fell on a long sigh. Her chin quivered, and he wanted to go to her, to wrap her in his arms. "I'm just sorry—for everything. For a moment, I let my past and my fears and my doubts get the best of me. I accused you of breaking a promise to me when I was the one who broke my promise to you."

Andrew's pulse raced. He didn't need her to say anything

else. He already knew what he wanted. He opened his mouth to tell her that but closed it when she held up a hand.

"When I told you I loved you, that was a promise." A tear fell from her eye. "A promise to be understanding, to be kind to you, to be patient. I promised to *hear* you, not just listen to you. And I promised to support you, to believe in you. I failed on all counts." Paige inched closer to him. "But I need you to forgive me."

Andrew had said those exact words to Paige at the lake house, when he'd told her he couldn't walk away. He couldn't fathom a life without her then. *I still can't.* He stood. "Paige?"

"Please," she whispered.

He wiped her tear away, traced a finger over her brow and down her nose. "You're not the only one who failed in the promise department. I should have called you. I shouldn't have let anyone convince me not to."

"You only did what you thought was best at the time."

"Still . . ." He caressed her cheek and her eyes fluttered closed. "I can't let you take all the blame for this."

She nodded, dropping her gaze. "I guess we messed this one up, huh?"

"And it won't be the last time," Andrew told her.

Xavier had brought up good points last night. As much as he loved Paige, they needed to have a serious discussion about expectations. For starters, he needed to know that she wouldn't break up with him after every disagreement. He needed to be certain they could deal with things as they came, without going to extremes.

"Baby, if we are going to be together, we need to *be* together. I have to have some assurance that you won't break up with me because we argued."

"I know. I'm sorry. I guess a part of me is still raw. I

freaked out about everything. My mind was running with all kinds of scenarios. Mostly, I'm just stressed out."

"I understand that. But you have to know . . . I can't live like that."

"I wouldn't expect you to."

Andrew sighed. "I guarantee that I'll fuck up again. You will, too. That's the nature of relationships between two imperfect people. Baby, I want to be with you. *Together* for me means talking things out, respecting each other even when we don't agree, and loving each other through everything. There's no middle ground for me on this. Either we're together or we're apart. Because—"

"Together." She pulled him into a kiss. "I'm sorry you have to ask that question. I'm sorry I made you doubt me."

"Do you still have doubts?"

She shook her head. "No." Biting down on her thumbnail, she asked, "Do you?"

"Since I promised to be honest, I'll admit that I've worried that I'm a rebound for you."

Paige blinked. "What?"

"It's not that weird. The divorce was finalized a couple months ago." She burst out in a fit of giggles, which surprised him. "Why are you laughing?" he asked.

"Because you're not a rebound. Andrew, you're everything I've ever dreamed I wanted and nothing that I deserve. You're not second choice. You're the *only* choice."

God, I'm so in love with her. Every hurt, every disappointment, every misunderstanding faded away in that moment. They'd risked a lot to be together, to take a chance on love, but he wouldn't change a thing. Because this woman had transformed him, she made him a better man.

Andrew closed his eyes as a surge of emotion welled inside him. There was no way he'd ever be able to let her go, no way he'd be able to live without her. "I don't think you understand what your words mean to me."

"If they mean as much as *you* mean to *me*, I get it."

"I choose you, too. I'll never not answer your call again."

A whisper of a smile formed on her perfect lips. "And I'll never slam the door in your face again."

Andrew chuckled. "You better not. Or I'm breaking that shit down."

Laughing, Paige wrapped her arms around him. "I love you so much," she whispered against his ear.

He pulled her closer, into a tight hug, burying his face in her neck. "I love you, too."

They stayed like that for a while, holding each other, whispering "I love you" over and over again. For the first time in days, he felt settled.

Finally, Paige pulled away. But he tugged her forward and kissed her. Like many times before, the kiss quickly turned into more—*more* tongue, *more* teeth, *more* moans. He backed her toward the kitchen table. Because he knew he wouldn't make it to the bedroom.

Gripping her waist, he lifted her and set her on top of the table. He lowered her back, untying the belt on her dress along the way.

"Drew?" she moaned, unbuckling his belt. "*Oh*. Oh no!"

Andrew jumped up, stepping back a few steps. "What?"

"We can't." Paige let out a low groan before she sat up and pulled her dress closed. "There's something I need to tell you."

Uh-oh. Andrew backed away a few more steps. "What is it?"

"It's about me firing you."

The fact that she'd fired him hadn't even crossed his mind. He'd been too focused on her, on them together.

He'd assumed he was reinstated in all ways when they made up. "What about it?" he asked.

Paige averted her gaze, tucking a strand of hair behind her ear. "Um, so I regret the way I fired you. Can you forgive me?"

His shoulders fell and he inched closer to her again. "Of course." He bent down to kiss her, but she turned away, causing him to connect with her cheek—not her lips. Pulling back, he scratched the back of his head. "Paige, just say it."

Paige met his gaze again, a worried look in her eyes. "You're still fired."

Andrew blinked. *That's not how I imagined this conversation going.* "Why?"

She slid off the table and stepped into him. "Although I regret how I did it, I realized it was the right thing to do. I talked to Xavier and he agreed that Vonda should represent me."

Frowning, he wondered when she had a chance to talk to X, and why X hadn't told him. "When?"

"This morning," she admitted. "You have been the best agent that I could have ever had. But if we're going to do this?" She motioned back and forth between them. "We have to concentrate on us. We can't do that if you're still my agent."

Admittedly, the thought had crossed his mind many times since they'd started seeing each other. His problem was that he could never bring himself to walk away from her—in any capacity—so he'd never broached the subject. But Paige was right. It would be best for them in the long run.

Grabbing his hands and holding them against her chest, she said, "Please tell me you understand?"

Nodding, he rested his forehead against hers. "I do."

"I want to be with you. Not as your client, but as your lover, your friend, your heart."

He brushed his lips over hers, cradling her head in his hands. "I love you." Closing his mouth over hers, he tilted his head and deepened the kiss. *Damn, this woman . . .*

With each brush of her lips to his, with every soft moan, she was taking him apart and putting him back together again. She was so soft, so warm . . . *so mine*. She tasted like cinnamon and apples, sex and love. He was drowning in her and had no desire to come up for air.

Opening her dress again, he pushed it off and lifted her in his arms. "Where do you want to go?" he breathed, nipping at her shoulders, her neck, her chin, and finally her lips.

"Anywhere," she murmured against his mouth. "As long as I'm with you."

He met her gaze again, searched her eyes. "You know what you're saying, right?"

"Absolutely." She kissed him again. "Now stop talking and do me."

Andrew laughed, carrying her to his La-Z-Boy, plopping down on it with her astride him. "Nah, I think I want *you* to do me."

Wrapping her arms around his neck, she winked. "My pleasure."

One month later

"Hm?" Paige moaned, sipping her wine. "This is so nice."

Paige scanned the dining room, smiling at several of the guests. Then she met Andrew's intense gaze. It was their first official—and public—date. After they'd reaffirmed their promises to each other, Paige had immersed herself in their life together. She didn't think she could love him more than she did yesterday, but her love for him grew every single day.

They'd settled into a new normal that involved her learning to navigate the industry without him. But she had a good team, and Vonda was perfect for the job that Andrew had filled so effortlessly before.

"I'm glad we decided to come here," she said.

He squeezed her hand. "Me too. I love that we don't have to hide anymore."

When they made the decision to finally "go public," Skye had suggested they leave the city. So, they'd taken the weekend off and headed back to their safe haven, the lake house.

After they'd spent the first day in bed, on the couch, against the wall, and atop the kitchen table, he'd surprised her with dinner reservations at a local Italian bistro. The food was delicious, but the company . . . superb.

"You're so beautiful," she whispered, giggling when he frowned at her. Andrew had always made her feel beautiful and treasured. But she had yet to tell him how beautiful she thought he was.

He eyed her over the rim of his wineglass. "That's nice."

"Nice? I tell you I think you're beautiful and you tell me it's nice?"

Andrew laughed softly. "I'm . . . I don't know what to say to that."

"You're such a man. Say thank you."

He leaned forward and picked up her right hand, bringing it to his lips and kissing her knuckles. "Thank you."

They shared another glance, and Paige shifted in her chair, crossing her legs. *My man is hot.* And the way he was looking at her made her want to climb across the table and sit in his lap. "I think you need to stop looking at me like that," she told him.

He blessed her with a wicked smirk. "Never." His gaze dropped to her mouth, then lower . . . lower. "I like the way that dress fits you."

"I noticed." She shuddered as she recalled the way he'd taken her from behind—on the staircase—before they'd left for the restaurant. "Stair sex was hot."

Andrew grinned. "Yeah, it was. Car sex might be even hotter."

She gaped at him, but the mild fluttering in her chest suggested her body liked his suggestion. Paige stroked her throat as her mind turned with the possibilities—back seat, front seat . . . hood. But her celebrity prevented them from being too adventurous with it. *Maybe in the driveway at the house?*

"You're thinking about it, aren't you?" he asked.

A blush worked its way up her neck. "Yes," she whispered.

"What did you come up with?"

Paige glanced at the couple behind her. There was no doubt in her mind that the young woman had recognized her. During dinner, they kept staring at Paige, and she could've sworn she'd caught the flash of a camera out of the corner of her eye earlier.

"I'm thinking the hood, under the moonlight."

Andrew leaned back, never taking his eyes off her. "I think I might be able to make that happen."

She trembled in anticipation. "Yes, please."

"The only thing is"—he leaned forward—"I want you naked on that hood."

Her lips parted and a shiver snaked up her spine. "Really?" she croaked.

Andrew nodded slowly. "But that can't happen in Michigan."

"Shit," she grumbled. She'd almost forgotten where they were. Late fall in Michigan might not be the best place to make her fantasy come true.

He finished his glass of wine. "But trust me . . ." The low rasp in his voice, the lustful promise in his eyes made her want to lean in to him, to touch him, to taste him. "I will have you there. Soon."

Paige jumped when the waitress came to the table. She pressed a hand to her chest, hoping to steady her rapid heartbeat. Andrew shot her one last glance before he turned his attention back to the waitress. The older woman asked if they were ready for dessert.

Andrew looked at her, a question in his eyes.

Smiling, she told the waitress, "No, thank you."

The woman set the bill next to Andrew and ventured to another table. "You're turning down dessert?" he asked her.

"Yes." She smirked as an idea started to take shape in her head. "I'm thinking of a different kind of treat."

Andrew lifted a brow. "What do you have in mind?"

"Something hot. Something sweet." She moistened her lips, watching as his gaze followed the motion. "Something private."

Andrew's gaze darkened. He pulled his wallet out, removed two large bills, and waved the waitress over. Once he settled the bill, he stood and pulled Paige to her feet. "Sounds like my kind of dessert. Let's get out of here."

"You read my mind." She placed a quick kiss on his lips. "We just have to stop by the market."

He froze. Frowning, he asked, "Why do we need to go to the market?"

"To pick up dessert, silly."

Paige knew what Andrew had been thinking and she'd done it purposely—to get back at him for teasing her about car sex. Of course, she planned to give him what he wanted, but she needed her sweet treat first. As they approached their rental car, she tried her best not to laugh at the sour expression on his face. But a soft chuckle burst free.

"What's funny?" he asked.

"Nothing," she lied.

It didn't take long to get to the market. As she walked the aisles looking for what she needed, she grinned at Andrew. He was still a little salty about this turn of events, and it was so funny to see him this way.

Turning to him, Paige asked, "Are you okay, baby?"

"Yeah" was his one-word answer.

"Then why are you pouting?"

"I'm not," he argued. "What are we here for?"

Paige peeked her head down an aisle. When she spotted her dessert, she grabbed it off the shelf. Turning around, she held up a bag of marshmallows. "S'mores!" she said with a grin.

He narrowed his eyes on her. "Really? You brought me here for s'mores?"

"I thought you said you wanted dessert." Picking up a box of graham crackers, she added, "I figured this is a good full circle moment for us." She felt him step up behind her and gasped. He was so hot—and hard—she couldn't help but back her ass into him. Just to ease the sudden ache in her core.

"What I want is you naked on any available hard surface," he whispered in her ear. "Specifically my dick."

Oh my. She let out a shaky breath. "I want that, too." She sucked in another sharp breath when he gripped her hips and held her against his hard length. "Oh, you're playing dirty."

"Turnabout is fair play," he tossed back, sucking her earlobe into his mouth.

Paige turned in his arms and kissed him. "Let's go."

He smirked. "That's what I thought."

"Excuse me?"

Paige turned toward the soft, shaky voice behind her. She smiled at the petite, gray-haired woman standing before her. "Hi," she said.

The woman grinned. "I don't know if you remember me. I ran into you at the apple orchard a little while ago?"

Recognition dawned on her, and she said, "Yes, I remember."

"I know you probably get this all the time," the woman continued. "My husband said I was wrong, but are you Paige Mills?"

"I am."

The woman clapped. "Oh my God. I used to watch you on *All of Our Lives* years ago."

Andrew chuckled. "Told you," he muttered under his breath.

"Oh, yes." Paige shook the woman's hand. "That was me. My first big job."

"I loved your character. I was so mad when they had you die in that explosion." The woman shook her head, a sad look in her blue eyes. "I wish you could come back."

"Aw, thank you," Paige said. "I appreciate your kind words."

"Can we take a selfie?" The woman held up her cell phone. "My book club will never believe I met you."

"Sure. Do you want my boyfriend to take the picture?"

The woman looked at Andrew. "Do you mind?"

"Not at all," he said, a soft smile on his face.

Paige wrapped an arm around the woman and smiled. Andrew took one serious pic and one silly pic. When they finished, the woman thanked her and rushed off.

"This is why I love you," Andrew said against her ear.

She smiled. "Because I take good pictures?"

"No, because you're genuine, kind, and beautiful. You made that woman's year. You're amazing."

Paige's heart opened up as his words rolled through her. "Thank you." She kissed him. "You're pretty awesome, too."

He squeezed her hand. "Let's pay for your *dessert* and go back to the house."

As they stood in the checkout line, Paige glanced at the magazine rack, eyeing the crazy tabloid headlines. But one in particular caught her eye.

JULIUS REEVES FACING UP TO 80 YEARS IN PRISON
AFTER MORE WOMEN COME FORWARD.

Even more eye-catching was the caption under the picture of a haggard-looking Julius ducking his head as he entered the courthouse:

CATHERINE DAVIS CALLS OFF THE WEDDING.

Paige shared a glance with Andrew. He shrugged and she grinned. No words were needed. Julius would get what he deserved for being a horrible person.

He paid the cashier and grabbed the bag. "Let's go."

Back at the house, Paige was giddy at the prospect of gooey marshmallows, graham crackers, and chocolate. "I'm so happy. I can eat two s'mores." She pulled the package out of the paper bag and opened it. "It's cheat day," she sang, doing a little twerk.

Andrew snatched the bag away from her and tossed it

behind her. Marshmallows flew everywhere. Before she could ask him why, he tugged her to him and kissed her. Hard.

"No, baby. S'mores are for later."

Her mouth fell open. "Later?"

"Oh, yeah." He lifted her in his arms, and she wrapped her legs around his waist. "We have unfinished business. Remember? Hard surface."

Paige burst out in a fit of giggles. "Drew, you're crazy." Her head fell back as he trailed a line of wet kisses down her neck. "But I love it when you're crazy," she whispered. "After this, s'mores. Okay?"

"No problem."

She brushed her lips over his. "I want them just like you did it the last time."

"Whatever you want. Always."

Paige ran her fingers through his hair, peering into his eyes. "I love you."

"I love you, too." He shifted her in his arms, pressing his erection into her. "Now, where are we going?"

The love she felt for him was so big, so consuming, she thought she'd burst open from it. She ran a finger down his cheek. "I told you. Anywhere. As long as I'm with you."

Epilogue

Two years later

"She's so beautiful." Paige's eyes filled with tears as she stared down at her little doll. *Khristina Denise Weathers*.

Andrew pressed a kiss to their daughter's brow. "She is."

After the longest pregnancy ever, thirty-two hours of labor, an epidural that didn't work, and lots of prayers, Paige had finally given birth to their little miracle. Given her age, it wasn't easy carrying a baby—so many tests, constant monitoring, and the awful pregnancy pics posted on the media outlets. But they'd made it through to the end. "I can't believe she's here," she said. "I love her so much already."

He kissed Paige's brow. "I can't wait to teach her everything I know—how to change a tire, when to stop a negotiation, and where to buy the best hamburgers—"

"How to roast a marshmallow," she finished with a wink.

Rubbing his finger over her cheek, he said, "Thank you for giving me this gift, Mrs. Weathers."

"Ms. Mills," she corrected. Peering down at her wedding

ring, she said, "In public anyway. In private, I'll be Mrs. Weathers."

Andrew laughed. "Whatever."

With their busy work schedules, they'd decided to table the marriage conversation, choosing instead to focus on loving each other and enjoying their time together. But a positive pregnancy test had changed everything. During a trip to the lake house—which they'd purchased from her uncle—he'd proposed to her on the patio, during a glorious thunderstorm.

They'd married at dusk, on a beach in Bali, surrounded by their closest friends and family—and the little bun baking in her oven. And Paige couldn't be happier with her life, with her man, and with her beautiful daughter.

Andrew took the baby from her, cradling her in his arms and staring down at her lovingly. "She looks like you," he said, running his thumb over the baby's plump cheek. "All these dark curls, gorgeous eyes."

"She has your nose," Paige said.

He frowned, peering at their baby. "She does." He smiled. "Isn't that something?"

The door swung open and Connie and Tina walked into the room.

Connie stopped, bringing her hand up to her mouth. "Oh, I finally have a grandbaby. She's so pretty."

"Let me see that baby," Tina said, pulling her sunglasses off. They both looked at the baby in Andrew's arms. "No, she's gorgeous, Connie. Pretty doesn't do her justice."

Paige shook her head. Some things never changed, and her mother was one of those constants. "Mom, why do you have on that hat?"

"Girl, I couldn't be recognized coming in here. I'm on a break."

Andrew handed the baby to his mother and sat down on Paige's hospital bed as the two women gushed over their granddaughter.

Connie swayed with the baby. "Aw, I'm your granny, beautiful."

Tina scoffed. "Granny? That's so old, Connie. She will not be calling me Granny. GG is just fine. Or, better yet, Glam-Ma."

Connie shook her head. "You're a mess."

"I can't wait to teach her how to do her hair and makeup," Tina said.

"Tina, she's a newborn," Connie argued. "That's a long way off."

Shrugging, Tina said, "Not really. She's so gorgeous, we have to put her in diaper commercials."

Connie frowned. "Not my grandbaby. She'll be a normal little girl. I can't wait to keep her over the summer."

Tina waved a dismissive hand. "Oh, I'll let you handle that, Connie. I'll fly in and visit during the holidays."

Paige giggled. "They are something else," she whispered to Andrew.

"That's an understatement." He glanced at her. "How are you feeling?"

She leaned her head against his shoulder. "Tired, but I can't sleep. I just want to look at her."

"Stop trying to teach this baby how to sing," Connie said, drawing Andrew and Paige's attention back to them. "She can't even keep her eyes open."

"Hey, I have to start early. I wish I had done this with Paige. That girl can't sing a lick."

Paige's mouth fell open. "What? I can sing."

Tina shook her head. "No, baby, you can't. Ask Andrew." She pointed at him. "And you better tell her the truth because you don't hesitate to tell me the truth about my career options."

Andrew averted his gaze when Paige turned to him. "Thanks, Tina," he said.

He'd taken over as her mother's agent after Jax retired. He'd also been promoted to senior partner at Pure Talent.

"Well?" Paige shot a pointed stare at her husband. "Drew? Tell the truth. You know I can sing."

He shrugged. "In theory."

She glared at him. "Are you serious?"

"Yes, honey," Tina cut in. "He's serious. But you can act your ass off. That's your gift."

Andrew snickered next to her and she elbowed him. "Whatever," she huffed.

Wrapping his arms around her, he said, "I promised to tell you the truth, baby. Stick to acting."

She swatted his shoulder. "Don't play me."

The last two years had been a whirlwind for Paige. While she'd continued to act, starring in a NetPix drama for two seasons and a variety of films, she'd also produced several projects. And her team had rolled with her through and through. She wouldn't have been able to do half of the things she'd done without them. And although Andrew wasn't her agent anymore, he'd still offered her advice and a shoulder to lean on when she struggled with decisions regarding her career.

"It's okay, though," he continued. "We can't all be good at everything."

"I'm good at a lot of things."

He met her gaze and smiled. "I'd agree with that. Last week, you did a particularly good job on that chair."

Paige's cheeks burned as she recalled their chair *sex*capade. Her belly hadn't stopped them from making slow love that night. "You are so bad."

Andrew kissed her. "I need a repeat."

"I think I need to move to California and live with them," Connie announced.

Both Andrew's and Paige's heads snapped up. "What?" Paige asked.

"Let's not get carried away, Mom," Andrew said in a calm voice. "We can definitely talk about you moving to California, but I'm not sure moving in with us is the best thing."

"We'll see." Connie handed the baby to Tina. "I just think you two need help. You're too busy."

"And you're no spring chicken, Andrew," Tina agreed. "You probably do need the help."

"We can talk about it later," Paige said.

The baby started to fuss, and Tina walked her back over to Paige. "I think she wants her mama."

"Your grandmothers are funny," Paige told the baby. "But you're blessed to have them."

Paige scanned the room, smiling at her mothers, who were now discussing the best way to make chicken and dumplings. Then she peered over at Andrew.

"You're watching me again," she said.

"I can't stop."

"Something on your mind?" Paige fixed the swaddling blanket and shifted the baby to her other arm. Time for a feeding.

He nodded. "Actually, I have a confession to make."

Raising a brow, she asked, "What is it?"

"I just love you." He moved a strand of hair from her forehead. "Your turn."

Tears pricked her eyes. The joy she felt in that moment made everything she'd ever gone through worth it, just to get to this slice of heaven on earth. "And I love you, too."

Don't miss the previous installment in Elle Wright's
Pure Talent series...

THE WAY YOU HOLD ME

*Dazzling, demanding mega-stars. Tabloid drama.
Brilliant, unpredictable creators. Viral rumors.
Ambitious, gifted newcomers. Internet-breaking
crash-and-burns. The Pure Talent Agency team
manages it all—even risking scandals of their own . . .*

Skye Palmer puts out the biggest publicity fires for Pure
Talent's top names. But when an A-list Hollywood
actress's dream marriage proves anything but, Skye
has to do nightmare damage control. Even worse,
her ex-lover, attorney Garrett Steele, is crisis manager
for her client's powerful director husband. Now for
Skye and Garrett, containing this disaster—
and keeping their reignited passion in check—
may be mission impossible . . .

Troubleshooting is what Garrett and his elite firm
do best. But saving his client from career-killing bad
news means battling the one woman Garrett's never
gotten over. And when joining forces with Skye leads
to one steamy night together—followed by another
and another—both their reputations are on the line.
Yet now that they've turned up the heat, can they
put a new spin on their future?

*Available from Kensington Publishing Corp.
wherever books are sold*

Chapter One

"I feel like my entire life is an overthought."

Skye Palmer let out a nervous laugh and shifted in her seat. A soft charcoal-gray plush chair. It wasn't the infamous chaise longue she'd expected her therapist to have. After all, she'd seen enough scenes—in movies or on television—of distraught people entering clean, nondescript offices to blab all of their troubles to a stiff person paid to listen and write prescriptions.

Making the decision to see a therapist, to reveal pieces of her life and detail her struggles to a stranger, had been difficult. Skye had always been the person who helped others, not the person who *needed* help. Somewhere along the way, though, she'd lost herself. She'd wrapped herself in the cloak of hurt, disappointment, and bad decisions. She'd suffocated under the weight of gut-wrenching heartache. Bitterness had replaced contentment. Doubt had replaced hope. So when her bestie, Zara Reid, encouraged her to take this step, Skye agreed.

Instead of feeling frazzled or even nervous, Skye felt calm. Still, she couldn't bring herself to embrace the peace she'd felt or the warmth of the woman silently watching her, waiting for her to complete her thought.

"How so?" the doctor asked finally.

Skye swallowed and gave the woman another quick once-over, noting the clinical psychologist's professional— yet relaxed—appearance and demeanor. Instead of a "Plain Jane" or a "Blah Betty," the woman before her was gorgeous, with smooth, brown skin, thick curls, and long legs. Again, she wasn't sure what she'd expected when she decided to make the appointment.

Dr. Sasha Williams stared at her, a polite smile on her lips and her black-rimmed glasses perched low on her nose. She'd come highly recommended from Skye's good friend Paityn Young, and had made room on her schedule that morning to meet with Skye. The least Skye could do was talk. *Right?*

Except, it had been fifteen minutes since she'd arrived, and Skye had only made the one comment. She *should* be talking. She'd paid for the session. Hell, she'd prepaid for several sessions.

"I . . ." Skye didn't know what the hell to say. *Damn that Zara for suggesting I do this.*

Skye's gaze swept the room. The ample space was impeccably decorated with warm colors, slate hardwood floors, a beautiful rug in the center, a vintage desk, and a matching loveseat. Artwork on the walls added a calm to the room. The owner had obviously spent time and money on the details. And if Skye didn't know anything else, it was her job to notice the tiniest of details. Even the smallest thing could derail a client's career, and she was paid to pay attention to everything, to be five steps ahead in every situation.

The bookshelf to her right boasted a variety of titles,

from classics like *Little Women* and *The Hobbit* to titles by Toni Morrison and T. D. Jakes. Several textbooks about a wide range of subjects from psychology to anatomy also lined the shelves. Scattered on the table next to her were a few issues of *Essence* magazine, along with P*sychology Today, Vogue*, and the *Atlanta Tribune.*

Skye's attention drifted to the Allbirds flats her therapist wore, the ones she'd been tempted to buy herself a week ago. "I like your shoes," she grumbled.

The beautiful doctor crossed her legs at the knee. "Thank you."

The clock to her left ticked ahead, each second echoing in the room, reminding her that she only had twenty more minutes to get something meaningful out. Blue Atlanta skies were visible out of the window ahead, which could be deceiving if one were expecting a warm day. The December temperatures were low for this time of year, a balmy forty degrees. If she were outside, though, she was sure she'd find Midtown bustling with people getting ready for New Year's Eve.

Speaking of New Year's Eve . . . "Thanks for seeing me today." Skye smoothed a hand over her lap and clasped her hands together. "I appreciate you fitting me into your schedule on the holiday."

The doctor shrugged. "It's not a problem."

"This is my first time."

Dr. Williams smiled. It wasn't a tight smile. It wasn't an annoyed grin. It was genuine, sincere. Like she actually meant it. Yet, she didn't say anything.

"I guess I don't know what to do," Skye admitted. "Which is different for me."

"Whatever you need to do is what we'll do."

Tears burned her eyes. *Oh God, don't you dare cry,*

Skye. She took a deep breath and let it out slowly. But one of those damn tears slithered down her cheek, like a cold, slimy snake. She wiped it away quickly. Glancing up at the doctor, she said, "I didn't mean to do that, Dr. Williams."

"Call me Sasha."

Sighing, she peered up at the ceiling to regain her composure. Once she'd taken a few seconds, she met the woman's unwavering gaze again. "Sasha."

"Why didn't you mean to cry?"

"Because I don't cry." *A lot.*

"Is it because you think you're not supposed to?"

Skye shrugged. "I've shed enough tears. Too many. I'm not going to cry anymore." *Yeah, right.*

Sasha tilted her head, assessed her with kind eyes. "Someday, I want to talk about why you feel you're not entitled to show emotion. For now, though, I'd like to focus on why you feel your life is an overthought. It's obviously on your mind."

Skye's watch buzzed and she peered at the screen. *Carmen.* The second time her boss had called her this morning. "Excuse me." She grabbed her phone and opened the Messenger app. Rolling her eyes, she typed out a hurried response. "I'm sorry."

"No problem."

"Overthought." Skye swallowed, attempting to continue her initial thought. "My life is an overthought because I can't stop overthinking everything I do. It's excessive and stifling. I feel frozen in indecision."

"At work?"

Shaking her head, Skye said, "No. Never at work. I'm good at what I do."

"Publicist at Pure Talent Agency."

"Yes."

"Do you love your job?" Sasha asked.

"My job is fine." Skye swallowed the lump that had formed in her throat. "It's everything else."

Nodding, Sasha said, "Tell me about it."

Skye opened her mouth to speak, but snapped it shut. What would she say? She'd already given the practiced response—*work is fine, I'm good at what I do, blah blah blah*. If she was honest with herself, though, she might be able to admit that work was part of her problem. Because she wasn't satisfied, she wasn't fulfilled, she wasn't challenged. But those feelings paled in comparison to the loneliness, the regret she felt about her personal choices.

"Skye, how about we start with a task?"

I can do that. Skye perked up. "What are you thinking?"

"Based on your questionnaire, and the little bit you've shared, I think it would help break the ice if you could focus on a small project before our next session."

Leaning forward, Skye asked, "What would that be?"

"Think about one thing that you're hesitant about, one thing that you tend to overthink."

Garrett.

The top of her list of regrets was always Garrett—her first love. They'd burned hot and heavy while together and blew up spectacularly when it ended. Well, not exactly. It just felt like a bomb had gone off in her chest, hollowed her out, and left her empty. The breakup itself was pretty tame. There were no hysterics, no broken glass, no harsh words. But it still hurt like hell, worse than any pain she'd felt before then, and even after. And that was saying a lot, considering her history.

She had no one to blame but herself, though. Because she'd walked away from him, even though it had ripped her apart. He'd done nothing but love her, take care of her. And she'd walked away without really even telling him the reasons why. Then she'd blamed him for it, not verbally, but in her actions toward him. Since he'd moved back to Atlanta, she'd kept him at arm's length. She'd mostly avoided one-on-one interaction with him at events and treated him with cool indifference when she did speak. He didn't deserve it, though. Yet, she couldn't stop doing it. Every. Single. Time. Hell, it was probably some sort of twisted self-defense mechanism she'd turned on its head. She didn't know. Hence, the need for therapy.

"Next time you're faced with this thing—or person— don't think about it," Sasha continued. "Don't tick off a list of pros and cons, don't question your motives or anyone's perception of you."

Damn, she's good. Skye had already started thinking of the reasons why giving it another try would or couldn't work, what he would think if she admitted she was wrong to break up with him all those years ago. *Does he even find me attractive anymore?*

"Allow yourself to feel your emotions in that moment and do what you really want to do," Sasha said. "Is that something you think you can try?"

Skye always loved a challenge. Even if it felt impossible. "Sure, I can handle that." She glanced down at her buzzing watch again. Once again, it was work. Because work never stopped for Christmas, for Thanksgiving, and definitely not New Year's Eve. "I have to go." She stood, wrapping her scarf around her neck and donning a pair of shades.

Sasha rose from her seat. "Two weeks, same time?"

"Yes. Thank you." She gripped Sasha's outstretched hand and squeezed. "It was good to meet you. Thanks again for seeing me on such short notice."

"I look forward to working with you."

Skye nodded and rushed out of the office. Frustrated, she pulled her phone from her purse to call her boss—who'd called her three more times since she'd responded to her text that she was unavailable.

"Skye, thanks for finally calling me back. I've been trying to reach you."

"Hello, Carmen. What can I do for you?"

"We have a problem with Paige."

Paige Mills was a popular actress and one of Pure Talent Agency's biggest clients. Usually when she had a problem, everyone jumped to her attention. Holidays were no exception.

"What's going on?" Skye asked.

"I need you on a flight to Los Angeles next week. The details will be on your desk when you get back to the office after the holiday."

"But, I have—"

"Skye, this isn't up for discussion. Everything will be finalized when you get back in the office."

Except Skye hadn't planned on going back to the office after the New Year. For the first time in her professional career, she'd scheduled a vacation to do nothing in particular. Her goal was plain and simple—stay home, go to movies, chill with herself and her family.

Closing her eyes, she took a calming breath. "Carmen, you know I'm scheduled to be on vacation next week. Can someone else handle Paige? Like her personal publicist?"

"No," was the short, curt reply. "And I don't have time to explain to you the reasons why that won't happen."

It was just like the older woman to disregard Skye's plans. The two had never gotten along, but Skye wasn't one to play the "I'm your boss's only niece" card. Even though her cousin, Xavier Starks, had offered on more than one occasion to step in and say something.

Massaging her temples, she bit back the curse itching to burst forward. She swallowed. Hard. And tried again. "Is this something I can handle *after* my vacation?"

Skye was no idiot. In fact, she'd spent a lot of time educating herself on a myriad of subjects outside of her chosen career, from horticultural science to Nietzsche to wine. She could talk to anybody, anywhere, at any time, about any subject. Since Carmen was promoted several years ago, Skye had attended every single conflict management training course she could stomach. Each of them had left her feeling extremely inept. Because no matter what she did, she still didn't like the woman yapping on about work like it wasn't New Year's Eve.

She wanted to tell her boss where she could stick her foul attitude, she yearned to give Stupid-Ass-Know-Nothing Carmen a piece of her mind in Tagalog *and* in English until she begged for mercy. And, damn it, she wanted to tell Uncle Jax exactly how that heffa had treated her since she'd traipsed into the office and told Skye she didn't care whose niece she was.

"Skye?"

"Yes," she bit out.

"Did you hear me?"

She didn't. "I'm sorry, can you repeat that last thing?"

"I said, I'm going on medical leave for two months, starting now. You're in charge. I'll leave my notes on your desk."

Skye's mouth fell open. "But—"

"Happy New Year."

Then Carmen was gone. And Skye was screwed.

Skye purposely arrived at Xavier's and Zara's house for their New Year's Eve engagement party half an hour before the ball dropped. After that phone call with her boss, she'd screamed in her car for two whole minutes. Once she'd effectively released her tension, she headed home to put her boss and work behind her and focus on the task at hand.

It had taken her hours to find the right dress for the occasion. Then it had taken her even longer to get the nerve to leave her condo. Because tonight was the night she would make her move. Tonight was the night she wasn't going to overthink her past or her future.

"What's up, cousin?" Xavier greeted her with a kiss on her cheek as he always did. Raised more like siblings than cousins, Skye had never known life without X. Her adoptive father and his father were brothers, and they'd grown up in the same Brentwood, Los Angeles neighborhood. Now they worked together at Pure Talent.

"Hey, X." She noted several familiar faces in the room. "Party is lit."

"We have a lot to celebrate."

Grinning up at him, she nodded. "You do."

Skye couldn't help but be happy for her cousin and her bestie. She'd seen the two of them fall for each other despite their own personal reservations about love and relationships. She'd rooted for them as they slowly realized their lives didn't work without one another. And she would be there with them every step of the way going forward.

"I need your help, though," he said.

She frowned. "What's wrong? And why didn't you warn me about Carmen?"

"Trust me, it was a shock to us, too." X had recently stepped into the role of heir apparent to the Pure Talent empire, so she knew he'd been privy to the details about her boss's leave. "We got the email this morning. I called you, but you didn't answer."

Skye grimaced. Her cousin was one of the calls she'd missed during her session. "Sorry."

"Zara explained where you were, so you're good. It's short notice, but I figured you'd be happy."

"I don't know how I feel," she admitted. "She's the head of publicity. Am I ready for this?" *Do I even want it?* "And her desk is a mess. I'm going to have to fix her shit."

He squeezed her shoulder affectionately. "You got this, Skye. I have no doubt. And if *you* do, I'm here to help."

She couldn't help but smile. There was never a time X didn't have her back, even if he didn't agree. Growing up together, a mere block away from each other, had ensured they would be present in each other's lives. But it hadn't stopped there. They'd built forts, played video games, and transitioned from precocious kids to determined teens to successful adults. They were family, but they were friends, confidantes. And she loved him dearly.

"Thanks, X. You're always there for me."

"That never changes." He smiled. "Now, I need you to find your girl. She's around here, panicked."

Skye looked for Zara among the crowd and instead

spotted a waiter carrying several flutes of champagne. She snagged a glass and turned to X. "Why?"

"The wedding."

"Ah. I'm not surprised." Her bestie was many things, but event planner wasn't one of them. "I got you."

He bumped shoulders with her. "Thank you."

Skye scanned the room again, telling herself she was searching for Zara. Not Garrett. "Where is she?"

X glanced around the room. His eyes lit up when he spotted who she assumed was Zara behind her. "Over there." He pointed toward the bar. "Talking to Garrett."

Turning slowly, she caught a glimpse of her best friend before focusing on the man that had haunted her dreams more nights than she'd even want to admit. He was dressed casually, in black slacks and a black shirt. His brown skin glowed in the dim lighting. He laughed at something Zara said, before taking a sip of his amber-colored drink, most likely cognac. Neat. At least, that's what he used to enjoy.

Before she could stop herself, she headed over to them, Sasha's words echoing in her head, playing on an endless loop. *Don't think about it, just feel, just do.*

"Skye, where the hell have you been?"

She stopped in her tracks, recognizing the male voice immediately.

"I know you're not going to walk up in here and not speak to me!"

Skye turned slowly, ready to shoot her best guy friend with her fiercest scowl. The smirk on his face let her know he didn't give a damn what she had in store. And the arch of his brow told her he knew exactly where she was headed when he'd intercepted her.

Grumbling a curse, she rushed over to him. "Why are you so damn loud, Duke?"

"I mean, damn. Can't get a call back? A hug? A Happy New Year? A *go to hell*?"

"Hi," she grumbled, noticing the three women standing close to him, eyeing him like he was prey.

Dressed in a crisp, white dress shirt unbuttoned at the collar and rolled up at the sleeves and fitted gray slacks, Duke Young didn't look like any personal chef she'd ever seen. In pure Duke fashion, his beard was trimmed and his wavy hair was mussed to perfection.

"Amihan." He grinned, holding out his arms. "Hug. We're supposed to be celebrating."

Amihan was her middle name, and it meant "northeast monsoon" in Tagalog. It was also her great-grandmother's name. As an Afro-Filipina woman, she was proud of her heritage. But only her mother called her Amihan, or Ami. Duke did it when he was trying to play the big bossy brother role he liked to play so much.

When she was a kid, her mother used to tell her stories that make up what is called Philippine mythology. According to the folklore, Amihan was a birdlike creature—the first of the universe—responsible for saving humans from a bamboo tree. For some reason, that story always made Skye feel special.

Unable to pretend to be mad at him any longer, she laughed and shoved him playfully. "I can't stand you."

"Hey, I figured I better stop you before you do something you'll regret." He pointed one finger at each of her eyes. "I know that look in your eyes."

Smacking his hand away, she told him, "Shut up."

"You look good enough to be dangerous tonight. Where's your date? Weren't you supposed to bring Kenneth?"

"His name is Keith, and we're just friends." Initially, she'd thought about bringing Keith to the party. They'd met at a fundraiser several weeks ago, and had gone out a few times. But she didn't consider them serious, even though he'd expressed interest in becoming more than friends.

"Friends, huh?" Duke studied her with narrowed eyes. Silently.

"Stop looking at me like that," she hissed. "You get on my nerves."

"Why are you so defensive?"

"Since you're so nosy, Keith and I decided not to ring in the New Year together. We're meeting for a nice break-fast tomorrow. An *innocent* breakfast."

"That's lame."

She smacked his shoulder. "Shut up. You're holding me up."

Chuckling, he held up a platter of mini desserts. "Try one of these."

Duke made a pretty good living as a personal chef, and had been hired to cater the party.

Skye bit her lip and mulled over the choices. "Did you make them?"

"What do you think?"

"Hm. I'll take"—she picked up a chocolate one—"this one." She popped it into her mouth. Groaning, she nodded and gave him a thumbs-up. "So good."

Duke set the platter down. "Thanks. Hug?"

Skye shook her head and finally gave him a hug. "You think you're slick," she whispered. "You just don't want those women to come and holla at you. I'm not playing your fake girlfriend tonight."

He barked out a laugh. "Damn, I can't get anything by you."

Pulling away, she pointed at him. "See! Dirty. Dog. I have to go."

"I can only be me."

Waving, she walked away. "Bye, Duke."

"Be good, Skye," he shouted.

Composing herself, she made a beeline for Zara—who just happened to still be standing with Garrett. X had joined them as well.

"Z-Ra, hey." Skye's voice came out more breathy than she'd intended. She hugged her friend.

"Hey, hun," Zara squeezed her hand.

"Garrett," Skye said in a clipped tone. The same tone she'd told herself she wouldn't use the next time she saw him.

Damn, Skye. She'd promised herself that she'd do better, that she wouldn't treat him the way she'd been treating him. The terse, one-word reply wasn't called for—at all.

With a heavy sigh, she amended her greeting, this time in a softer tone. "Hi, Garrett."

He smiled. "Hello, Skye. How are you?"

I can do this. "I'm well. You?"

"Good."

Step one complete. On to step two of Operation: Do Not Overthink. Turning to Zara, she said, "You look amazing."

Zara grinned. "Thanks. Can you believe I let X pick my dress?"

Now, that shocked the hell out of her. With wide eyes, she asked, "What?"

"I know, right? I must be in love."